AN ISHMAEL OF SYRIA

SYRIA

Asaad Almohammad

First published in the United States in 2016

Copyright © Asaad Almohammad 2016

Asaad Almohammad has asserted his rights under the Copyright,
Design and Patents Act, 1988, to be identified as the author of this work.

All rights reserved.

ISBN 978-0-9974815-0-1

Cover Image © Judy Almohammad

FOR SHARON,

WITHOUT A DOUBT IN MY MIND

Contents

Prologue

Petrea King preached that *the pursuit of happiness is making us miserable*. She claimed that our hunger for that emotion unveiled a pre-existing internal unease. Her thesis emphasised the illusion of this holy grail of human experience. She laid plausible arguments; uncovering the dangers of the mantra, *I will be happy when…*

I'd believed in her logic; I'd lived by it. But on that day she couldn't have been more wrong. For upon reaching his destination, a man with a past full of misfortunes can both taste the bitter drops of his sorrow and grin in triumph despite them. In reaching the desired end of his voyage there is an outbreak of joy. Even in a pyrrhic victory, a man of past and present tragedies experiences the sweetness of that elusive emotion.

****

I was fully aware of having two left feet. Still, I danced from the door to the living room. I couldn't care less about the disapproval in my housemate's eyes. He kept on staring, while I gambolled closer to him. Seated on our only couch with his toes gripping the edge of the table in front of him, Sami needled, "What's wrong with you?"

"Feet off the table asshole!"

"Stop, you sound awful. Are you on something?"

I continued to belt, "Because I'm happyyyyyyyy! Clap along if you feeeeeeel like a room without a roof! Because I'm happyyyyyyyy! Clap along if you feel like happiness…"

"You're an even worse singer than dancer. Stop it man! Are you on something?"

"Noo, noo, no, no, noo. Happyyyyyyyy!"

"What's wrong with you?"

"You mean what's right?"

"Why are you happy?"

"I just am!"

"Happy for no reason?"

"No, but I don't have to justify myself to you. Not tonight anyways."

"Just stop!"

"Nope!"

"Just so you know, your voice is annoying."

"I don't care!"

****

My exuberance dissipated later that same day. Mad as hell, I found myself haranguing my brother Nyhad. We were on a video call. Before that day, I hadn't seen his face for over six years. The twenty-three-year-old was dumbstruck. I remember lecturing, "I am sceptical about many things. I don't get the raison d'etre of faith. I doubt most people's, if not everyone's, altruistic drive to personal triumph. I don't get hope or wishful thinking. In fact, I have come to assert those emotions as a most lethal and dangerous fallacy. Scepticism and cynicism, on the other hand, have been growing on me. For one thing, they serve me in repressing that hazardous state of hope. It's the most destructive of all human emotions. It keeps us in the places we are frightened by the most."

Nyhad followed several moments of awkward silence with a pitiful look, wondering aloud, "What happened to you to be this way?"

"What way?"

"A man of no ambitions."

Part I

Chapter 1

The Brand of Victimhood

For some reason, notwithstanding the alienation and utter rejection, I consider myself a global citizen. They say misery calls for company and I've always been a man of funerals. The companion of the misfortunate, until they are not! As a citizen of the world, it's my instinct to keep the fallen and the suffering in my thoughts. The human brain fascinates me; its limitless bounds of empathy. You see, in my mind there is logic to it: do no harm, prevent harm, help, support, care for the harmed, face the harmer. My stupid idealist conscience considers sympathy, not pity, at its worst, the most basic and the least negotiable civil duty. Of course as a citizen of the world, I should strive to do more. That said, I am only a man and so I often do the least.

I have to admit that I feel sad for Ban Ki-Moon. The guy is in some fucked-up shit. I think he cares but, like me, find himself quite helpless. It must take a lot of sleeping pills to put his burdened conscience to rest. Syria, Ebola, Somalia, Nigeria, CAR, Mali, Iraq, Rohingya, Ukraine, Yazidis, human rights abuses, ISIS, Hezbollah, Yamane, sinking immigrants' boats, drug cartels, among other more or less pressing items. The man has to deal with warlords and dictators. The man has to pretend so he can get some shit done. He has to deal with genocidal maniacs. He has to deal with devils who almost always deceive him. His tenacity defies all logic. I guess even for a man in his position, denouncing acts of aggression gets tiresome.

Sometimes I think there is a part of me that craves to know of the harmed, when unfortunate events unfold. Sometimes they keep me up at night; sometimes I have the usual nightmares. Though, being an exhausted workaholic usually has the power to put me to sleep. Eyewitness accounts are the most excruciating; of course, after those who went through the fucked-up shit first hand. Getting hold of the latter version of events isn't that simple. Death, shame, honour, and fear, among countless reasons, are strong forces, preventing us from taking the bitter sip of their tragedies. I never miss victims' and eyewitnesses' accounts of the horrors of war: raped underage girls and women, beheadings, summary executions, refugees' hardships, suffocating babies. The aftermath of technology-based and motherfucking natural disasters often leave a deep scar and thus, I owe it to the harmed to help, assist, or care, to say the least. See, I know that

I'm fucked-up real bad but it's no excuse. I've been told that I cannot change shit, so I might as well stop torturing myself. My emotions are ridiculed and branded as childish. I have been told that the world has given up on my people. I have been told, and realise that on many occasions, I myself am viewed as an outcast by some of those suffering. I've been confronted and my answer is always the same: I care even in my most fucked-up moments. I care even when gates of shit pour open to drown me; I care because I am a citizen of the world. This citizenship is something nobody can give you; it's gained by a force of will and keeping it is worth all the struggles.

I have been told that I've always been this way. Maybe so, maybe not. What matters is that I intend to keep fighting for this citizenship. I know my limits but foremost I know where I came from originally. With that brand on my forehead, a reduced status is assigned, courtesy of the more developed world. Even for the most oblivious Syrian on earth, the look on the stranger's face when you have to do the unspeakable that is apply for a visa to their country – subconsciously removes all sense of pride. You are there and to their ears, being a Syrian sounds like you're unclean, shameful, indecent; it's like you owe the world an apology for your very existence. For I'm neither a submitter nor a hating retaliator, I acknowledge the boundaries of my existence; yet, I still care. I care regardless of the way they choose to reduce me to the brand that is the birthmark of the accident of my conception. I care less about what that brand signifies in terms of my character, potential, and intentions. For the harmed I care. For the real victims. It's the most basic of my mandatory civil duties. Only in caring, am I a citizen of the world.

I have to stress that my duties towards victims of all sorts, be it helping, taking their side, or caring, ends the moment their status becomes a bargaining chip. The moment the victim becomes a righteous sufferer. For in my short time on this planet, history and on-going affairs are full of those competing in victimhood. You see them recounting the horror their groups had endured, giving it more or less of a competitive edge. Its logic that I-suffered-more,-therefore,-I-need-something-in-return. But I am all for justice. The aggressors and those inflicting pain and agony on others must endure judicial repercussions. I am not denying the existence of villains who strong-arm the law. I cannot claim that the perpetrators of genocidal acts can always be charged for their psychopathic crimes. The world is a fucked-up place. I read a study somewhere; I guess it was on the competitive victimhood of the Hutu and

Tutsi of Rwanda and its role in delaying and preventing post-conflict reconciliation. Competitive victimhood doesn't hide itself; you can hear it in the Palestinian-Israeli rhetoric. It's there, everywhere! And somehow, it's used to legitimise unjust demands, marginalise a group with connections to aggressors; even justify the elimination of innocent people.

On the individual level, victimhood, by many, is recognised as some form of political experience. I am not making the claim that victims don't have political experiences or lack the required skills. My argument is that victimhood in itself is not indicative of possessing the credentials to lead such central positions. For victims, my duties are to help, support, take their side, and care for them, not to reward them. For me victims deserve justice; the notion that a reward of any sort would erase their scars is the most ludicrous idea of all. Being a victim doesn't define you or entitle you to anything but justice. It doesn't give you the right to "cleanse" certain people from the face of the earth, it doesn't make you righteous, and it's not indicative of your expertise except for in the sociological and physiological senses.

The lowest of all lows are the self-proclaimed victims. Competing in victimhood is one thing, but deceiving others, and maybe yourself, into the violation of the self is a grave abuse of many. It doesn't take an expert in human motivations or much critical thinking to deduce its desired ramifications. Thinking of it, whatever the number of operational cells in their skulls there may be; victimhood appeals to them as a legitimisation tool. Beyond an instrument of legitimisation of the pursuit of basic rights, the self-proclaimed arrogantly and ruthlessly have the audacity to demand inflicting upon those, of whom their imaginary aggressors belong to, the endurance of their 'suffering.' For in them, being perceived to carry the bargaining chip of victimhood qualifies for the same privileges.

****

After things went south in Iraq, a number of Iraqi Shiite terrorists abandoned the "protection" of Sayeda Zainab's "honour". One might think that the woman was a spiritual leader of some sort. But the fact of the matter is that most of Shiite terrorists justify their aggression in terms of their victimhood. Extremist of the sect have long cultivated support and recruited fighters on the notion of shared misery. I strongly stress that I cannot apply this logic to the global Shiite population. It is rather limited to organisations like Hezbollah and Filaq Bader. Their rituals are centred on keening their lost. They moan and hit their own backs with chains to show grief. It's their claim that a caliphate ordered the killing of one of Ali's sons. Their fights from that point onward have been to avenge the killing of that son. Sayeda Zainab was the daughter of Ali and the granddaughter of Muhammad, Islam's prophet. So you see, the lady is long gone. How on earth can you defend the honour of the dead? How does it justify the killing of thousands of civilians? I cannot submit to the rationale that a man who got eliminated unjustly and for whatever reason, makes a whole sect of victims – righteous victims, I might add. Foremost, how and on what fucking planet does it makes the killing of innocent children, women and men a divine duty? Not only deceiving others and themselves in calling themselves victims, but also competing in victimhood, using it as an inner justification for the most horrendous of all crimes. I am not saying that all Shiite are supporters of those lunatics' aggression – though I have to admit, I haven't once heard them denounce the savagery. What I have heard is a denial of these groups' involvement, or the placing of blame on Sunni terrorist organisations.

I choose to believe that there are Shiites who denounce the radicals in their midst. That said, the

Sunni population, to a large extent, brands as terrorists those involved in heinous acts of aggression in the pursuit of intimidating other sects or other faiths. It's easier to reason with the non-self-proclaimed victims. For in the absence of that mentality, actions toward a peaceful and just society are for the common good. Of course this is with the exception of those preying on hatred, as for them, nothing is more dangerous than a life that is just for all.

I remember this time when I provoked the utmost rage in Yamen. He had contacted me days before his arrival on the island of Penang, though I had never met the guy in Syria. I didn't pick him up from the airport but my apartment was his first destination. He asked me for a prayer rug so he could compensate for the number of missed prayers. "I am not Muslim; can I get you a clean towel instead?" I offered. Yamen opened one of his bags and got what appeared to be a wrapped rug. He placed a small brick on his rug and prayed without folding his hands. *There it is; he is a Shiite,* I realised. I might be wrong and politically incorrect but I deduced, *supporter of Iran, Al-Assad, Hezbollah, and Hamas, righteous, entitled*. I knew that I should strive to neutralise my implicit prejudices.

That was in August 2010. I hoped I had misjudged him. Unfortunately though, it turned out I was right. The memory of me eliciting rage in him is still vivid. I voiced my disgust, "Fuck them and fuck their forty-fuckbag-whores!" It was my way of denouncing an act of terrorism in Iraq. He frowned and his tone couldn't have sounded less disciplinary, "Don't insult my religion!"

"Come on, how is that insulting? Are you telling me that fucking lunatic isn't a terrorist?"

"Don't call them whores!"

"I see. So which one angers you more: my 'insult'," I made quotes with my index fingers, "Or the asshat who killed more than seventy people?"

"They are not whores!"

"I am intrigued! But our tone is quite loud and there are a lot of people around." I pointed to the café patio.

Yamen was not confrontational. In fact, he would give anything to avoid a confrontation. He had this mysterious desire to be liked. He was one of the most narcissistic characters I had had the pleasure of making acquaintances with. Nonetheless, he fixated on proving me wrong or at least taking the opposite side of any argument on which I had a stance. So

15

there we were, sitting together. It was long before the Arab Spring became a term of interest. I lit a cigarette. As I exhaled the smoke, I asserted, "I have to be blunt with you. I won't be diplomatic. I will say what I believe. I won't patronise you or lie to you; you are too smart to recognise when I bullshit." The last sentence *was* a diplomatic tactic to put myself on the offense.

I continued, "Al-Qaeda and Hezbollah are both terrorist organisations; both are sectarian and both intimidate people for their political agenda. That said, the governments of Syria and the Islamic Republic of Iran are involved in terrorism by proxy."

"Al-Qaeda is a terrorist organisation, but not Hezbollah!"

"Why, is it because al-Qaeda is made up of Sunnis?"

"Hezbollah is fighting Israelis!"

"Indiscriminate shelling, kidnappings, attacks on embassies, intimidating Lebanese; I wouldn't use the term fight. I would say terrorise. Besides, training extreme Shiites from Iraq; fuck man, who knows of the atrocities they wrought when they got back to their country?"

"So any organisation against Americans and Israelis is a terrorist…"

"That's not entirely true."

"They hit themselves to attack Muslims!"

"What does that mean?"

"The twin towers were an excuse to take Afghanistan's gas. *They* did it!"

"I see. How do you know that? I mean, based on what?"

"There are companies that examined the towers; there is even a book on it."

"Please give me the title of that book and show me how you got these companies' reports."

"Do it yourself!"

"No, you are using arguments which I believe you either heard somewhere or made up…"

"They are real!"

"I see, on the hinge that there are reports and many books pointing the blame on Americans, I will continue this line of questioning. I am not saying that they are to blame; by the way, I am just entertaining your argument." I put my laptop on the table and asked him to look up his sources. He struggled for almost half an hour. Finally, he referred to some book. It was open-source and you could get it for free. We scanned through it for a while. Bored and with my intelligence severely insulted by the contents of that fiction, I broke in, "So conspiracy theories!"

"I don't know!"

"How do you believe in something, when you have no idea of its validity?"

"You believe in something and I choose to believe in something else. Why the double standard?"

"Yamen, foremost, in a state of full knowledge, there is no conspiracy. A conspiracy is projected when one lacks knowledge and certain clues are used to prove the malicious intentions of others. You are better than that man," I didn't mean it. I continued, "My argument is built on existing information and I have no access to hidden intelligence. Don't you wonder whether that person is biased and made up things so he or she gets your support?" Yamen cracked his mouth to say something momentarily, but I put up my hand to pause him. In Malaysia that gesture translates as *by the power invested in my hand, I command you to listen.* The sign means a lot of things. Sometimes we joked about it. We would say, the hand stops cars from going through. We imagined it could stop wars. I certainly hoped the last part was true.

Yamen gave me the chance to continue my lecture. Looking at him I preached, "Now, if the Americans, as you have had yourself believe, have inflicted that tragedy upon themselves, then it's part of their crusade against you."

'"I am a Muslim!"

"Humour me, please! Can you tell me how does that make that war against you?"

"Because I am a Muslim!"

"Oh, I get it. That makes you a victim by association. Sometimes it's hard to get something through my thick skull, but Bin Laden admitted and took credit for the attack, didn't he?"

"He is an agent of America."

"Oh," shaking my head as if I was trying to chase the idea away, "Americans are killing themselves and wasting billions of dollars in their crusade against Muslims. Man, I wish I could be half as confident about something, anything!"

"I didn't say that Americans are killing themselves. There are Mujahedeens who are fighting the Americans."

"You mean al-Qaeda and the Taliban."

"You don't get it!"

"Maybe not, but why you are so confident that the whole world is conspiring against you?"

Yamen was about to say something before I stopped him, "It's a rhetorical question, you don't need to answer. Though, I am wondering about suicide attacks in Israel."

"You mean Palestine!"

"No, Israel, where Hamas' suicide squads often carry out attacks killing civilians."

"It's justified! The whole world is taking their side. Palestinians are the victims of Israeli aggression and they have the right to retaliate."

"Retaliate! You mean terrorise civilians."

"Everything is not terrorism! It's a righteous struggle."

"It's to instill fear in civilians and has so far brought their people nothing but misery."

"You don't understand; you won't because you are not Muslim."

"I understand that you are not a victim and even on the off-chance that you are one, I don't how that justifies the killing of civilians. You fill your mind with conspiracy shit maybe to feel better about yourself. You're victimising yourself to give yourself a free pass to terrorise."

To date, to Yamen, Al-Assad is the victim of the worst conspiracy in the history. To him, all rebels are terrorists. The children who suffocated to death after they were struck with sarin gas are Shiite children, staged to bring legitimacy to those opposing Al-Assad. Though to him, Sadam's atrocities are recognised as such; the uprising of Bahrainis is legitimate; however the one in Syria is to cleanse Shiites, from start to finish.

****

So again, after some Iraqi Shiite terrorists abandoned Al-Assad to fight ISIS in Iraq, his forces started aerial attacks on Ar-Raqqa. ISIS was fighting other rebels. Even Yamen admits that they were left alone as a strategy to defeat the terrorists, terrorists that for him are those trying to topple the Al-Assad regime. With ISIS in the picture, getting news of the city is really tough. With every capable and sane person fleeing the scene, it made it nigh-on impossible to get the latest from any credible sources. It was a time when phone calls became a luxury. I had to wait for my father to contact me. Every time I got a call from a strange number I would stress. I knew two of my cousins and my childhood friend had been killed. In the few seconds between noticing the strange number and answering, only dark thoughts would come to mind.

So there it was, a strange number. My mood changes, anxiety rises; my face clouds with worry and fear. "Hello, Allo…"

"How are you son?"

"I am fine father, what about you?"

"I am fine."

"What about mother, sisters, brothers? How are they? Are they okay?"

"Yes, son, all of them are fine. I just missed your voice!"

I grinned, as my father isn't in touch with his emotions. The man had never given me a hint of care, let alone love. I knew he had had it tough; even before shit skyrocketed. I asked, "Tell me how things are going? How are you getting by?"

"Really, things are good. Your brother left to go to Aleppo yesterday. Your sisters will take their high school exam next week. Your mother, Nyhad, and your sisters are in Der Al-Zoor. They left last week.

You know ISIS banned girls' education. I mean, they allow them only to study until the fifth grade."

"I read their latest announcements. After the aerial attacks, I got worried."

"Figured…"

"I read that five barrel bombs were dropped in the centre and to the east of the city. One of them was really close to where you're staying now. You tell me if anything happens! I don't want to hear from somebody else, like when grandmother passed."

"Don't worry about us son, your worry is misplaced. See, we are really fine. Around the country people are putting up with things even I cannot even comprehend. We are fine, don't worry son. Let's hope that we wake up one day and the barbaric regime is gone along with the darkness that has overtaken the city and the region."

My father probably just said that to spare me the churning thoughts. But it was the way he said it – he sounded so sincere, I knew he meant it! I have no idea how to explain it. The man was in deep shit; he cried every time he asked me for some cash. He had recently lost his nephews, mother, job, and was living by very humble means. I wondered how he could sympathise with the losses of others. It amused me that he weighed his hardships close to nothing, thinking about those more miserable. His misfortunes were not bargaining chips. He didn't compete; he didn't justify atrocities against Shiite, Alawite. Most of all, he didn't mark himself with the brand of victimhood. He just wanted peace.

Chapter 2

The Leftover

A few magazines had been put on the side; two of them were on the seat of a chair. Scattered over the table were dog-eared copies of Time, Newsweek, and Bloomberg, all of them this week's edition. My cup of coffee was in one hand and in the other I had the book, *Mad as Hell*. I was half way through. By the time I finished reading about the evolution of the Tea Party, I couldn't focus any longer. I put my cup on the table and reached for my old backpack that was placed to my left on the ground. Its colours were faded and torn just above the main pocket's zipper. I opened the front panel and put the book inside.

Gazing at the picture-perfect view from the café's patio never failed to evoke old memories. As I studied the panoramic view of the island and its sea, a fragment of memory began to come back to me. I found myself back some twelve years ago. Vividly, I recalled standing on the pavement looking down at some fancy resort. Bassel and I were out for a walk after a long day at work. During my time in Beirut, I had come to look up to him. He was the handyman, the craft-master. Bassel had helped a woman from a town in the vicinity of Aleppo in getting a place, moving around, and securing a job. I knew he wanted to talk about her. Her name was Sara. Bassel told me all about her ordeal.

We lived with six other Syrian workers in a room on the top floor of an elderly Lebanese woman's home. The room wasn't large. There was no privacy; everybody was a part of everything going on under that roof. Bassel and I made a neighbourhood bench our home away from home. Actually by my current standards, it was our home. That is to say, the place you enjoy peace of mind and comfort.

Not long before that day, he told me all about Sara. She was a petite woman with a pale face, sharp features, dark hair, and green-coloured eyes. Her family's misfortune had forced her to leave school. To make ends meet, she worked at a minimarket. It was the only shop in town. Despite its size, you could manage to shop for anything there, from groceries to basic electrical appliances. Abo Mahmood, a distinguished man in the town, owned and ran the business. He was in his late forties. Once a week, he would go to Aleppo to purchase supplies for his shop. It was a successful business, considering. Abo Mahmood's customers were not limited to his town. Prior to his weekly trip, customers could order anything they needed or desired, from pharmaceuticals to electronics. For the special customers, even alcohol.

It was one of those hot summer days when she first met Ramez, the school's assigned teacher. For newly graduated teachers, it's mandatory to serve couple of years in a remote town. The young teacher became a regular customer of the Abo's. Well, it was hard not to be. After all, it was the only minimarket for the town and its surroundings. For the sake of a conversation with Sara, the young teacher sometimes came to the shop only to get change for five Syrian pounds.

She knew of his affection. Five Syrian pounds change! Who was he fooling?! Sara did not realise that she felt something for Ramez until he stopped coming to the shop. During his week of absence, she noticed the pupils playing around the shop during school time. With the cheapest candy in the store, she approached a seven-year-old girl.

"Hey sweetie, close your eyes."

The little girl closed her eyes, pursing her tiny lips strongly. "What is it?" she asked.

"I got you a treat," Sara unwrapped the candy.

The little girl smilingly wondered aloud whether it was strawberry.

"Ooh, will mango do?"

"I love mango!" The little girl opened her mouth with her eyes still closed. Sara gently put the treat in the girl's mouth. Chewing the gum-like candy, the little girl couldn't hide her ear-to-ear grin. Looking at the girl, Sara was overjoyed and for few seconds forgot that she was bribing the young innocent. She placed her hands over the little girl's straight red hair and kissed her on the forehead before proceeding.

"Sweetie, it's Wednesday, why aren't you at school?"

"Teacher Ramez is ill. We are off for the week."

Sara was upset by the news. She went back to the shop and sat behind the desk. Anxiously she moved around the shop trying to do anything to keep her mind busy. Abo Mahmood couldn't help but notice her distracted state. Turning a fruit container upside down, she made a seat for herself in the corner of the shop, just by the pile of second-hand clothes. Quietly she sat like a sad child. For Abo Mahmood, it reminded him of the silent treatment his son used to do back in the day, when he wanted a toy or more allowance. He decided to break the ice.

"Sara, is everything okay? Is your father okay? What is it, my child?"

Ashamed and scared to reveal her affection she tried to keep to herself. As Abo Mahmood's endeavours failed to cheer her up, he brought her her favourite ice cream.

"No, no! I don't want it," Sara muttered. He lifted his arm a little bit and spun his hands while his lips thinned, displaying some disappointment and sadness. Sara considered Abo Mahamood a father figure. Her own mother had passed when she was four and her father lost his sight after an accident in the cement factory, last year. Since her mother died, he seldom talked to her. He wasn't around much and she didn't know much about him.

In that patriarchal town, having feelings was a sin. Sara wanted to tell Abo Mahmood but her fear of disappointing him kept her from venting.

Sara's situation reminded me of the sad violin soundtrack typical of a Syrian series. Thinking about it in that moment, I saw through some of the cheap and deceptive means of conditioning through my country's controlled media. A variety of sad tones that could bring sadness to even Pharrell singing *Happy*. I recalled all the scenes whenever a girl was swayed by a guy, the fucking sickening music would go on and on. Somehow, it reinforced the fucked-up twisted taboo of dating. It didn't take a psychologist to associate the torturing sound with an attempt to induce shame and guilt to female viewers. Hypocritical as it sounds, Syria's Channels One and Two were notably incongruent on the issue. Channel Two was in English. One might safely argue that in one way or another, the language of Channel One could increase patriarchy. However, a male main character was approached in a totally opposite way. Just the good old double-standard of the deeply-rooted and fucked-up value system.

Abo Mahmood, in his turn, considered Sara like the daughter he never had. He sat behind his wooden desk and kept looking at Sara. He even went behind the cashier's desk to do the work Sara hadn't bothered to do. Abo Mahmood took a plastic bag and put in some tomatoes, cucumbers, eggplants, onions, potatoes, and a five hundred gram bag of cooking oil. In a smaller bag, he put some biscuits, chocolates, and ice cream. The vegetables were not fresh, two days old. He headed toward his downcast assistant, tapped her on the shoulder and said, "My child, please take the rest of the day off."

"It is only eleven; we just opened!"

"You are of no help to me like this. Please get yourself together and come back tomorrow."

"God bless you Abo Mahmood," Sara said with a doleful grin as she took the bags and headed out of the shop.

Her town was small, the kind where everybody knows everybody. She walked aimlessly for around fifteen minutes before she sat at the edge of some pavement. *Ramez has nobody to take care of him and attend to his needs*, she thought. *The poor man might be hungry; he could be seriously ill*, she kept wondering before she made up her mind to pay him a visit. His rented abode was on the outskirts of the town. Reluctantly, she stood by the old wooden door before collecting enough courage and strength to raise her little hand and knock.

"Come in, come in!"

Sara froze for a few seconds. She hadn't planned to go in. The thought of somebody seeing her kept her from entering. The idea of going in seemed akin to grasping the forbidden fruit, expelling mankind down from heaven. Hoping Ramez would spare her from this sin, she knocked again.

"Come in; it is open. Please just come in."

"It could be really bad, he could be too weak to open the door," she mumbled to herself. She stood by the door for a while, before making her way in.

"Sara! I didn't know it was you." He put a jacket on his shoulders as he graciously invited her to take the only seat in the one-room house. "I am sorry for the mess. If I only knew you were coming, I would have made some arrangements. Are you comfortable? Can I get you some tea? Coffee, perhaps?"

"No, no! I didn't mean to inconvenience you. I am sorry, I didn't. How are you feeling? Just go back to your bed. Have you eaten anything?"

"I am getting better, but not out of the woods yet. Actually, I haven't eaten anything."

"Please let me prepare something. Just let me know what you have so I can fix you a meal."

"Should I go to Abo Mahmood to get you stuff for cooking?"

"No, no! As it happens, I've brought you a little something. I'll cook for you an upside down vegetable mix." It might not have been the ideal meal to serve an ill person, nevertheless, it was the only dish she could have prepared, given the ingredients to hand.

Ignoring his distaste for this oily meal, Ramez enthusiastically replied, "That's my favourite!"

"I am glad to hear it. Just lie on your bed and let me do the rest. Try to sleep, if you can."

"I'll try."

Sara gave Ramez a gracious smile as she moved toward the stove. It took her a while to find her way around the space designated for cooking. She started by peeling, cutting, and marinating the potatoes and eggplants before throwing them piece by piece into the sizzling oil. She placed them on a plate full of papers to dry. As the tomato sauce started to boil, she emptied the plate of fried potatoes and eggplants inside and mixed them gently, so they didn't lose their shape. She looked around trying to find something. She covered the pot and lit the fire before placing an outdoor rug at the foot of his bed.

Sara touched Ramez on his forehead with two fingers and moved them toward his left eyebrow, leaning in so she was only a breath away from him.

"Wake up Ramez, lunch is almost ready!"

Ramez opened his eyes quickly to pay his gratitude. "Thank you, Thank you! I really appreciate everything you've done."

"Don't worry about it, please sit here on the rug; you can lean your back against the bed so you don't feel tired." Sara said as she moved toward the stove. She turned it off and filled a large plate.

"I didn't add much salt. Would you like more?"

"No! This is great."

Sara took the plate and placed on the ground as she said, "It is getting late; I'd better go. This should be enough for today. I'll come by tomorrow afternoon. Would you like me to cook you something in particular? Maybe, chicken soup?"

"No need to bother yourself."

"Don't talk like that. I will take care of you. I have to. Now, I have to leave."

"Please join me."

"I cannot, I have to leave. I'll come tomorrow."

Sara moved closer to Ramez and kissed him on his left cheek without laying a hand on him. As she moved toward the door with a pleasant grin, "Take care of yourself," she said. With her back against the door, she looked at him as she parted. In her state of euphoria, she did not notice the pedestrians until she glimpsed the disgust in their eyes.

"What were you doing there, whore?" a man in his fifties shouted.

She froze. It was a fight or flight kind of thing. For several moments, she just looked them in the eyes. As she stood, trying and failing to think of an excuse for her "unforgivable sin", let alone a defensive word, she was interrupted with one of the men displaying his utmost revulsion. Loudly, he spat on the brown soil instilling in her a mixture of guilt and fear. Suddenly she felt clammy, and as she looked down to her left side, noticed she was dragging one foot before the other with a weakness she had never experienced before. Several paces away from them, Sara's lumbering changed into a stomp. From a distance, a now weeping Sara could see her father sitting on the porch of their house.

"Are you hungry, Father?"

"No, no! Have you brought me some batteries for the radio?"

"Baba, I replaced the batteries yesterday."

"Oh, bring me the radio."

"Sure, father."

"And tea."

"Give me few seconds."

"Bring me the radio and then make the tea"

Sara rushed in to get him the radio. She noticed that the radio had been moved from where she had put it last. Her distracted state cut her short from giving it much thought. She took it out to him. "Here it is. The tea will be ready in no time." He took the radio without a word. He brought it close to his right ear and started listening. In few minutes Sara brought him a large mug of hot tea.

"Not the mug!"

"Baba, once you finish it, I'll get you another one. I just don't want you to burn yourself again."

"You're disrespectful!"

Sara did not dignify his words with a reply. She just went inside. The downcast little thing literally went into a corner and began whimpering, mourning her pride. Without a doubt, she knew that by the dawn of the next day, her town would strip her of her honour. Keening over her lost reputation, she couldn't hear her shouting father. To her surprise, one of the pedestrians had allowed himself into her house. That was when she started to hear her father's poisonous words streaming forth. Distracted by the venomous premonition of the ordeal to come, she felt the blind man's presence before seeing him. The excruciating pain of his heavy cane only amplified her sense of self-loathing, marking in her thoughts the end of her life, at least in this town. Sara managed to push her father away and run to his room. She grabbed her identity card and some cash she has stashed in there.

Bassel spotted her couple of days after she fled the country. In an attempt to end a quarrel between her and a guy from her hometown, Bassel stood between them, his hands stretched to their fullest, but without touching either of them. Trying to prevent any attempts of physical contact, he took the guy aside. "What is your problem? You are causing a scene", Bassel spoke loudly. He kept looking at both of them.

"Tarek, what is it?"

"Take the whore outside."

"Lower your voice."

Tarek's face and demeanour showed all signs of shame, failing to make any eye contact with Bassel. His shame was replaced by rage, every time he looked at Sara. Sensing Tarek's heavy breath, Bassel whispered, "Calm down... calm down! Whatever your issue might be, this is no way to solve it. You are just causing a scene. Lady, what's your name?"

"Sara," she replied as she lowered her head.

"There is a shop over the corner. Can you wait for me over there? It won't take long, I promise," Bassel gently instructed.

She shook her head slowly, sighing with disappointment, her tears of sadness dripping faster and faster as she walked toward the thrift shop. As so often happens, her story had travelled faster than her. Tarek told Bassel the town's exaggerated and dishonouring tale of Sara and the teacher. Without much thought she had come to Tarek seeking help. He finished her disowning with "Whoring is a better business for her!"

"Let me handle this", Bassel said. Tarek gave him a sickening smile as Sara's apparent defender rushed to meet her. Walking on the brown soil of Subra Street, he made his way, avoiding any eye contact with those he knew to be Palestinian street thugs.

"I heard you are trying to find a place to stay and a job. Let me make some calls, I know a few families and ladies staying at San Mishael. Are you hungry? Let's get something to eat. Let's get some thyme pies." Sara followed him, keeping a snail's pace. "Is it your first time here? I mean in Lebanon."

"Oh, yes. How long have you been here?"

"Ha… ha, since I turned twelve."

"So I guess, I could ask you about everything in the city."

"I won't say that I know everything. I know what I need to know. I am going to help you, don't worry. We are here! In Lebanon they add onion to thyme pies, it sounds weird, but believe me it is really good. I'll get you one."

The pie shop was barely big enough for the two men already inside to move around. A long steel table was fixed on the shop door to prepare batches for baking.

"Can you get me two thyme pies," Bassel said as he handed one of the bakers a thousand Lebanese Liras. Bassel's mouth was watering and he looked at Sara excitedly. Sara couldn't help it but give him a gentle smile. The other baker placed the two pies on the table. "It is better hot," Bassel said as he got two papers. With the tips of his fingers, he pulled each pie over the papers. Hypnotised by them, in a gentle tone, "Sara please take yours; it is better hot!"

"Yum, it is surprisingly good!"

"See, I told you."

Sara did not like it, though she collected every ounce of self-control to suppress any hint of rudeness. She even complimented his choice.

I had known Bassel for a while then. He didn't get sarcasm. He couldn't read people. In fact, he never had a clue. You couldn't be subtle around any issue, you had to be as blunt as possible. Since their meeting, Bassel had gone out of his way to help Sara. He made a point to dine with her every day. It was clear to me that he really liked her. I went out with them a number of times. He tried to hide his affection toward her. The funny thing was, his feelings were very obvious, even to strangers.

I recalled a day – by that marble seat, Bassel put his arm around my shoulder as he kept going on and on about Sara's first day at work. I was telling myself, please not *The Shopping Tale*. The shopping tale was the most boring. I had heard that story more than five times. I never hid my lack of interest in that day when they went shopping together. He took her to two malls. They ate at a fast food restaurant. For Sara it was by far the fanciest restaurant she had ever been to. If memory serves it was KFC. Long story short, they ended up buying clothes from a thrift shop.

I was really tired that day. My train of thought was broken and I couldn't help but look absent-minded. Tightening his arm around my shoulders, excitedly and with a hint of triumph, Bassel loudly and pleasantly enquired, "Adam, isn't she beautiful?"

"Are you kidding me? Beautiful does not begin to do her justice!" Now Sara was pretty, but knowing his affections toward her, I had to exaggerate. My words were music to his ears. He smiled and started to tell me about her roommates, her cooking skills, the colour of her eyes, the way she ate thyme pie, all the little details, and of course the shopping tale.

"Bassel, I think you like her. You know she is innocent. She didn't do what they think she did. Are you in love with her?"

"Love?! Are you fucking with me? I can only love the one I marry."

I should have known better and pretended to accept that insolent mentality but instead I asked, "Why don't you marry her?" He suddenly lifted his arm and glowered at me menacingly. I knew that look. I have angered many in my life before.

"Adam, I think of you as a brother. Why are you disrespecting me? They all lie! Do you think I believe her? Of course she'll claim innocence. She is a whore and I thought you knew what I am after. How can you accept somebody's leftovers for me? You told me that I am like a brother to you. How dare you? She is a leftover and I deserve an honourable woman. Not a whore!"

41

Thinking back, I have always questioned my friendships. I am certain if I was then the same person I am today, I would've done things differently. I might've made different choices or at least elicited some change in his mindset. Bassel would have been an easy case. I would've conditioned him in less than a month. I would've stripped him from all the idiotic impulses, making him willingly revolt on that fucked-up value system.

Turning from Bassel to the ocean, my mouth couldn't help but spell it out, even then, "Leftover, my ass!"

Chapter 3

Barricading the Roads to Jesus

"Hey *Sadiki* Adam!"

"Hello Mr Smith. Your Arabic pronunciation is quite good, my friend! Hey Sami," I tried not to show my irritation of meeting Sami, "you are out at this hour. It is early for you," I noted as I looked at Mr Smith.

Mr Smith placed a hand on my right shoulder and grinned, "You are an easy man to find. I hope you're not starving. I am sorry, I am not on time. I was in Butterworth; it took me almost an hour to cross the bridge. Where is Mustafa?"

Observing the downcast Sami, my mind lingered on keywords like *starving, not on time, sorry, where is Mustafa*. Thus, I deduced that it must be another one of Sami's moments; eventually, I realised that Mustafa and I had been invited to lunch. Yet another time he intentionally didn't pass on a message. *Tactless, self-righteous, self-conscious, sectarian, racist, misogynistic,, judgemental, envious, shameless, ultra-materialist, bottom feeder, and backstabbing coward*, to name a few, are the adjectives my subconscious mind transferred to my working memory upon encountering Sami. For in recent days, I had discovered that Sami was also a Shape Shifter. In other words, he could master the theft of your identity, character, personality, and individuality. I overheard him crediting himself for my opinions and telling past stories of mine as his.

I still remember the time Mustafa called me at around two in the morning. He woke me up and pressed me to check Sami's post on Facebook. It was about a Syrian dessert for which I kept my recipe a secret. Through trial and error, I had managed to develop a technique to make it soft and moist. I even had a unique topping for it. My compatriots would gather at my house, waiting for the *Harisa* to cool down. Sami would take the most, yet he was its biggest critic. It wasn't only me; nobody seemed to be good enough. He knew that I used Facebook merely to read the news. I told Mustafa, it is not the first time for Sami to credit himself for something he didn't do. I laughed a bit. Then, Mustafa said he hadn't just claimed that he made it, he had also shared some of it with his local friends. He continued, "There is a comment by one of his friends, telling him how much she liked it and wants a bigger portion next time." I replied, "You know Sami, man." Mustafa couldn't forget that incident.

Sami also tended to forget his own opinions, arguments, thoughts, and probably what he claimed

44

to be his past. He would use my position on a number of issues and, in contrary to actual events, would claim that it had been the same all along. I confronted him on multiple occasions and his only response was to diagnose me with dementia. With him, I had nothing to prove and thus I let it slide, mostly. Nonetheless, sometimes I get carried away and recount the course of previous events. For in some positions, one is distinguished by some pattern or footprint of some sort. He wouldn't steal your ID card, but he'd be you in the superficial, intellectual sense. He'd copy classmates' ideas and claim authorship. He'd use your pick up lines. He'd claim your achievements, even the deepest, most personal tragedies. His personal style was copied from a friend of his. From his choice of the colour to his accent, be it Arabic or English, all had been stolen. Foremost, his life before we met and his past had changed too many times; he would take over yours, in your absence, when it served. Like the one-celled amoebae's ability to change its shape, the douche would change his past in heartbeat.

"Mustafa is busy," Sami shamelessly replied. I had known Mustafa for ages; he wouldn't miss such an event. A lunch on somebody else, he preyed on such ceremonies. I was not a big fan of Mustafa though. One time I told him that it was fortunate that he was good-looking. He didn't get it! He even asked me to be direct with him; he couldn't dissect any subtle messages. Even in the most direct and oversimplified manner, he almost always missed the point. He had certain expressions for his idiocy. He would stare down at you as if to emphasise some sort of intellectual supremacy. I have to say, it didn't do him any favours. He was by far the most legible face of idiocy. Seeing that face, I'd shake in my seat, gripping the table edge in fabricated fear. "Fuck off, man! You are scaring nobody," I'd say. I remember he was angered by a friend once and claimed that he would explain it to us but our lack of sophistication would make his efforts fruitless. To him, we were all very primitive.

Mr Smith led the way out of the café and made a few suggestions. He was a pacifist in all senses of the term. He had spent years in Oman. He seemed to be captivated by Arabian cultural norms. Mr Smith fascinated me; he was a very spiritual man. Hearing him talk, I imagined myself touching his face and going around him before asking, *what are you?* Growing to be a sceptic of human kindness, I couldn't get him. I thought, nobody could be this caring and sympathetic. Besides his generosity, Mr Smith really listened, a quality for which I often yearned. I had made his acquaintance through Bob.

Bob and Donald were old friends who shared two common denominators with Mr Smith, namely, Americans and Christians. I came to name Bob and Donald *The Christian Battalion of Proselytisation*. Mr Smith was a little different. A very proud Christian, but I hadn't witnessed his preaching in the explicit sense. Thus, I could not associate him with that battalion. How dare I to make such claims, especially after I had developed a tactic to make those preachers stray from their inevitable *Road to Jesus*? After all, I could not accuse him of that without him explicitly preaching to me.

I was not an atheist chauvinist myself; opposed to theological supremacy and absolutism. Mr Smith and I had many philosophical discussions that always escalated to an intellectual argument. It was like we had an unspoken agreement to have our say and then clarify why we agreed or disagreed. He often ended up agreeing with me, leaving me in limbo, not sure whether he was convinced or just patronising me.

Being the shortest, I avoided walking in the middle. We strolled for a while before Sami shamelessly picked the most expensive restaurant. Again, it was free and for Sami the music was playing to his ears. The restaurant was too pricy, even for Mr Smith. Since the day I first met Sami, he had never invited a soul unless there was something in it for him. Mr Smith's shyness prevented him from objecting. On Sami's request, the hostess led us to the smoking area. We seated ourselves and scanned the menu, except for Sami of course. He studied every item and ordered the most expensive ones from the appetiser to the main course to the drinks. The wine was very expensive and I gave him a look before voicing my disapproval. He looked at Mr Smith but couldn't decipher any encouragement. "Fine," he said as he shrugged, displaying his irritation. I took a single espresso and Mr Smith picked the cheapest salad on the menu. He pressed me to order something but I claimed to have taken my lunch earlier.

As Sami greedily consumed from the surplus of dishes, I made a few inquiries in regards to Mr Smith's father's health. He had been diagnosed with Alzheimer's. We drifted from one topic to another as Sami devoured Mr Smith's salad. Staring at him I recalled one of my town's old sayings that goes 'nothing fills his eye but soil.' It implies that nothing fills a greedy man's void except for death. The restaurant was more of a dating place. For Mr Smith and I, it didn't feel right. Sami wanted to order another drink but Mr Smith insisted on going elsewhere. For reasons beyond my comprehension, Sami was angered by my welcoming of Mr Smith's suggestion. Actually, it was more of a decision. I was out of my natural habitat and the extravagance of the place had started to poison my mood. Besides, I couldn't care less about Sami's desires.

We seated ourselves in the café patio. For a while Mr Smith studied the array of superbikes that were parked on the sand by the ocean while the barista served us our coffee.

He drew us out, enquiring "Who are we? Really, who are we?" Sami was silent most of the time. How couldn't he be?! He was smart enough not to wear my skin and tell its tales in front of me. When forced to get by on the bare minimum, from things of material value to emotional investments, one's personality and individuality might endeavour to compensate for all their misfortunes and fill her or his void. But there is a fine line between being inspired by someone and copying that person's past.

If it wasn't for Mr Smith being here, I would say "You're full of shit," I thought. Immediately, I realised if I kept quiet, Mr Smith would start to preach. I knew whatever road he was about to take, it would inevitably lead us to the Saviour, Almighty Jesus. I wanted to avoid my inevitable annoyance that would follow that trite cliché, that is, *Jesus spoke to me*. So I figured it was time for a grand diversion.

Barricading the Road to Jesus was an awesome tactic. Being calculating and aware of subtle clues helped keep me vigilant; for in the position of a potential argument or a debate, my odds would improve. I knew that allowing him to elaborate his point would put me on the defensive. Defence was a losing position that inclined toward investing too many thoughts and being persuasive; the best odds were getting permission to be yourself. Barricading the road to Jesus would reverse that state of affairs.

Bearing in mind his most probable intention, I contended, "Firmly, I believe that one shouldn't be reduced to gender and sexual orientation, ethnicity, nationality, clan. There is a lot to an individual. We might be to some level the products of our environments. Still, the sum of our experiences, in reconciliation with the context, shapes our perspectives. I am what I have control over and I am the choices I make. I am the sum of my tragedies and triumphs, achievements and shortcomings, wrongdoings, ideologies, flaws, conscience, ethical and unethical conduct, political correctness and incorrectness, allies and enemies, intellect and backwardness, open-mindedness and closed-mindedness, levels of empathy and psychopathy, and much more. Maybe what makes us alike can come in handy but what defines us is a tally of our differences; all of them, not reducing any of us to a uniform character." I had lost Sami at "Firmly." Mr Smith eventually agreed with me. After all, I had barricaded the road to Jesus and he couldn't spot a single turn to his desired destination.

Mr Smith was not willing to give up just yet. He looked at me and asked, "Have you ever thought why we keep going? What is it that makes us do the right things?" I broke in, "For long, I have wrestled with that question," I was giving myself the time to plan my offence so as not to find myself on defence.

"It is one of the most central questions of all. You see, man is good and man is bad. Still man has a void. Man can't claim his good deeds yet he might strive to own his wrongdoings. A religious man might do what he believes to be good, fearing god, or collecting the required points for heaven. Man, for some reason, is not wired to admit his good deeds; it has to be for something divine. Man expects warmth and comfort; but he needs someone to acknowledge it, even if he has to imagine it. One time I told a friend that I admired his patience with his wife, who was bipolar. He claimed, 'God spoke to me and gave me the strength.' That man just could not admit to being good for no reason. I would have taken 'I love my wife.' any day. But no, he had to do it for Jesus. You want to know what keeps me going? It is very simple, I have tons of responsibilities and I do my best to fulfil them. Acknowledging the fact that I have done all I can, in itself, lessens my burdened conscience. Unlike religious men, I don't do what I do fearing god or collecting points so I can go to heaven. A religious man is an ass." Mr Smith laughed. I grinned and continued, "I have to say that over time, the act of helping and doing the good deeds, becomes automated. It doesn't make me feel happy; it just doesn't make me feel bad. Not feeling bad makes me sleep at night. I wake up in the morning and work my ass off to lessen what might make me feel bad at night."

I have been preached at too many times to count, by Muslims, Christians, Buddhists, and Hare Krishnas. I don't know what it is in me that calls to "saving". It's not just that I don't believe in a god or gods, but on the off chance that I am wrong and the "Almighty" does exist, I can't submit to him or her and follow their ways. For me, Richard Dawkins' definition of God of the Old Testament applies to all gods, on various levels. He, She, or It is worse than all the psychopaths of fictional and non-fictional characters: an ill-minded, sexist, homophobic zealot who could prevent all manmade and natural catastrophes and yet chooses to only watch; a maniac who creates the desire in paedophiles to rape children; a totalitarian dictator who's more ruthless than any regime or terrorist organisation known by man; a narrow-minded narcissist who preys on self-actualisation. For me, this delusional douchebag is everything that is wrong with us and is precisely what I don't want to be. Yet, I am not an atheist preacher. I am not an absolutist or chauvinist whose ways are immune to evolution. My core philosophy is that I might be wrong.

Chapter 4

In Racism We Trust

It will only take few seconds to get down using the elevator, I kept telling myself. It took forever and I started sighing impatiently. Lifting my head up to see my way through the door, I caught a glimpse of some of my fellow tenants. The middle elevator doors always opened so slowly that you needed to rush in while they were still opening. Then they closed too fast. You couldn't make your way in unless somebody pressed the button to hold them. Having learned not to count on the residents' kindness, I shouldered my way in sideways. My brown skin, tattooed arm, and muscular physique seemed to frighten some people, especially the ladies. In that claustrophobic, clammy space, Malaysian Chinese ladies were commonplace. The Malay women of my block were only programmed for flight, not fight. There was no hiding the Arabophobia. Six years ago, it would've pissed me off. Now I just found it hilarious. Sometimes, the dark side of me craved it. Rolling my eyes I muttered, "Run, Forrest, run!" Six years ago I would've gone ballistic.

Over time I had come to the realisation that, against my impulses, I should maintain my manners, even if it made for more work. I would keep to my personal space and say, "Excuse me", "Thank you", and "I appreciate it", even greet them. Politeness was part of my code. Observing my compatriots, I had realised that tactfulness was a dying art. So I looked these neighbours in the eye, wore a fake smile and nodded my head. I knew it; I knew that I shouldn't expect a reply. I should've known better but I still expected it! Sometimes it happened, though not often.

My back was facing them and my fingertip was on the glass cover, just over the "open door" button. When the door opened, I pressed and held it hard. Everybody rushed out. Not a single thank you, of course! Before leaving the elevator, I caught a glimpse of a handwritten note on the bulletin board. It said, "A white, tall British man is looking for a cheap, fully furnished master room." We have an old saying in my town; "One knows which side to eat a shoulder from." It implies that one knows how to get things done. That saying later came to my mind as I recalled one of the Chinese ladies writing down his number.

The noticeboard was opposite the lift. I don't know what came over me; I just walked towards it.

Displayed was a full-page announcement made for property owners in the condominium. There was no header. It displayed twelve pictures, aligned in a grid. The images were poorly photo-shopped and each surrounded by a white frame. The faded photo in the top left corner showed a convertible, with a black dude taking a selfie in the lower right of the picture. The next image displayed a black man being escorted by law enforcement officers. The third showed a similar scene, except the man was of an Arab descent. The fourth, seemingly unrelated, was a blurred panoramic view of the island. Then two more pictures, one of another Arab and the other of black dudes. They were handcuffed with their backs bent and police smiling from behind. There were three policemen in each picture.

I couldn't make sense of these or the photo of the black dude taking a selfie, and the car. I guess the last photo was inspired by the movie, *Taken*. It had four ladies with messy hair kneeling before a couple of Arab dudes and "Human Trafficking!" in blood-spatter font. Under the pictures the announcement stated:

Please be more selective and conscious if you wish to rent your unit to these people as aspects of safety and peace in the

environment plays an important role in N Park.

You might end up finding yourself 'busy' with the Police or immigration dept. should you rent to them.

Thank you

The stamp of the condominium's management was on the far left of the page.

Admittedly the announcement pissed me off at some subconscious level; for in recent days, only horrific tragedies had been capable of arousing minor emotional responses in me. I felt my firm grip on each side of the board's frame as a smirk started to wear away at my anger. That said, my grasp on the box outlasted the smirk on my face. For reasons beyond my control, another self-defence mechanism provoked an obvious sardonic smile, which eliminated any hint of the mirthless grin that may or may not have existed before. For in the realisation of disappointment, one can find an inner refuge distanced from the aggressive impulses of anger. Sighing I muttered, "Man, it's gonna be tough for my people to rent a room here, let alone an apartment."

As I lumbered toward my bike I vividly recalled a recent encounter with the lady in the management office. I wasn't sure if she was the manager. In the short period I had been staying at the condominium I had noticed that many of the things I threw into the trash were being removed and left on the side. Things like old jeans, pizza boxes, and broken clothes hangers. I had ignored it for a while, though the growing pile was by an emergency door just opposite my apartment. After studying my neighbours, I figured they were either students or foreign workers. So I decided to pay our management a visit.

From behind the glass door I could see a fifty-something elegantly dressed lady reading. As I made my way toward her desk she lowered her stylish glasses and stared at me. I wore the usual pleasant mask of graciousness. "Hello," I said. She frowned at me and shouted, "What is it now!" *That's funny*, I couldn't recall a prior visit. Actually, I'd never been there before. *Maybe she confused me with another member of my community.*

Still plodding towards the bike, I drifted into another memory. It had happened three days before. It was in Professor Anus-Mouth's office, a name I had deemed appropriate for the bigot. Seated in his office he noted, "You came highly recommended by Professor Zainul. Is he a good client of yours?"

"I cannot talk about my clients."

"Very well. What's your name again and where are you from?"

"My name is Adam and I am Syrian."

"Oh, are you ISIS?" he enquired smugly.

"What?! Do I look like an ISIS member to you?"

"How can I tell? You're all brown and have hair on your arms. Oh, and of course you have big brown eyes."

"No sir, I am not an ISIS member. Can we get down to business?"

****

Oh, that explains it, I said to myself as I reached into my pocket to get my keys. I didn't care about correcting the management lady; I'd never been in that office before so who cared. I had clenched my hands and put them against her desk. "I hope I am not causing any inconvenience; I can come later," I spoke softly.

"Take your hands off the desk. What is it now?"

Growing irritated, I sighed, "I have a complaint. The rubbish bin is opposite my door and the waste collector keeps putting some trash by my door. I confronted him once; and for that one day only he didn't put them by my door; after that day, the trash has continued to block my entryway. I cannot stand by my apartment all the time to prompt him to do his job."

"He is only responsible to collect regular rubbish."

"Regular rubbish! What is that? There's a pizza box that has been by my door for almost a week. I think there is something inside. Ant colonies from the whole neighbourhood are by my door."

"You should take it yourself; it's not regular rubbish."

"You keep saying 'regular rubbish', but I have no idea what that means."

"You are all troublemakers."

"I don't know who 'we' are. You don't have to be offensive."

"Troublemakers and stupid!"

"Please stop insulting me." I remained calm despite my rising temper, "I just asked what you meant by 'regular rubbish'. I really don't understand the term."

Glowering at me she yelled, "Get out… GET OUT!"

"I will respect our age difference and leave. You need to calm down."

Louder and even more outraged, "GET OUT! GET OUT!"

By this point I abandoned any effort at diplomacy. "Take it easy madam, I am leaving. You need to see somebody; I mean to treat your rage episodes."

I laughed a bit and shrugged my shoulders as I left. "Poor lady!" I muttered, filling the bike's gas tank. As a master's student six years ago, she would've got under my skin.

****

It was hard to forget that day from the third week of my studies. I had arrived a couple of minutes late. For some reason, they had changed the hall that day. Research methodology wasn't virgin territory for me. Before enrolling for the course, I had done some readings on my own. I have to say, prior to my third class, I had found Drs Zainul and Amirul's teaching styles interesting. However, it was hard to be objective after our classroom altercation. I remember pushing open the new door and observing the other students, looking for any familiar face. Dr Amirul was walking between the seats.

"I am sorry; it took me a while to figure out which hall is AC018," I said as I took my seat.

Dr Zainul fixed the projector while Dr Amirul was talking to students in the last row. Finally, the two lecturers stood by each other; Dr Zainul stated, "We'll be covering quantitative research methods, descriptive methods in particular." After almost half an hour of covering the main elements of that sort of research, "Now it's time to put theories into practice," Dr Amirul announced. "The campus is full of Arab students. So I want you to conduct research on Arab behaviour," growing excited. "I realise that we have Arab students in the hall, five maybe? A descriptive researcher can approach many topics, like an investigation into the aggressive behaviour of Arabs. No offence!" adding the last words as though to tick the invisible box of political correctness.

Already familiar with quantitative research methods, I had been absent-minded for most of the session. However, that statement got my attention. Dr Amirul's fascination with Iranian culture and body language had become obvious in the first weeks of the course. I had nothing against his affections; I still don't. But this was the first time I had heard him compare them to Arabs. Curiously the subject was descriptive methods, which doesn't actually encompass any comparative elements.

63

Nevertheless, as his criticism of Arab students escalated, he also became increasingly animated in his characterization of Iranian body language.

Dr Amirul announced, "In general, one can conclude that Arabs' aggressive attitude is elicited by their pre-existing socio-cultural artefact. They lack tactfulness! I'd rather pick an Iranian student over an Arab. They are generally respectful and hard working. Now, I'll open the floor for your contribution."

There was only one student raising her hand. "We'll take questions later, it's time for your contributions." The Iranian student nodded her head in agreement. Dr Amirul smiled, remarking, "In Iranian culture, a nod means yes."

I couldn't help it but say, "I thought it was universal!"

The woman who had raised her hand glowered at me for a second and said, "I think you should know that we hate them and they hate us."

As she finished her thought I replied, "The feelings are not mutual." It was practically impossible to stop myself from responding. I continued, "Lady, last I checked, you are not representative of the people of Iran. Now I know it's not a democracy over there. As such, I won't take your word for it. Let me be clear, I don't hate you. I heard that there are five Arabs in this class," I looked around the hall, "Please raise your hands if you happen, by any chance, to have any prejudice against the people of Iran. The people of Iran, not their government."

"You imbecile!" As the giggling voices became louder, her mouth gaped in disbelief.

I enquired, "Did you have something else to add?"

She was speechless for few moments. As her mouth dropped in sorrow and her eyebrows arched outward, she continued, "No! Dr Amirul, I wanted to say that you can tell an Arab from the way they walk."

"What!?" I stood up and pointed my thumb at my ass and laughingly enquired, "Do you see a tail over here!"

Dr Amirul interrupted me, stating, "It is time for questions."

"Not yet doctor, I have a real contribution."

"Firstly, what's your name?"

"Adam."

"Go on."

"Very well. First and foremost, all your offences have been received. It's ludicrous to say no offence and then start ranting. Back to the main issue. Descriptive methods, I suppose. As the textbook goes, and in reconciliation with published scholarly work using that approach, a researcher should start with a title and a background of the selected study. See, the thing is you neither picked a theory nor presented any previous work on the issue. Instead, you assumed that a problem existed. Now one might argue that researchers are allowed to use their observations. Fine! But not actually. This isn't exploratory research. Moreover, there has to be compelling evidence that a problem exists. You just assumed the nature and the pattern of the phenomenon. There is no mention of the literature on, and I quote, 'Arabs' aggressive behaviour on campus.' Research of this approach is deductive by nature. Yet, you have no theory from which you inferred your hypotheses. The essence of any scholarly work is the method utilised and the techniques employed to test the underlying premises. I guess anybody in this class with a single cell in their brain, would tell you that your exemplification lacked, as with the earlier sections, this element. It goes without saying that you've no data to examine. You just concluded with, and so I quote, 'In general, one can conclude that Arabs' aggressive attitude is elicited by their pre-existing socio-cultural artefact. They lack tactfulness! I'd rather pick an Iranian student over an Arab.'

"With that stated, I am obliged to suggest to everybody that your premise was 'Arab culture is leading Arab students on campus to be aggressive.' Psychologically, attitude and behaviour are distinct constructs. Even a below-average layman can dissect the difference between these two variables. My point is that in no way can your premise lead you to such a conclusion. You might be able to empirically present evidence that supports or rejects your hypothesis. But not another hypothesis.

"Last but not least, the scope of the study you've illustrated is Arab students on campus, which by the way you did not cover, not Arabs all over the world, which you then addressed. As such, your generalisation is a blasphemy against research methodology. Or against any field of science! So if you were my student, you would've failed the subject. In conclusion, you sir, are racist! Plain and simple, you are racist! If you like, I can research prejudices and discrimination against Arab students on campus. Judging by your attitude that might be a worthwhile. So if you will excuse me, that's enough for one day. I am not interested in apologies,"

While walking out I continued, "I just hope that next time you can be more civilised." Everybody seemed dumbfounded; he kept shouting my name as I reached for the door.

An administrator for the school called me the next day and summoned me to the dean's office. I was expecting an apology. The funny thing is he had the audacity to put the blame on my English proficiency. I knew I had no rights, but I didn't let it slide. I responded, "As a prerequisite of enrolment, one has to present evidence of English proficiency. I believe attending any class implies the attendants' English proficiency. Dr Amirul was offensive, so please don't insult my intelligence with such evasive claims. I demand no apology, just fair treatment. And of course not to be offended again, that's all."

After that awkward meeting he became very friendly. Until the end of that semester, I enjoyed my classmates' respect and many privileges. I even received a written apology from an Iranian student, though not the same one who made the racial remarks. I guess this other student felt the urge to demonstrate that she was not like her fellow Iranian classmate.

****

As the nicotine rush rose, I decided to move to the café patio. I took the table close to the road; I could see almost all the other tables from there. Having to pay my tuition fees, make end meets, and transfer my family a monthly allowance, I had to put every second of my day to good use. It might sound a bit extreme but I often skipped breakfast and lunch. Of course, sometimes there wasn't much work to do but I wished that particular day could have lasted forty-eight hours. For some reason, I found myself on Facebook. My mind drifted to a conversation with two Malaysian acquaintances that had taken place in that café, I found myself typing a post on my wall:

I think it would be better if people chose to be explicit about their preferences. Well, in Malaysia it's not a choice; almost everybody I've interacted with is implicit about nothing. Many people believe negative stereotypes to have been scientifically proven. These premises (stereotypes about Middle Eastern and Africans) could be theological scripture; science is only for the ignorant. So either you submit to such politically incorrect sentiments, assimilate to a culture of negative generalisations, and consider

yourself inferior, or alienate yourself to retain whatever is left of your dignity.

The most ridiculous thing you might hear is what I call the "social liberal idiotic talk": Here I am quoting Z from X ethnicity. Z claims that "sometimes I give people the benefit of the doubt so therefore I cannot be a racist". Z gives us the benefit of the doubt and Z was looking at me as if it was time for me to contact every Middle Eastern and African I know, so we could celebrate Z and reward Z for Z's contribution in civilising the savages' universe. So I was wrong; it is way better to patronise and be implicit about your ignorance than to deliberate it. Anyhow as a Syrian in such interactions, although I don't believe in souls and curses, I curse Assad's soul and I move on; I bet other people have other souls to curse too.

So as usual, I had written a lengthy, not very personal status. I was thrilled to get two likes and a comment. Carl liked it and wrote, "Douchebag, we should meet!"

****

Not long ago Carl and I were close; he was a narrow-minded ass, but my options were limited. He set me up on a date with his friend, Anna. I had gone with him the day she arrived on the island. That day, she'd spoken to me in Italian. Eventually she'd asked if I spoke the language. Carl was a know-it-all kind of a guy. Upon your first meeting, he'd cut the formalities and lecture you on how to lead a better life. He had an opinion on everything and expected conformity. Either that or you would get douchebagised.

I still recall the day Anna and I had invited him over for dinner. That day Anna stayed over for the night. Eating twice his usual intake, he lazed around. He also had too much to drink. In fact, Carl finished three quarters of our stock of cheap wine.

I had met him downstairs as he was on his way up. He was wearing an old white shirt that looked yellowish around the shoulders. I cannot recollect a time he ever changed his torn brown sandals. His accompanying frayed jeans were his trademark. Those jeans could've survived a nuclear apocalypse. In financial terms, Carl was the most fortunate guy I knew. He owned a house in Florence. He had a steady income. Above all, he stayed in his girlfriend's house. Never spent a penny on that poor little thing. Anna told me that among their mutual friends his was called "The Short-hand Man"; apparently, it was too hard for him to reach into his wallet. Looking at the dirt on his shirt and feet, I couldn't help but ask, "Where have you been?"

"I was at home. I smell like a nigger after a long day working on the cotton field ..."

"That is utterly offensive. Don't be racist man!"

"You and racism," Carl shrugged, "everything I say is racist!"

"Not everything. But sometimes you go over the top."

"I have to be blunt with you, Adam, I am a realist..."

"There is a fine line between realism and prejudiced mentalities. May I add, what you say is not only stereotypical but utterly offensive."

He sighed his irritation and continued, "It is scientifically proven that they smell worse."

"Shut your face, asshole! I doubt..." giving him a glare, "I am certain that you made that up."

"I am..." sighing in devastation, "Are you calling me a liar?"

"Get over it asshole..."

"We *are* racist!"

"Man," I scoffed, "you don't speak on behalf of your nation, let alone your race."

"You are arrogant." Carl shook his head, "It's impossible to have a fruitful conversation with you. You always have to be right."

"That's me, righteous old Adam!" With a sneer I placed my hand on his shoulder and invited him in.

Without a doubt I had eagerly waited for Carl to make such remarks. For on each occasion, the opinion was deliberate. What bothered him the most was that I never let it slide. Among friends, peers, acquaintances, and even strangers, I made it a point to ridicule his self-perceived European supremacy. He was an insular, stereotypical, entitled xenophobe. Over time, I had realised that if it wasn't for such qualities, he wouldn't be a part of so many social circles, including my own. After all, psychological research supported that the use of stereotypes, in certain settings, is associated with a welcome sense of humour. The lowest of all jokes are stereotypical. But that's only my opinion. Unfortunately, there are those who look up to certain nationalities and their peoples. Carl knew that well. Seeing him around people, I always felt he abused such ignorance.

From an observer's perspective, racism takes the form of a pledge of allegiance. In a country divided by ethnic backgrounds, you often find yourself in situations where you are urged to pick a side. Such a choice is strongly associated with the submission to all prejudices and negative stereotypes. Carl had mastered the skill of pledging such allegiances. One might expect submission from those of weak character, but Carl was not a submitter; he was an initiator.

Carl made a good first impression. He was my plus-one on numerous occasions. Familiar with my attitude, he often begged me not to pick on him. My reply to his request became a cliché. I have to admit that the sight of Carl shrugging his shoulders in his attempt to mimic me saying "Political correctness is no joke." always brought me pleasure. It was his demeanour and obvious Italian accent, I guess. He just couldn't hold it in! My Pavlovian approach had conditioned the poor guy to anticipate a reprimand following his impulsive remarks. Sometimes he would look at me frozen with fear from anticipating a punishment, unsure of whether he had transgressed. Eventually Carl fell into a state of political-incorrectness paranoia.

Sami was a different case. I had to be more subtle with him both in public and private. By far, he was the most irritating character I had ever met. He lacked any sense of tactfulness and was highly critical of even the tiniest of flaws. The forbidden scruples! The most subtle admonishment was enough to arouse in him the urge to tear you to shreds. He would harangue you with his ethnocentric ways. Dare you go against his never-ending externalisation of every problem that came his way! Sami's externalisation of problems coupled with his generalisation was the root of his prejudices. A victim of his own interpretation of events. Though, I have to confess that he too suffered race-based injustices. Nevertheless, an encounter with one Chinese girl would be sufficient to derogate the whole Republic of China. However, notwithstanding his immunity to direct pressure, his scrupulous attention to another's slightest ineptitude in handling a matter opened the door for confrontation. In private I wouldn't confront him with my take, unless he sought it. I wouldn't partake in his conversations, preferring instead to show all the non-verbal signs of disapproval. Though, it was nearly impossible not to lecture him in public.

Sami's meticulous care in his pursuit of pointing out others' flaws was the key. As long as he was not the subject of criticism, you might have a chance to elicit a lasting attitudinal change in him. My belittling of Carl woke him up to the danger of prejudices. I still remember the time we got acquainted. Back in those days, he shamelessly used the N-word. One Malaysian person was a representative enough sample for him to generalise a nationwide behavioural pattern. Witnessing the public denigration and castigation of those making race-based remarks disciplined him to avoid falling for the temptation of externalising his problems through generalisation.

****

On Friday nights the café would often get packed after nine. That night I worked until they closed, as recently more Saudi students had been hiring me for my usual ghost-writing services. Looking at my watch, I realised that it was a quarter after eleven. I'd have to get myself some dinner as it's my only meal when I am swamped with work. I hadn't cooked for ages. Last time I did was after Christmas. My girlfriend, Jennifer had insisted I make her siniyah kebab. To this day I can't tell whether she likes that dish or just likes the idea of me cooking for her. Before she moved back to Korea we used to cook all sorts of things, but not on Fridays! Before things went south between us and our Iranian friends, we used to dine at their place every Friday. Despite everything, they were very generous. Harris and

Hannah would serve many courses. Sami would always fix an unending flow of drinks for himself and Carl, no permission asked, of course. Sami functioned by "if it's not lethal and it's free, it's a win". Usually his face portrayed all the signs of self-inflicted hard alcohol. Our Friday night hosts' facial expressions of irritation at Sami's manners didn't take an attentive person to decipher. The rest of us would always get embarrassed. Sami would notice our hosts' disapproval but choose to be oblivious about their annoyance. Harris and Hannah were aliases. Their actual names were Arabic and didn't fit their desired self-image. A common misconception is that Arabic names are Islamic. Harris had a superficial charm that came in handy on many occasions. We became close after I used the line, "agonistic at the corner of atheism," when he asked me about my faith. The odd couple defined themselves as atheists.

"Hannah told you that they only talk when we visit them. Beside we've no other plans," was what I told Jennifer before we went to their place a month before she left to Korea, the first time since she had moved in with me. Jennifer was not thrilled to willingly bore herself to death. "Is everybody going?" she disappointingly enquired. "Yes my love!" As I pulled her head closer, kissing her on the neck just below her right ear, I purred, "Everybody." Sami, from the balcony seat shouted, "Guys are you going or what? I won't if you won't!"

"Yes we are! Jennifer needs some time though."

"Just fifteen minutes!"

"Hey, should I call Mustafa?" Sami asked as Jennifer walked to our room.

"No, I already called him," I shrugged, "he said he'll be on time. Maybe less than three hours late this time!"

"That guy..."

"Yah! Carl will be there too. Harris told me he invited this guy. Some Turkish PhD student, I presume. I don't want to say it in front of Jennifer but I have to admit that I am not thrilled. The gloomy atmosphere in their apartment has started to put me into a minor state of depression. I don't know why they are still together! I don't know why they keep insisting on inviting us! Hannah made Jennifer feel guilty because we ditched them the other week. She told her that the only time they talk is when we visit. Harris is obviously using Hannah, but she is deeply in love with him."

"Besides, he's run out of topics and keeps repeating the same tales every week."

"Not a smart liar I would say! Have you noticed the discrepancies…?"

"I guess everybody does!"

I gave Jennifer a gracious grin as she made her way out of the room. "What do you think," she smiled. I grinned, "Elegant, yet sexy!" Beaming her satisfaction she enquired, "Shall we?"

"Yah it's better to be on time," I smirked, "I don't want to hear another of Harris's made-up tales of Australian punctuality. If we go now, we'll be there in five."

We could hear their dog barking the moment we got out the elevator. Giggling, Jennifer noted "There isn't much sex happening in their apartment. You can even sense their dog's frustration." We all laughed as we made our way towards their door. We didn't need to knock as their dog jumped and voiced his excitement from behind the door. I could see the table from outside; it was covered in numerous dishes. Harris shouted, "Come on in guys!"

"I see everybody is here, except of course for Carl and Mustafa," Sami sighed as we seated ourselves on the couch that faced the balcony.

Harris noted, "Mustafa called to ask whether it is ok to bring his friend along? I don't think he'll be on time. He never is…"

Sami interrupted, "Don't tell me it's his Chinese lady friend. I can never tell the nature of their relationship. I don't know why he keeps bringing her around. Until this day he hasn't introduced us…"

Looking at Harris' friends' face, I said, "Speaking of which, Harris why don't you introduce us to your friend?" I shrugged and smirked, "I am Adam by the way! This is Jennifer, my girlfriend, and the guy pouring the whisky before eating or greeting today is Sami. He is my housemate." Harris went to open the door as their dog began to jump, marking the arrival of somebody. As Harris opened the door, I caught a glimpse of the three remaining guests. "Ah," pointing my right index finger at the guests I continued, "that's Carl and Mustafa. Just an FYI, this the first time ever Mustafa has come on time. As for the lady, I have no clue who is she and whether she speaks at all. Yourself?"

"Rezeg, PhD candidate at UPS."

"Nice to meet you Rezeg from UPS," Jennifer grinned.

Carl's demeanour, his facial expression and Italian body language, conveyed his immediate excited response to the many dishes, making the whole room chuckle. Observing us on the L-shaped two couches, Hannah said "People, I am sorry, I was on the phone with my sister. The food is still hot and you don't need an invitation." We all sat around the table. By the time we had finished and paid our gratitude to the host, we had complimented every single dish, a tradition our host had grown fond of. Sometimes, you could see the burning desire to rise to the not-so-sincere compliments. As the ritual came to an end, I collected the dishes and started to clean them. Others felt obliged to do the same, though our host always begged me not to do it. It took us around ten minutes before all of us returned to the living room. The kitchen and the living room were not separated. The dinner table was in the middle, dividing the two spaces.

On the couch, Mustafa's special friend was captivated by something on her smartphone. For the whole evening she didn't say a word. Carl asked her few questions though. She'd whisper in Mustafa's ear and then he'd answer Carl's inquiries. After dinner I sat beside Jennifer and Hannah. I tried my best not to get involved in any political or science-based conversations. I could not recall what we were talking about but the ladies seemed entertained. Despite the many temptations, I prevented myself from getting involved in my favourite topics. It was not for the ladies though. I had kind of made a pact with myself to avoid such topics with the guys.

There were times when I was forced out of my silence by saying, "Stop mixing your shit with cream." Responding to baseless, self-proclaimed, and conspiracy-based socio-political notions, as always, led me to harangue and lecture all parties involved. It brought them pleasure to debate such topics. Then they extrapolated on the aforementioned aspects for the sake of winning an argument, especially when they grew short on concrete evidence to support their stance. Their poor political interest and knowledge combined with nonsensical ethnocentric rationales often led them to mix their shit with cream. Cultural and philosophical-based subjects were approached in the same fashion. Nevertheless, for some reason, they almost always engaged in such conversations. I explained my detailed opinions, but only if asked. Unless their mixture of shit and cream splattered onto me or topics of deep value to me were brought up, I kept to myself. That night Harris interrupted, "Stop talking politics with them! Why don't you join our conversation?!"

"I am not talking politics. Hannah's been telling us about her sister's wedding plans. She is explaining to me and Jennifer the Persian ways. I can talk about things beside politics. What are you talking about by the way? Maybe the ladies and I can join you!"

"Yes, please!" The Turkish guy said excitedly and continued "I was responding to Sami's troubles with Asians…"

"What kind of troubles are you talking about?" I cleared my throat, "Maybe Sami would rather I didn't get involved. I don't want to cause any fuss!"

Sami couldn't hide his annoyance, yet he felt obliged to respect our host's wishes. He murmured, "No, no. Please join us!"

"If you insist! So Rezeg, you were saying."

"I was telling him, it's not his fault, as Asians have shortcomings."

I was surprised by his choice of words so with an irritated tone I exclaimed "Shortcomings! Would you care to elaborate on that?"

"Asians are materialists with no sentimental sense and conscience…"

"Are you for real man?!"

Sami seemed to be taken by Rezeg's notion. With a smirk, he said "Allow him to explain; he has a compelling argument."

Calming my nerves, I sighed, "Sure, go on, go on."

Rezeg irritatingly continued "Um, I was explaining the reasons behind their shortcomings. Harris and Sami have had their share of bad experiences. Harris has tried hard to get close to his colleagues. He has invited them out countless times. But their backstabbing nature just pushed him away from them. It's obvious that they lack even the faintest sense of etiquette. Sami is disgusted by the way they eat. His friend only contacts him when she needs something. After inviting his classmates to a dinner, the Chinese girl asked him to pay for the gas and parking. Their concern is merely pecuniary."

"So is that all of it?" my voice conveying my anger as I started to stare at him.

"No. I did my research and they don't have these words in their languages."

"Is that right! Well, Jennifer speaks Korean and Chinese. I am sure she's outraged by your…"

Rezeg sighed, "Can you listen until the end, please?" he continued, "It is because they don't function in a way that requires a sentimental sense and conscience; reflective words don't exist in their languages."

I derided, "Well it's no shocker that Sami is amused by such rationale. Apparently, he seems to agree with you and find your justification compelling. I for one, find it preposterous!"

Harris mumbled, "You always have to disagree but we have our own opinions. You speak as if you don't have a clue what those people put us through…"

Shaking my head in disappointment, I expostulated, "What I hear is a bunch of drama queens and self-centred generalisers venting their social misfortunes. Please give me couple of minutes to explain myself. I have been the confidant of everybody in this room. Except for the new bigot. You've all bewailed to me your social hardships in this country. I am not saying that you haven't been ill-treated by some idiots. However, the sum of your troubles can occur anywhere, at least the issues you have brought up tonight. In Iran, Syria, Italy, and Turkey!

"Sami, the girl is not into you. You are offering your services and she is reciprocating to those demands. By the way you're forcing these words out of my mouth. I don't want to criticise you, as later you'll have yourself believing that you cannot be wrong and it has to be me. At this moment, I don't given a flying rat's ass. Instead of accepting that she's not into you, you retaliate by belittling every single citizen of the Republic of China, Taiwan, Singapore, the Malaysian Chinese, and everybody of Chinese descent. That's fucked up man! Harris, I have never been to Iran and, honestly, I don't have any intention of going there. I have to say, I know shit about your country's office politics and how competitive things can get between colleagues. The fact of the matter is backstabbing the bottom feeders is the bread and butter of office politics. Furthermore, you have to consider that you might not be as interesting as you think and thus, befriending others could prove difficult. These kinds of horse shit are global; I still don't know about your country, but they happen to all of us, even in our countries." Turning toward Carl, "Stop anticipating me to discipline you; you haven't said anything yet. You, new guy, look at me and stop ogling the ceiling! I just checked on my phone, China and India, alone, account for around thirty-seven percent of the world's population. I cannot make the assumption that everybody on the Asian continent is Asian. Just an FYI that makes approximately sixty percent of the world population. Your theory strips Asians from any sentimental sense and conscience."

Staring at Harris, he conceded, "I meant only Malaysians…"

Berating him, I broke in, "Don't you fucking interrupt me. You said Asians repeatedly, so shut your face and listen. Foremost, I am not trying to cajole you here, so listen! Your main thesis is that the lack of certain expressions or words in a given language is indicative of its native speakers' absence of any awareness of such concepts. Now I doubt that anybody in this room is able to speak all Asian languages." Laughingly I continued, "Jennifer here speaks Korean and Chinese; let's disambiguate that in regards to sentimental sense and conscience! Love, can you tell us whether those concepts exist in each language…"

Jennifer chipped in, "They do exist, in both languages."

I gave her a grin and thanked her. "Back to you, you half-assed theorist! For the purpose of this argument, I will assume that the scope of your theory is Malaysia. Given that the Chinese comprise around twenty-two percent of the population of this country and the fact that the Turkish guy's complaints were limited to people from this ethnic background, your theory holds no ground whatsoever. But that's for the sake of argument; you said Asians. I will go further, in fact I challenge your whole notion. The fact that etymology of some word in language X derives from foreign language Y is not indicative of their usage in language X. In fact, they are used and their meaning sensed. Take the word 'etiquette' for instance. None of us are French but we still comprehend its meaning. Evidently, it's more important for some of us than others.

"Conscience, man! Asians' shortcomings! How dare you?! Hearing your hypothesis doesn't only insult my intelligence, but it's utterly offensive. The unfortunate fact is that your bigotry," I frowned at Sami and Harris, "was music to their ears. You all pretend to be friends of Jennifer and thus you all owe her apologies."

I raised Jennifer's little hand and kissed it. Then, "I am sorry for putting you into this situation, let's go." I purred into her ear, trailing kisses across her face. Harris shouted, "Please stay; we didn't mean to offend you." Sami, Carl, Mustafa, and his special friend followed us. Sami did not say a word. That night, we sat in our living room. Harris and Hannah came by later. They both apologised to Jennifer and me.

****

88

At three in the morning, I left my table and went to bed. Staring at the ceiling fan, I started contemplating, *Martin Luther King Jr. said "There comes a time when one must take a position that is neither safe, nor politic, nor popular, but he must take it because conscience tells him it is right... On some positions, cowardice asks the question, is it expedient? And then expedience comes along and asks the question, is it politic? Vanity asks the question, is it popular? Conscience asks the question, is it right?"* The position I often take is silence, not outward cowardice, politic, or popularity. Conscience is a tricky concept and I have to admit that speaking out against injustice is popular. To me, it's an information-based moral compass that directs my action toward guilt reduction and righting what I perceive to be wrong. Thus, conscience is a tricky concept! Over the too-many encounters I have had and the offences I have taken, an interest in the subjects of racism and prejudices has emerged. My interest has led me to the sub-cortical regions that activate the impulses of prejudice. See, the fact of the matter is there are a lot of ways to confront the blind faith in stereotypes. Even reverse it. However, for my conscience, that comes at a cost. That is to say, freeing the self-proclaimed slave masters and the genetically and socially supremacist beings from the dark cages of ignorance. A loud devious voice in my head, shouts *that ain't right son, that ain't right!* I have to admit that my conscience speaks in a Southern accent.

Still, is silence a sign of cowardice and indifference? For long, I have struggled with this question. You are a coward when you flee from your battles. There are those battles where I have fought fiercely. I have belittled vast battalions of supremacy. Admittedly, I made them confess the menaces they are! But I have to acknowledge, it has been an endless war. Endless like an intractable conflict that has forced me into a prolonged state of self-alienation. After all, I am no King Jr. But, again I've caused change across the circles wherein I rotate. Sure, some pretend and keep appearances, but over time, many of them have changed. Even better, some of them now look down on those suffering self-proclaimed supremacists.

To date, I've never hesitated to display my utmost disapproval of race-based entitlement among my peers. Deliberately, I lay down my diagnosis, "Oh, you're racist!" With my offensive, they retaliate viciously. Tallying against their defensive claims, I start my course of treatment. Among those suffering this illness are the retaliating generalisers. For in my experience, this escalating state is quite common. Racism can be a contagious disease. Well, not always! It depends on one's immunity to derogatory stereotypes. It starts as a defence mechanism; which in turn and later time, transforms the victim into a perpetrator. Upon the diagnosis of this symptom, I will declare, "Oh you're racist now!" As the denial of the illness is voiced aloud, I become all ears. The sardonic smile never fails to amplify an aggressive tone of dissing the new victims. From that point on, a subtle dose of antidote is given at my expense. Now of course I've lost a lot of patients. But who cares! In my town there is an old saying that goes "Tell me who you befriend, I tell you who you are." The implication is clear and thus, my conscience says, *Son they ain't right for you.* If only I were on a civilizing initiative, I would've been an atheist apologist against the faith in genetic and social supremacy. But I am no preacher. So as the voice of their priests chanting, "In Racism we Trust" and their applause gets louder, I find myself in a limbo of conscience, out of my depth, just an exhausted heretic, in a purgatory, yet denying submission.

Chapter 5

The Whore

Lying down on the bed, spooning Jennifer, I started trailing kisses from the nape of her neck to her dimples of Venus and back to her neck, yet again. Our fingers were intertwined, forming a moving fist that gently went back and forth from her thigh to the arches of her backside. The irresistible temptation of her long, curved back, rekindled in me the recently sated desires, taking me to places beyond my physiological limits. My automatic, yet well-calculated touches and the absence of rhythmic breathing had the power to awaken in her a growing feeling of need and hunger.

"You're killing me," she breathed, freeing her hand from mine and, with it pushing the back of my head towards hers. "Darling, please sleep by my side tonight," she pleaded.

"I am really sorry, sweetie. I've got some work to do. You know the time difference. I'll get back to bed, once I am done."

"I will wait for you."

"No, sweetie, please don't. It'll take a while. Besides, we have to wake up early."

"Take a shower first," she distracted.

After finishing my shower, I wrapped a towel around my waist and leaned on the bed. I kissed her few times before whispering, "I'll go to the living room. I might have to speak loudly. I don't want to disturb your sleep." Jennifer kissed me a few times, as I carried her to the bathroom. I lowered my arms so her feet landed balanced on the wet, tiled floor. Standing in front of me, she grabbed my hands and stood on the tip of her toes to give me her goodnight kisses.

After dressing myself, I carried my laptop to the living room, seated myself, and lit a cigarette. I downloaded a file from an email. There was no subject, no text, just a video file. After it had downloaded, I fixed my earphones so the sound came only to me. The video appeared to have been captured through a hidden camera, though the quality was fine. Marzooq and a ginger-haired young woman were the only two in the room. The room seemed to be so small. It had a single bed and a closed window just above it. The video started moments before the redhead seated herself on the bed and persuaded Marzooq to sit closer to her. She spoke in a Damascene accent. She was probably seventeen or eighteen. She looked too young. Marzooq was sixteen, the oldest former Jihadi in the group.

The redhead didn't have much in the way of skills. She put an arm on his shoulder and rubbed his thigh with her free hand. I couldn't hear what she whispered in his ear, not that it was important or that I cared for it. He looked away. I was afraid he wouldn't do it. She undressed herself. He didn't make any moves, though he didn't leave the room. I thought either he or she would flee. However, he didn't seem to mind. *It's a good sign*, I kept telling myself. Without any sign from him or indication from her, she knelt, and unzipped his fly. "Ohh hoo," I clapped my hands, "Finally," I laughed. He was erect before she gave him what she thought was oral sex. I guess she got bored and wanted to get it over with. I stopped watching the moment his animal took over, placing himself on top of her.

I lit another cigarette and hunched over, sighing with my elbows anchored on my thighs and my hands rubbing my face. "That's fucked up, real fucked up shit," I sighed. With the cigarette between my index and middle fingers, I found myself opening a file in a folder titled academic. I scanned it quickly.

The notion that individuals' exposure to and memory of politically motivated and sectarian violence manifests in powerful emotional episodes that elicit a gamut of negative attitudes and behaviours, that such states justify hostility and violence, prompts a critical question: What can be done to overcome such barriers to peace? Extrapolating on political, psychological, and marketing research, an eclectic answer to this urgent question is described. This new answer hinges on the idea that marketing concepts and applications might be useful in reducing emotions that hinder peace and post-conflict reconciliation. Moreover, the current endeavour pursues addressing two complementary objectives. On the concrete level, it builds on recent trends in social cognition, political psychology, and marketing, aimed at describing conscious and unconscious information processing in shaping an individual's assignment of emotion-based brand equity of out-group. In a broader sense, theoretically it demonstrates the process by which the exposure to marketing applications manifests in the elicitation of

> implicit and explicit emotion-based
> brands of out-group, and thereby
> enhances political attitudes that facilitate
> efforts toward peace and post-conflict
> reconciliation.

Ten months ago, I started that little project. I admit that, since then, I have strayed from following up on it. In reality, I ended up in an endeavour to de-radicalise former child jihadis. If you want to reach out to the poor, middle class, former rebels, real activists, victimising, self-centred, self-proclaimed activists, real activists, real victims, victims for benefits; boy, even former and wannabe jihadists, Şanlıurfa is the place. It's easy to tell a real activist from the Facebookers. The Facebook victimisers believe themselves to be the only true activists without whom nothing can be achieved. Yet they've done nothing except tell lies that don't add up outside of their twisted heads. They have the ability to drill a vagina in your skull just to rape it afterwards. I was fortunate enough to have made the acquaintance of two real activists, not your go-with-the-flow kind of people.

Akram and Hothefa stood against the regime not only in demonstrations; they also carried arms. When things went extreme Islamic bananas, they organised demonstrations against the al-Qaeda affiliate Jabhatu Al-Nusr; then against the ways of ISIL. They held their ground and ideals until they had no choice but to save their necks. The old law of an eye for an eye didn't make them blind to the fact that another man's terrorist wasn't their freedom fighter. They knew the dangers of ethnic separatists, the bottom-feeding Muslim Brotherhood who'd been thus far hiding behind the assigned leadership of the Syrian National Council, even after being forced to rebrand as the National Coalition. They were not part of the mainstream that hadn't wanted a foreign intervention but then cried for it; Akram and Hothefa had wanted it all along, before Sunni terrorism started to sweep the country. The guys weren't deceived by the Ponzi Scheme of Moderate Islamist Opposition that everybody kept hearing about, yet when names were named, they were no better than the regime or the radical Islamists. They didn't cry for some buildings or ancient sculptures more than the worst humanitarian catastrophe of the twenty-first century. They knew the actual definition of terrorism and thus, the regime, Iran, ISIL, and all those who used the tactic of civilian intimidation for political purposes were branded as such. Foremost, they weren't some half-assed-Middle Eastern-conspiracy-theory-submitters; for them information was there and analysis was extrapolated on it. I respected them and picked their brains on many occasions. They were a reliable source of information.

It was their support that I sought when I started my academic project. I wanted to train them on how to conduct the required experiments, recruit participants, and register data. We talked about it for a while. Hothefa brought to my attention the names of sixteen former child jihadies. The children were from my city. They had been, as Akram put it, brainwashed by ISIL. I asked the guys to persuade the children's parents of the immense need for some sort of psychological intervention. A Rehabilitation Program is what we called it. For everybody, even the kids themselves, it was an English course and I was the tutor. You'd think of the power of persuasion necessary to convince parents of such a need would be enormous. However, it was quite easy. In fact, most parents facilitated the thing and even paid for outdoor trips. Twelve out of the sixteen enrolled in the 'English lessons.' Three were not convinced and instead forced their kids into child labour. There was this one parent who cursed the guys for trying to make his child an infidel. The parents sat in that same small room where Marzooq would lose his virginity. I explained to them the steps involved in the treatment, its behavioural and cognitive components. I could sense some cynicism at the beginning, but they were desperate and willing to do whatever it took to rehabilitate the shit out their children. Even when I said that there might be side effects, they gave me their blessing. I told them that their kids might never enter a place of worship again and that they should give them all the freedom needed in order for the program to succeed. I demanded avoiding all topics of Islamic nature; still, they gave me the go-ahead.

****

Some of the children had been smuggled out of Ar-Raqqa right after graduating from ISIL indoctrination and training camps. Some of them fought for ISIL. Hothefa shared with me the account of a veiled kid who recounted the course of ISIL recruitment, their theological courses, their morning exercises, their army training. He talked in length about the money they paid: Two hundred dollars, he claimed. In comparison, that was the monthly pay of a degree holder. He showed the smartphone given by ISIL. He claimed that they distributed Galaxies and iPhones to all the kids. On his phone the kid played a number of ISIL's non-melodic songs and audio messages of their caliph or spokesman.

The kid told a story of a child recruit who had ratted on his mother. She disobeyed the ISIL ban on smoking. The poor woman was lashed twenty-six times. Another former jihadi account was that those who were too young and from Ar-Raqqa worked as informants on the residents. Kids no more than ten years old making sure that residents were following the ways of ISIL! He claimed to know a child who took revenge on a shopkeeper who had slapped him. Apparently, the fifty-something-year-old didn't take it well when the kid hit his daughter for not displaying ISIL's code of repression. Eventually, the man was blindfolded and seated on a white plastic chair before his executioners threw him from a building in Karnak square in Ar-Raqqa. He was stoned to death after his fall.

****

I sighed with the smoke going out my mouth and nose. Marzooq was one of the children undertaking the rehabilitation program. He was the oldest kid. Through the English Skype sessions, I gave them all the support that I thought they needed; I befriended them on and offline. I contributed some cash to pay for the cost of dancing and drawing lessons, weekly pizza lunches in the city, transportation, movie tickets, et cetera. I did teach some English though. For in these classes, I found ways to cultivate in them a sense of admiration to the American ways, sympathy toward the victims, and most of all identifying with empathetic and intelligent figures. The kids were too mature for cartoons to be an option; besides, they didn't like them. Movies provided a wealth of characters that could induce changes in the kids. I sent those dubbed movies, or ones with Arabic subtitles, always selecting movies with sympathetic and empathetic individuals. The children's homework was to tell me about those figures; why they did what they did, their motivations, their impact. I took these people and glorified them, eliciting an admiration towards them.

War movies, like the Lone Survivor, The Pianist, The Hurt Locker, and Beyond Borders came later. The characters under the scope were those who displayed heroic humanitarianism, the musician and victim of Nazi brutality, the marines. Upon my request, before screening any movie, Akram screened movies of all sorts of political and sectarian motivated violence, be it state-sponsored terrorism and Shiite-based terrorist groups or Sunni-based terrorism. No villain was spared, even the Kurd separatists. All the screened videos started with the attack, execution, and humiliation, followed by the aftermath, and ended with the humanitarian scars. The lion's share was on brutality and its victims; the story of victims and terrorised eyewitnesses. The children had experienced first-hand real fucked-up shit. But there were no psychopaths. Some of them wept. We had prolonged conversations about the victims, their suffering. The brutality of all villains, the tragedies. I made a point to convey the political motivation of parties causing civilians misery, be it with the regime or against it. I made it a point to strip them from any good for the people of Syria. I outlined their agenda and deceptive tactics. I showed the real hypocrisy between what they claimed to be and what they actually did, creating an incongruence of belief in the children. Then, it was war movie time!

Be Smart was the part in which emotional regulation and critical thinking training took place. I hid behind the title to nurture within them all sorts of implicit and explicit emotional regulation. Empathy towards the victims was the aim. Increasing their hatred of the villains was central. Increasing the humiliation and shame of being identified with ISIL was also at the heart of the intervention. Improving their critical thinking and problem-solving abilities was the key to achieving such objectives.

Outdoor activities, dance, and drawing lessons helped introduce the kids to regular children.

Sharing things in common and mingling with the Turks elicited a notable desire to adapt and the urge for some sense of belonging. Going out for lunch or that trip to the sea assisted them in relating to regular kids and gave them some perspective of what their lives could be. Of course, I wouldn't have been able to do that without the help of Akram and Hothefa.

Our rehabilitation program seemed to work. Some of the kids went back to school. Some of them stuck to the art classes. I was asked by a fourteen-year-old kid to get him the photos of some Korean, female singers. Korean drama and K-Pop are quite popular among Syrian kids. In the last months of the course, whenever I brought up the subject of ISIL, a strong river of juvenile insults poured out the kids' mouths. Marzooq or the jihadi name he went by, Abo Hamza Ar-Raqaouy, was the exception. Masood, his father, called me. He applauded our success with the other kids and hoped we could manage to elicit a lasting change in his child. His father reminded me of how his eldest son had escaped to Syria a couple months before he started the course. His friend, a commander in the Free Syrian Army, held him in a town in the vicinity of Aleppo for few days before getting him back to Turkey. Marzooq threatened, "I am going back to fight for the Islamic State, no matter what. You're all infidels, my mother and sisters. You've lost your ways." His father cried begging for help. I assured him that I'd do my best. He gave me permission to do whatever it would take.

****

I sent Akram a message to video call me through Skype. Marzooq was not there yet. We smoked and talked about the news making headlines; mostly about the Ferguson shooting. It was a while before Marzooq arrived. I demanded a private conversation with him. Akram left the room singing one of those Raqqan folk songs. Marzooq and I laughed. He seemed calm. "How are you these days?" I asked

"I am fine, what about you teacher?"

"I've been better."

"God bless you teacher."

"No, there is no god. You can thank me and tell me of your good wishes but please don't insult me with this god shit."

"I pray to Allah to put you in the right path. I pray you can see the light."

"Save me the bullshit…"

"Is there something wrong? Did I do anything wrong?"

"I don't know, you tell me!" I let it hang for a while.

"I think I should go," he broke in.

I requested, "Please stay; don't go. I need to talk to you."

"What about, teacher Adam?"

"Is there anything bothering you at home?"

"No, things are fine, nothing out of the ordinary."

"Do you need anything, some allowance maybe?"

"I don't understand…"

"If there is anything I can do, do let me know."

"Did my father talk to you?"

"Actually, yes; he did talk to me. Your father is concerned. You're breaking his heart!"

"What did I do?"

"You want to go back to ISIL…"

"The Islamic State, you mean."

"Islamic State, my ass. Rapist-slave masters-bloodthirsty thieves and idiots."

"Teacher don't insult my religion."

"If your religion is ISIL, I'll fuck it and after I am done, I'll shit over it."

"I am going out…"

"Give me just a second, two more minutes."

"Okay, but you don't say shit."

"Okay. Shit I won't say. Can I ask you something and please humour me; maybe I will be convinced. Why are you going back? Why ISIL? Why not others?"

"Because Jihad is my duty. It's called the Islamic State not ISIL. The FSA is a group of liberal infidels! The Islamic State is the only true Islamic caliphate. Defending the state is my duty."

"Liberal infidels, FSA; I really wish so. So your father said that in few days you are going back to Ar-Raqqa. Are you?"

"Yes. The Islamic State not Ar-Raqqa. There is no force under the sky that can prevent me from doing so."

"Don't be so sure."

"If it's the last thing I do; nothing but death can prevent me."

"There is a video on the desktop. Please open it."

He clicked on the video and I could hear its sound. He closed it immediately. I remember telling the guys to say that it would take them no less than an hour before they got back before leaving Marzooq with the redhead. The kid's expression showed humiliation and anger.

He sat speechless for a while. I expected him to shout, *what are you going to do?* The camera went off. I thought he had ended the call. I tried to call again but I couldn't get through. I tried to reach Akram and got a little worried after the sixth time he hadn't picked up. When he finally answered, everybody was swearing. Hothefa's voice sounded as though he was struggling to control the kid. Akram and Hothefa recounted the way Marzooq had reacted. He'd been about to smash the computer before Hothefa punched him, launching the kid onto the bed. Akram dragged Marzooq to his parents' house. The guys told me that Marzooq's father locked him up in a room for a few days. My guess was that the father had been too scared of his son making a run for it.

When I saw Marzooq the next time around, his face was a mess. Akram had slapped him and threatened to call the Turkish police, should he leave the room. But it would take more than a slap to put a black eye on his face; Akram claimed that it was the kid's father.

From the moment Marzooq caught a glimpse of me, he used every demeaning expression in his arsenal. Swearing at me, he called me a bastard, twink, and kept going on and on. I actually giggled when he described me as sucker of crusaders' cocks. Hothefa was double the volume of the kid. I heard him shouting before he made his way past Akram to kick the kid on the hip. Hothefa gripped the kid's face and forced him to sit.

The first words I heard were, "Fuck you, I don't give a fuck."

"I see! You don't give a fuck but if you dare to leave Turkey, I'll send the video to all activists' Facebook pages. I'll upload it on ISIL's supporter pages. You don't need to be smart to know what ISIL will do to you. They will stone you to death; lash you if you're lucky. I cannot stand by idly while watching you fuck your life, let alone branding your parents and sibling as a terrorist's family."

"Dare you bring up the subject again, I'll put the video on the internet. Stop taking the lessons, I'll put it on the internet. Meddle with your sisters' way of dressing, I'll put it on the internet. Raise your voice, talking to your father, I'll put it on the internet."

Marzooq left without saying a word. Nine days later, the kid and his father were waiting for me. I was a bit late. After greeting the father and the guys, I requested to have a one-to-one conversation with the kid.

"Please let's talk…"

I could sense his fear before softly he asked, "What do you want?"

"Should I repeat what I told you last time?"

"That's it?"

"Yes, that is it. We all want what's good for you, I hope you understand that."

"I won't go back. I don't want to talk about that again. I will start working tomorrow. I won't bother anyone."

"No, you'll go to school. That's what your father wants."

"I will."

"You can go now, but don't forget that we all want what's best for you."

"Thank you, teacher Adam." Shackled by his shame, Marzooq wanted to get it over with. At that moment, I realised that the kid would go to extreme lengths to put the whole thing in the past.

****

Instructions were given to the parents to ensure a lasting effect on the kids. Our rehabilitation program took almost a year; three times a week. Except for Marzooq, for whom the course stretched for more than two years. After my last conversation with the kid, Akram noted, "When your science failed, it was the whore who saved the day. Is that what you call political marketing?" I laughed and argued, "I wouldn't use the word 'whore'."

Chapter 6

God's Narration

Before Jennifer was in the picture, there was Anna. She abused the filthy habit more than I; she was the only person I knew who smoked more than me. She was a great cook though. Out of almost nothing, she'd prepare wonders. We had nothing in common whatsoever, except for one person. Carl was an old friend of hers. A self-righteous punk singer, whose shortcomings brought Anna and me closer to each other. She had a fucked-up past. At only thirteen years of age, her mother passed. The big fucking C had murdered a few people I admired; my grandfather, my friend's father, the nicest, and the most cultured neighbour of mine back home. Her mother survived its agonising pain for years before the merciless fucking disease put her to sleep. Little Anna then had to endure her drunken father's abuse while raising her younger sister.

She spent a year in Australia before she made it to the Island. You could tell that the woman was broken, at many levels. Even by Middle Eastern standards, the tales of her ex-Australian douche of a boyfriend made the vast number of misogynistic men I have come across look more like progressive feminists. Before our affair started, she and Carl would come to my place at the weekends. Anna would cook a meal for Carl and me, while I cooked for her. No honey, milk, or eggs, let alone meat; it didn't leave me too many recipes to choose from. On occasion she'd teach me how to make Italian.

We didn't go out on a single date. The first time Carl ditched us for some dinner, we ended up in my bedroom. I had something of an obsession with that flat stomach of hers. Man, that sex was so aggressive, even by my standards. Not that I was complaining! She was kinkier than me, far beyond your most kinky fetishes. I loved it! Before her, I thought the human body was only capable of so many things. There was no arrogance, no guilt or full submission; it was a fight of some sort. Bruised, breathless, showered in sweat in that arctic room of mine was the aftermath of two savages' affair.

I still remember when I laid out my lifelong philosophy. I guess my anxiety at the time had to do with me waiting on the results of the university's fellowship programme. She comforted, "Adam, be positive, I hope you're lucky enough to get it." I challenged, "Anna, good luck is only an illusion. I work three times as hard, yet there is a chance that things might go south. In fact, things have the habit of going that direction. For in bad luck, I am a believer."

She responded, "You're probably right. I should rephrase. Adam, you might not get it, but you need to be resolved to cope with that. What I'm saying is that luck isn't about getting what you want. It is about surviving a bad situation and making the best out of it." I was not sure whether she had read, heard, or come up with that by herself. But I have to admit, it sounded compelling to me. I realised, *there might not be things like good or bad luck. I might've been lucky all along, figuring things out in the worst of situations and passing through different stages of grief in a short span of time.*

Anna was a lot of things, though I doubt she ever understood the impact she had on me. She was not intelligent in the scientific sense. But her life experiences compensated for all of that. She had reinforced in me a desire not to relapse when overwhelmed by the aftermath of severe misfortunes. Acceptance and looking forward, no matter how shitty the impact of falling short in the face of hardship, were the keys to her happiness.

For long I'd wrestled with that notion. Though, I have to say that living by her code somehow made me less miserable. In her words, "I live day by day.

115

Things could go extremely wrong." At times I'd hit a wall. In the morning, I was a new person with the right to be happy, like a newborn. Happiness is a state of mind and I'd choose to be positively moved by the little things. Happiness could be a smile from a stranger, a funny joke, a nice meal. Happiness for me was the absence of misery. Ever more, I actually tried to live by her philosophy. However, half a day in I'd relapse. After too many trials, I reckoned, I lacked the tenacity needed for finding that elusive emotion. Ever since I'd known her, she'd been a puzzle, an oxymoron of some sort. As broken as she was, Anna was by far the person most capable of happiness I knew.

Maybe I still endeavoured to change people around me, even after Anna taught me how to fully accept others. Although part of me had always known that she was right. I wasn't oblivious to how I could sometimes be a tool. After her, I revised my understanding of my own sapiosexuality. Science and literature might be at the centre of an individual's intelligence, yet sometimes all it takes to be intelligent at the logical and inter- and intrapersonal levels is first-hand experience.

I recalled a time when I asked her, however subtle, to behave in way I thought was more mature. Her natural response was to rush out of my place. I knew at the time that I had no right to ask such a change of her. Barefoot, wearing short pants and an old tank top, I followed her to the bus stop. The bus driver took pity on me, allowing me to ride without paying the fare. Obviously, he thought I was a smelly unstable homeless beggar. He forced me to sit away from Anna, scared of what I might do. I am sure I saw her try to hide a smirk. She didn't have to hide it, I had that one coming.

I knew her station but got down a stop before. I was scared of the bus driver's reaction. I thought he might chase me away from her or not allow me to get off at that stop. She might've thought that I'd given up and decided to retreat. It would've taken me hours to walk back to my place. Towards her place I scurried. From afar, I could detect her figure. Furious but concerned she slapped me. "Don't do that again asshole," she yelled at me. She took my hand firmly and led me to her apartment. I'd failed to come out with a proper apology and tried to gather my thoughts. Meanwhile, she gave me the silent treatment all the way to her room. In there I shred myself to pieces. It was the only way I knew to pay my sincere apologies. I realised the mistake I had made. It was one thing to compromise; it was another to change your whole character.

Despite the little she had, she always gave to those she thought deserving of help. As a cook she had access to the restaurant's leftovers. It was a kind of ritual for her to give them to the homeless men in the touristy parts of Georgetown. Thursday was her one day off. On Wednesday nights, she used to buy Tesco's discounted meat and vegetables. We agreed to cook for the homeless of Georgetown weekly at our expense. On a couple of occasions, we hadn't had much luck finding those in need in that area. We figured out that the poor had a habit of setting up by places of worship. We would fill the tank of Carl's girlfriend's car so he could drive us around town. She was one of a kind. Somehow, she never failed to bring out the best in the people around her. Before our thing became mechanical, it brought me some joy.

During my short time with her, she tried to uncover my most tragic emotional scars. Every night after sex, she'd bring about tales of hardship. Then it would be my turn to talk. She would recount the stories of her ordeals in third person narration, as though it had happened to someone else. She had a term for it. God's narration was what she called it. It was like the marks her agonising past left on her were war scars. She was proud of them as though they were medals of honour. For her, surviving them affirmed how lucky she was. I admit that it felt weird having to pour out my personal tragedies as bedtime stories. For in me, it was like that lyric in which the singer describes the emotional walls he used to cover all his vulnerabilities. I have no idea how to describe it, but witnessing her willingly expose herself brought forth in me a desire to break down my walls, stripping myself of all armour. After all, I had my share of depressing tales. I'd follow the narrative style she employed. I'd thought, *this will distance me from my emotions*. I was wrong.

Part II

Chapter 7

Our Values

When he woke up in the common room in the cold of a grey early morning, Adam rose, pushing off the thick edge of a neatly sewn blanket. "Good morning mama," he yawned, placing the palms of his hands over the sides of his slack-jawed face, like Munch's Scream painting. At that sight, sullen Warda's pale doleful face transformed into a grin, though it still didn't manage to hide her wan eyes. "Good morning son," she said. Adam's older brother, Fadi was still sleeping peacefully. Warda pulled the blanket off him and gently touched his bruised cheek as though casting a healing spell on him. Fadi opened his eyes to see his brother eagerly waiting for him to get up. Through a grungy scratched wooden door, Warda walked the two shivering children across the brown soil of the side courtyard that bleak winter morning. Warda sensed her children's fear as they stared at the ghastly frosted water tap.

Their house reflected poverty; it would have made the most unfortunate character of Victor Hugo's *Les Misérables* pity whoever resorted to it seeking shelter. It was old and unpainted. The roof was made of thin transparent plastic sheets that were covered with rusting tin sheets. These were placed over the top layer of the walls' concrete bricks. Some large bricks were placed on the top of them to hold the roof from falling when wind blew. Looking down on it, it resembled one of those Sumatran houses in the aftermath of the 2004 Christmas tsunami. It had only two small rooms facing the tiny side courtyard where an unfinished, roofless bathroom and toilet connected the parents' room with an unfinished concrete brick wall. Through surface wiring, each room had a plug and two switches fixed to their right walls. A bulb in each room dangled from the ceiling. There were no luxuries, not even a chair. For sleeping, Adam's family shared three thin mattresses and two blankets. They were six in all.

The rusty, unpainted front door split the full-length wall. There were two metal windows, one for each room. They were made for seeing the yard, not the outdoors. The only water tap emerged from the wall that linked the bathroom and the toilet.

Warda filled a plastic red kettle and handed it to Fadi. "Go to the toilet," she instructed. Meanwhile she'd stood with Adam on the square metre of unpolished concrete that covered the ground under the water tap. While waiting for Fadi, she washed, then dried Adam's face and hands with a faded blue towel that was placed over her left shoulder. Warda rubbed her cold pink hands against each other and looked at Adam's light brown shivering face, "It's too cold, go inside son." As Adam ran toward the common room his brother walked out of the toilet.

A heavily built, herculean middle-aged man, with arms like sledgehammers emerged from the parents' room, making his way toward Warda and Fadi. Hazem had a receding hairline, an angular tanned face, and a Greek nose. Hazem bent toward Fadi until his five o'clock-shadowed face was a breath away from his eldest son. Fadi pursed his lips with a gracious smile, "Good morning father." "Good morning son," he replied as he kissed both his son's cheeks. His piercing black eyes caught a glimpse of Warda's almond-shaped, brown, sorrowful eyes. "How are you feeling," he muttered. "I have been better," Warda mumbled. He leaned against the toilet wall, near the water tap, and lit a cigarette. He sucked on it as if it was his only source of oxygen. Inhaling deeply, he waited for Warda to finish washing Fadi's face and go back to the common room.

Warda picked a pair of jeans and a burlywood school uniform shirt from a clothes stand hanger. She dressed Fadi. "Go be seated next to Adam," she instructed after she'd finished fixing his hair. Fadi turned the TV on before he sat close to his brother.

Their black and white set was placed over a large, blue plastic fruit container. Through the door, into the room, Warda carried a metal kettle and walked toward a steel table with a stove on top. The stove was connected to a gas cylinder below via a black hose. The children and their mother were barefoot. The ground was unpolished concrete and partially covered with plastic outdoor mats.

Adam was only five years old. It was the first time he'd seen graphic scenes on television. It was Channel One of Syria's state television. The anchor reported that a Palestinian man bombarded himself in a bus, killing eleven Israelis. Adam and his brother sat by the old small stove to witness the scene of the paramedics treating the injured. Meanwhile, the anchor had kept chanting, "Victory!"

Warda came back with a large chrome tray on which she carried a kettle of tea, empty glasses, a plate of yogurt, jar of olives, and few loaves of bread. Then she put the tray on the ground. "Kids stop watching that horrendous bloody scene and come to eat," she instructed.

"In a second," Fadi replied.

"Right now!" she insisted.

A few minutes later, Fadi was eating. After several minutes of observing his brother, a confused Adam wondered, "Do Israelis have children?"

"Okay."

"Okay what?"

"Yes they do."

"Do their mothers feel sad when they die?"

"I don't know."

"All parents love their children," a frowning Warda replied.

"They are sad. Is killing people wrong?"

"But Israelis always kill Palestinians," Fadi interjected.

"Why?"

"I don't know, my teacher says Israelis should be burned."

"Don't Israelis and Palestinians have children?"

"What is confusing you Adam?" Hazem queried while exhaling the smoke.

"The anchor said 'Victory'. A Palestinian killed by Israelis. Why?"

"Son. The killing of innocent people is in no way good news. It is terror, no matter who commits it."

"What's an innocent person?"

While breastfeeding her youngest daughter, their mother yelled, "Adam that's enough! Go play with your sister. Fadi it's getting late, you should be going to school."

Hazem looked at Warda and told her that Adam was a special kid. "This boy will bring us a lot of troubles," he laughed.

"What a life!" Warda sighed deeply, after Fadi and Adam had left and continued, "It is such a cold long winter. Adam wears Fadi's old sweater and jeans. My mother bought Heela a jacket. She has been talking about what a burden we've become. She never fails to stress her philanthropic deeds. Such a bitch! And I don't know how to describe your mother. The other day, she told Fadi how useless both of us are. She told him that she gave us three tomatoes. She is something. She asked a seven-year-old why doesn't he find a job? Despite all of her trashy jewellery, she couldn't get over three tomatoes. You need to get a job and stick to it. It is not fair that you still support your younger brother's studying expenses, let alone the monthly bribes you're paying to get your mother the weekly visit to your imprisoned brother. Your other two brothers are working in Saudi, saving their money, buying houses, and cars. Nobody appreciates what you're doing. Your brothers always get the credit. And for what? They do shit, yet they are the saviours. Somebody has to teach your imbecile family that giving is not equivalent to lending. I've been ill for months and everybody knows. What the fuck is wrong with people, a visit won't cost them anything. I'm a villager and no matter what, I will always be an outcast to them!"

Hazem listened, smiled demurely, and kissed Warda on her forehead the moment she'd finished venting her fury. Her eyes were watery on the brink of dissolving into tears. Warda raised her hands and looked up. She sniffed, cursing, "God where are you? God tell me in which casino you will be having your orgy. In the name of whores, what for? Why? A sadist bastard, that's who you are! Just tell me where are you? Son of a bitch." Warda kept going on. Hazem waited until she had stopped swearing, before he wiped away the tears that were coursing down her cheeks.

"Fairness is a childish concept," Hazem preached. He took a cigarette out of his shirt pocket, tapped it against the lighter, put it in his mouth and lit it. He continued, "Not everybody has the stomach to do honourable things. It might seem unjust. I might look like a waste of human sperm." He inhaled the smoke deeply, paused, and looked at Warda. As he exhaled, he affirmed, "We are damned poor. This is not a place to call a home. We live in a shelter. My kids slept hungry yesterday and my wife has been ill for a while. It kills me to see you suffer, it really does. However despite this, I cannot abandon my young brothers. I have a code. My other brothers might be selfish; might get all the credit. They might be laughing at us. But I want my children, our children to live by this code. I want Fadi and Adam to be men of dignity and honour. They will be, you will see. They will sacrifice anything for one another. They will be spoken highly of by everybody. They see me, they will learn. I know they will. I don't want my mother, your mother, my brothers and sisters to spare them the belittling of their parents. I want them to learn that in the worst situation, they have to be principled. I want them to take care of one another. I don't want them to seek recognition. I want them to help and stand by each other because it is right. Because they are family. Not in name only."

Hazem put down the tin can that he was holding and smashed his cigarette into it. He lifted Warda's pale, soft face with his rough hands. "Look into my eyes, honey." Her pink eyes reluctantly rose to his.

Hazem said, "Smile my love. We will be okay, we will be fine." He kissed her dry lips. He placed the palms of his hands on her thighs and rubbed them, whispering, "Our values must always be immune to unfairness. We must not allow any force to hijack our endeavours to do the right thing. Because if we surrender without a fight, what's the point?"

Chapter 8

The Orange

"I need books," a sobbing Adam pleaded to his mother.

It was the autumn of 1990, the year Adam turned six. Warda was breastfeeding Solaf. The whole family was sitting inside the common room, in a patch of light from the open window, on an outdoor plastic rug.

"Please try to understand… I cannot go to school without books," Adam tried to make his case.

"Today I will go to the public book store but don't do it again," Hazem harangued as his eyes glowered with anger.

Four days earlier, Adam had gotten his weekly allowance of one pound. On his way to school he bought an orange from a street vender. At the time, he thought he was in love with his teacher's daughter. Amira was very kind to him. In fact she was the first girl to sit beside him in the last row. Adam's face was as weather-beaten as a construction worker's in a hot and dry country. He had short black hair, an oblong face, and brown heavy-lidded oval eyes. He had his father's nose with a pointed tip and narrow nostrils. He was not the kind of kid found in unbought picture frames. He more closely resembled the face of an anti-child labour campaign. Amira was a classic Syrian cutie. She was as beautiful as a Disney princess. She had light brown, wavy hair, an oval face, a button nose, and large close-set green eyes. She was allowed to wear jewellery and dresses to school. Her favourite colour was pink.

"I got you an orange," Adam grinned, "I got you the biggest, the sweetest, the most juicy." With both hands Amira took the orange as the upper corners of her thin-lipped mouth quirked upward. Looking at her, the euphoric Adam couldn't help but blush.

"Silence! Be seated. You in the back, sit down!" Khadeja, the teacher yelled announcing her entrance to the classroom. "I am quite tired. Kids place your foreheads on your desk," she instructed as she took her seat.

After resting for several minutes, Khadeja asked the students to sit in a so-called ergonomic position. Half way through the math class, a younger teacher escorted Amira to her mother. "She's so beautiful," the younger teacher graciously smiled, kneeling to kiss Amira. "Thank you Farah, you didn't have to do that," Khadeja grinned.

"Do what? Oh you mean the orange. I did not, it's from one of your students," she smirked as she made her way out. From his front row seat and perhaps urged by the Syrian snitching genetic disorder, Mazen shouted, "It is Adam! I saw him stealing it from Abu Saleem. The street vendor was selling some to me when Adam stole it."

"Adam! You dirty boy, come here!"

With his head held down, Adam walked toward the front of the classroom. With a face full of shame he glimpsed his angry teacher. "I bought…" Adam tried to explain as he received the first slap on his face. She slapped him several times; each time harder than the last. She yelled, "Take your orange. A dirty thief, that's what you are." It was a shoot-first-ask-later kind of a situation. Adam couldn't take the humiliation any longer. In a brittle tone, he broke in "I bought it, I bought it, I really did. I love Amira!" Gratingly Kadeja lectured the little boy, "You will never be her equal, dirty boy! I know your family. Coming from that neighbourhood, what will you be? A waiter, maybe a thief. You're already there, little thief. Dirty boy, pick up the papers in this littered class; you might earn a career of it one day, if you're lucky."

The mortified little boy carried the trash bin and did what was asked of him. He sat silently until school time ended. Once the headmaster rang that reverberating bell, he sprinted away as fast as he could.

Chapter 9

The Thief

The summer of 1991 was quite hot. School holidays had started in early July, a month before. It was the year Adam turned seven. On that Tuesday morning, Hazem and Fadi had to leave home early. Adam's daily duty for several months had been to go to the bakery at the earliest hours of dawn to get the bread. Occasionally, Warda would ask her boy to shop for thick lamb yogurt. Not on that day though; they had some left over. Adam would wake up early to avoid fighting his way through the melee of rude, heartless adults. Some bakeries in Ar-Raqqah managed to coax their crowds to line up through fixed steel barriers. This method was not employed in any bakery in the immediate vicinity of Adam's neighbourhood; the closest on foot, was around forty minutes away.

Zain, the neighbour's kid, had been his journey companion; they had been friends for two years. Zain's father had always gotten his family the bread. He worked in a barbeque restaurant. Whenever he'd finished work, he would get it from the central bakery. Zain didn't need to join Adam on that long walk, but he usually did.

Adam was asleep beside Fadi. Adam was an early bird. He woke up at half past five. He was wearing shiny blue athletic pants and a white tank top. The pants were made from polyester. Adam raised himself and anchored his elbows, looking at Heela to his right and Fadi to his left. His mother had given him fifteen Syrian pounds before he'd gone to bed, so he wouldn't wake her up.

Adam pushed open the wooden door of his father's room and tiptoed toward his sleeping parents. Hazem's arm was over Warda's shoulder and his left knee was just above her right thigh. They both were snoring in rhythm; a duet of some sort. Adam tapped Warda on her shoulder and repeated, "Mama, mama, mama…"

She yawned and mumbled, "I told you not to wake me up!"

He stared at her for few moments and enquired, "Can I get a pound?"

His mother fell back to sleep and he studied her face for few seconds before he reached to her arm again. She muttered, "What do you want?"

He nagged, "I want a pound. Just one pound! Please mama, just one."

Irritated, she impatiently she ordered him, "Go and get the bread. I'll give it to you tomorrow." She fell asleep in few seconds. Adam stared at her and muttered, "That's what you said yesterday." As the sound of his mother's snoring rose, he made his way to the water tap in the centre of the courtyard.

After washing his face, he walked toward the other room to fetch his football shoes. He was very fond of them. His mother had got them from a thrift shop. They were red. Adam shuffled out of the house and to the right. He stood by the steel door of their second neighbours and shouted, "Zain, Zain, Zain, Zain…" He kept going on for several minutes until his friend came out. Zain's clothing style was almost identical to Adam's. They both wore blue athletic pants and white boys' tank tops. Their shoes were different brands, but both were red.

Placing a ball the size of a tennis ball under his right shoe, Adam excitedly announced, "On three we shall start! One, two, three!" He took the lead for couple of minutes until Zain brilliantly tackled him and gained possession of the ball. Zain juggled the ball from one foot to the other, as he was running, then passed it to Adam. While for the most of it they played against each other, they also practiced some team-based techniques. Their game lasted for almost half an hour. Zain was more skilled than Adam. He had even attended a number of matches between local teams with his father. Zain had often played with the older kids. Of the five-against-five street matches, he was the first to be picked and thus, players of the rival team sometimes bargained for six players to have a fair match. He was by far the most talented of the neighbourhood kids. Zain had acquired an obscure position on his team. When the match started, he was a defender, midfielder, and striker. On penalties he often became the goalkeeper. For the neighbourhood matches, football rules were meant to be broken. There was no referee. Zain earned the right to pick some of the players; especially, with the younger teams. Adam, against other players' desires, was selected by him.

The children walked between several alleys heading to Aum Mazen's house. She was in her late fifties, which seemed ancient to Adam and Zain. She had met them a number of times while queuing to get bread. She had made a deal with the kids. She paid them two pounds every day they got her the bread. Zain pointed, "There she is!" Aum Mazen was carrying the end of a water hose and with her thumb she closed almost half the halo ending to strengthen the water pressure. She was splashing the water on the brown soil in front of her door. There was a plastic chair on the pavement by her door.

Adam and Zain started giggling as they squeezed their bottoms on the chair. Zain laughingly asked, "Where is the tea, Aum Mazen?" She turned her head towards them and lowered it as her eyebrows went down. She stared at them, "Under the chair, bastards," she said in a shaky quivering voice. Once the words came out of her mouth, the children had belly-laughed until their eyes watered. Zain poured himself some tea. They had been looking at her splashing the water for several minutes before Adam elbowed Zain and queried, "What does bastard mean, Aum Mazen?"

The old lady, shakily teased, "You know, little fuckers! I know you do, dirty little shits!" The boys just cracked up. It was her voice that stimulated laughter in them.

Salma, Aum Mazen's youngest daughter, came out of the door and stood behind the chair. She was a twenty-six-year-old natural blond. Salma was quite tall. She tapped Adam on his shoulder and handed him twenty-seven pounds and greeted the children, "Good morning." Salma leaned her back, holding the chair's top rail.

Adam shouted, "Aum Mazen!" Once she looked at him, he continued, "Aum Mazen, I was thinking about a new deal…" She interrupted, "I am not going to pay you more. Forget about it, rusted, black street boy!"

"I am not a boy," Adam stood up and walked a pace towards her, "I am a young man. That's not the new deal. What say you that you keep our two pounds? Of course, as part of our deal! Say, fifteen years later that will be a lot of money. Under our new deal, you'll save me the money. Salma," he cleared his throat and looked back at Aum Mazen, "I love your daughter! So, Aum Mazen, consider the savings her dowry. Of course, if you agree to marry her to me." Salma and her mother cracked up. Adam tried his utmost effort to prevent himself from laughing. Aum Mazen, directed the water at the two kids and splashed them from head to toe, as they went in stitches making noisy giggling sounds. Adam and Zain started to run away as the old lady started calling them names.

"Oh, it's bad," Zain noted as they caught a glimpse of the crush of customers. The fixed steel barriers were hardly effective for organising the crowd. People would line up for hours, but if only one person pushed himself through, the rest almost always followed. Adam pushed his way through the messy crush of angry customers and found himself close to the window. It was very hard to breathe as his chest was pressed against the edge of the bakery window. He shouted out loud, "It's my turn!" placing his hands on both the edges of the concrete window frame and pushed as hard as he could to allow himself to breathe, "It's my turn, son of the bitches, it's my turn!" The bakery workers never bothered to cajole the crowds to be orderly. Occasionally customers would get very aggressive, leaving Adam with minor bruises. For his age, he was physically strong. Not as much as his older brother, though he compensated with courage.

Adam divided the bread. He carried theirs and Zain carried Aum Mazen's share. Before going to their neighbourhood, they made a turn to deliver the bread to the old woman. At the corner of their street, the minimarket owner was arranging the vegetable containers inside his store. Their pace slowed as the delivery truck faced them on its way toward the main street. Zain stopped by the shop to buy a cone of vanilla ice cream and Adam waited for him outside. Adam's mouth watered as he observed his friend licking it. Before parting ways, they agreed to meet after breakfast.

"Adam, you are here finally," Warda grinned from her place. His father, mother, and brother were sitting on a plastic mat around a few dishes, drinking some tea. It was like they were on a picnic in their courtyard. Adam laid the bread to his right and sat between his brother and father. He gave each a loaf and started dipping it in the yogurt plate. Adam took an olive and chewed before dipping a little piece of bread into the yogurt again. His mother conversed with Fadi. She cautioned, "Don't carry heavy stuff that will stop your growth."

"I just wash and hand them the brushes, soften the concrete wall with the glass papers, and get them food. There is no heavy stuff, Mama."

Adam broke in, "Show me your muscles, Fadi! Please, please show me."

"Fadi show him your muscles," laughingly Hazem said as he lit a cigarette. Proudly, his brother flexed his biceps. Adam exclaimed, "Ooh, very strong! I want to have them." Hazen laughed and announced, "Fadi get ready. We should be leaving." Warda walked her husband and son to the door and came back to collect the dishes. As she reached to the bread, she queried, "Don't you want to play outside with Zain? Your sisters are sleeping." Adam jumped to his feet and stared at his mother for few moments. "Tomorrow I will give you a pound," she noted. "You always say tomorrow," he complained. "Son, I promise," she assured. As he left, his mother carried the bread and two plates before disappearing into the common room.

Adam opened the door to see Zain sitting on the doorstep. He sat beside him and put his arm around Zain's shoulder. Zain claimed, "I waited for hours!" Adam laughed, "Don't lie! I have only been inside for forty minutes." "Ha, ha," Zain continued, "forty minutes," he grinned wider, "not forty-one, not thirty-seven, exactly forty minutes." Adam gave him an elbow. The children sat for a few minutes waiting for other kids to come out. Zain cautiously pulled a lengthy green elastic tube and pushed it from between his feet while distracting Adam with the passers-by. Zain succeeded in making Adam unaware of the object over his shoe's outsole. Zain waited patiently for a few moments for Adam to notice the object over his shoe. But his patience soon grew thin and he pushed and pulled the object until Adam spotted it. As he did, the child jumped with a frightened pale face and for a moment was breathless and unable to say a word. The youngster almost wet his pants before he shouted in a terrified voice: "Snake, that's a snake, that's a snake!" Looking at him, Zain broke up in a deep belly laugh and kept sniggering as he leaned his back to the door. He chortled as he pointed at the snake and assured him, "It's a plastic toy, you idiot!" Zain gloated for a while before Adam ran to him and started wrestling his friend on the doorstep. Sitting to his right, Zain noted, "I scared you."

"It wasn't scary," Adam claimed. Zain repeated rhythmically, "I scared you. I scared you. I scared you." Adam frowned and sat silently.

Adam and Zain knew it was still early for the other kids to come out and gather in the neighbourhood. Adam held out his hand and requested, "Let me see it." Zain handed him the toy. Adam noted, "It looks real," while inspecting the toy, "it looks very real."

"How do you know?"

"Last year, I saw one!"

"You didn't tell me."

Adam shrugged and continued, "It was a big black, male snake with horns."

"Horns?!"

Adam recounted, "Two; one to the right, and one to the left."

"Oooh!"

"It was very big and scary!"

"Adam, how could you tell it was a male snake? Did it have a penis?"

"I don't know," he shrugged, "I didn't see a penis."

"How did you know?"

"My uncle told me. He slithered by my legs; he was too fast; he didn't bite me."

"Slithered?!"

"Snakes cannot walk or run because they don't have legs. My uncle told me that snakes slither, not walk or run." Studying the toy, Adam continued, "It looks real. Nobody is out yet. Your snake is very scary. Do you want to scare somebody?"

"Nobody is out yet!"

"The Metraq's have already gone to their shop. All of them! So, they left Angry Dalia alone. Let's scare her."

"My mum grounded me once because I threw the ball at Dalia's window."

"Let's scare her. She won't tell anybody. We can tell them that we were playing with your toy. We can laugh at her. Let's do it, let's do it.' Adam stood up and dragged Zain with him.

Dalia felt persecuted by the children. She was in her late thirties and still unmarried. She was bipolar. On her best days, seeing Adam or Zain agitated her and aroused in her extreme outrage. The children were not aware of her condition; not that it would have changed anything. Her room had two doors;

one through a veranda and the other from across the living room. It was open to the street; with an entrance that marked the end of a low concrete fence. The entrance was in the middle and was connected to the street via three flights of stairs. The veranda was a gathering place for the elderly women of the neighbourhood. During summer, they sat and socialised there, from dusk until the early hours of the night.

Adam pulled Zain to climb the stairs and whispered, "Let's do it. Let's do it!" Giggling, "Let's do it," answered Zain, in hushed tone. They tiptoed gleefully towards Dalia's door. "Keep a look out," Zain instructed as he kneeled, slapping his hands against the tiled floor. Adam leaned forward and put his elbows on the low concrete fence.

Adam's patience ran out in a few seconds and he playfully stood by his kneeling friend. Zain pushed the plastic snake from under the broken bottom rail. The door had side stops but, for some reason, a threshold hadn't been installed. Zain kept hissing as he pushed and pulled the toy, trying to lure Dalia. He even knocked on the door. At this point, the children started to wonder whether she was even at home. But they hadn't given up on their prank just yet. Adam hissed louder and knocked on the door while he pushed the snake to its fullest length.

148

"Maybe the door is open," Adam said as he pushed it and continued, "See I told you! She is not here, maybe she's in the other room. Let's make some noise so she comes here." They stepped inside and started yelling loudly, "Dalia, Dalia, come here, Dalia, Dalia, come here." They ran toward the door and started to move the snake from under the bottom rail. Dalia did not come so they decided to attract her attention by entering her room again and yelling her name louder. The children were on the veranda for the third time, hoping that she would hear them and come to her room. Zain kneeled and put one hand on the floor and with the other pushed the snake. Adam was standing and looking at his friend.

"What are you doing boys?" A deep and croaky voice alerted the children to turn their heads toward the street. On the veranda behind them, stood a tall plump man. He was wearing a dirty uniform. Black and brown patches of oil and grease were all over his pants. Their original colour was probably dark grey. Large patches of industrial dirt made it hard to determine the shirt's original colour. He had a long beard with a few grey hairs emerging from under his chin. His hair was razor-shaved. Caught off guard, Adam and Zain looked at each other before Adam claimed, "It's our house. We are just playing!"

The man asked, "What's the game?"

Zain replied, "We are playing with a snake. It's plastic!"

"Ha, ha," the man laughed as he put his thumbs in his pockets. He enquired, "Is there anybody at home?"

Zain looked at Adam and answered, "No, my mother just went to the bakery."

The man inspected the street before turning to the children. He held out his hand and requested, "Let me show you how to play with it?" He took the snake and sat beside Zain. He shook the snake and placed his hand on Zain's thigh. "Give your uncle a kiss," he grinned. Zain acquiesced. Adam was standing and looking at his friend giving the strange man a kiss on each cheek. The man stood up and pushed the door as he instructed "You stay here," he pointed at Adam, "Knock on the door if anybody comes." Pulling Zain's hand, he led the child inside the room and set the door ajar. As instructed, Adam stood outside.

The man led Zain towards the centre of the room and asked him to sit, while he was still holding the plastic snake. Sitting opposite Zain, the man put four fingertips under the child's chin and demanded,

"Open your mouth." Studying the man's face, he shook his head in refusal. "Just open it," he insisted.

"No, no, I want to go," the child stammered. The man blustered in a louder tone, "Open your mouth!" The child silently shook his head and tried to stand up. The man pressed his hand against the child's thigh, forcing him to stay seated. Then, he dropped the snake and reached with his left hand to his right pocket. He pulled out a flick knife. With the tips of his fingers he held its handle and flicking his wrist in a speedy motion, opened the knife. He stared down at Zain as he pressed the blade against his shoulder. The knife was sharp enough to evoke a combination of pain and fear in the child.

Looking at the predator's eyes, Zain detected all clues of danger. The mixture of regret, pain, and helplessness alerted the innocent child to what the brute might have in store for him, stoking his fear. The anger that followed Zain's fear failed to enable the prey to flee. He was in no way a match to the aggressor facing him. Distressed, the child shed tears, pleading for mercy. With the side of the index finger of the hand that was forcing the innocent child's thigh onto the ground, the aroused man gave the subject of his desires a signal to stop and continue in silence. The strengthened force of the knife's edge scared the prey into submission.

The man kept the knife on the child's shoulder as he reached to the snake. "Be a good boy and I'll take the knife off you," the man purred into the child's ear, trailing the tip of his tongue across the child's earlobe. The child wept silently as the knife lowered. The aggressor kept the knife under his hand while he spun the elastic toy in pleasure. He loosened his grip, allowing the snake's head a shorter distance from his grip before holding it firmly. "Open your mouth, pretty boy," he instructed. The shivering boy nervously followed his instruction. The predator pushed the toy in strongly, hurting the child. The choking victim gagged. "Do you like?" the man whispered as he put his hand on the side of the child's face.

The tears were dripping onto the predator's hand and across the child's naked cheek. "You will enjoy it, if you stop crying," said the brute before his tooth reached the right vermillion border of his lower lip. He then unzipped his fly and pulled out his erect penis. 'The period of sickening grooming was now done'. "Do the same thing with it," he stared down at the terrified child. "Come here," he continued, pulling his prey. "No, no! Open your mouth wider and hide your teeth with your lips," he instructed while placing his grip on the crown of the child's head. Forced to give the brute oral sex, the child's tears coursed his cheeks while a mixture of mucus and tears was draining out of his nose, toward his lower lip and around the predator's penis. The liquid snot bubbled as the child struggled to breath.

"You're good! A fast learner," he breathed. "That's enough," he ordered, after pushing and pulling the nape of his suffocating prey's neck, back and forth in a fast manner. The aggressor unbuckled his belt and unbuttoned his pants. He held the child's hand and moved a few paces away. The child was now standing opposite the predator. Shivering, young Zain could not have anticipated the next course of brutal abuse. At the age of seven he couldn't comprehend the word sex, let alone rape. The disturbed aroused man placed his hands around the child's hips, turning him to the opposite direction. "Now, kneel on your knees," he insisted while applying force, "and put your hands on the ground." With the tips of his fingers he pulled down the child's pants and underwear. He held the child's hip in one hand and lowered his back by pressing the blade of the child's left shoulder with the other, in his attempt to penetrate the little boy.

The rapist pulled the child's hip strongly, failing to ravish him. The pain was excruciating and the child started to call out, shouting out loud "Adam, Adam..." The predator fumed, "Shut up! Be quiet and it'll end soon." At that moment Zain realised that his friend was not guarding the door anymore. The pain escalated and the child shouted his friend's name more times. The brute became more aggressive as the child kept shouting. "Shut up, shut up, shut up, shut up, shut up," he exclaimed, banging Zain's head against the ground every time he repeated his instruction. The first bang broke the child's nose and the next almost smashed his forehead. Over the unconscious victim's body, the outraged predator breathed heavily before he continued raping his prey.

Adam had left the veranda when Zain and the strange man entered Dalia's room. He'd caught a glimpse of his mother going to the grocery store. Craving a cone of ice cream he'd followed his mother. He'd stood by her while she picked the tomatoes, potatoes, and cucumbers. With the growing desire for vanilla ice cream, the child stayed at the store for a while. Warda was distracted by Dalia and Ahmad. Dalia was Ahmad's younger sister. The siblings made their way inside the shop. Ahmad walked towards the cashier's table. "Get me a pack of Marlboro," he requested. "Are you going to pay your condolences," Dalia asked Warda.

Looking at Dalia, Adam remembered his friend and ran to warn him of the Metraq's arrival. He pushed the door slowly, looking at the tiled floor. He noticed the knife and the streams of blood, almost two steps from the knife. There was too much blood. Looking at his friend trapped underneath the aggressor and the slow streams of blood emerging from Zain's nose and head, the petrified Adam froze. Standing there, the child felt the heaviness of the inhaled and exhaled air, while observing the back of the assailant and the side of his friend's face. Adam's eyes went dead and his legs slowly dragged him to the knife. The rapist was preoccupied; unaware of the child who was holding the knife just a few steps to the right and a couple steps behind him.

Adam moved toward the rapist with the knife in an ice pick grip. At a breath away from the aggressor's back he attacked, stabbing twice above the collar bone. The surprised brute straightened his back, turning towards Adam. The knife hadn't cut very deep. He threw the child a strong punch. Holding the knife while buckling his belt, he noticed a man standing by the open door and made a dart, pushing Ahmad to the ground. He jumped over the concrete fence and kept running. Ahmed hadn't noticed Zain's head but he recognised the gruesome scene of rape and saw the bruises around Adam's left eye. He rushed to the veranda, closing the door. Adam heard

Ahmad blurting, "Thief, thief, thief, thief!" before he re-entered and closed the door.

Adam's memories of the event grew fuzzy over the years. Some parts of it more than others. Even at the age of thirty-one he could still vividly recall Zain's mother moaning over her son. The woman keened over him with no care of the ancestral noise of her deepest grief. Her confused eyes and the way she pulled out her hair had haunted Adam for years. There wasn't anything left to be saved and, thus, nothing seemed worth repressing. She wailed without whimpering. The way she fiercely pushed Ahmed, trying to get to her son to hold him, left a deep scar in Adam's memory.

Days passed and Adam didn't leave the house. He didn't say a word. He only ate and stared at the empty courtyard from the living room. His parents tried but failed to provoke him to break his silence, until the day his father brought ice cream. It was a kind of a family tradition; Hazem would buy a lot of ice cream late at night and Warda would get two spoons for each. They would finish it all. That night, Adam didn't join them. He sat and observed the smoke his father had exhaled. With a confused expression, Adam suddenly enquired, "Why he shouted a thief?" Warda jumped on her feet and seated herself next to her son. She put her right hand on his thigh and rubbed it in support. The child looked her up and down and studied the movement of her hand for few moments. Her hollow-eyed child gave her a dead look, and moved her hand off his thigh. In a flat voice, "I am okay," he said. Something about the way he looked at her, or the way he sounded, or the way he rejected her support elicited grief in his mother. Her brimming eyes wept, mourning the loss of her son's childhood innocence. With the dangling ends of her scarf, she dried her falling tears. She stared at her husband who thinned his lips and closed eyes as he shook his head from the right to the left and then to the right again. From that day onward, Warda associated that signal with helplessness in the face of the deepest of loss.

Hazem mirthlessly grinned, "Who shouted 'thief', son?"

"Ahmad."

"Oh, that!' He thinned his lips and continued, "Son, it is complicated. Son, we live in an ocean of shit. Ahmad is a good man! Smart too! Son, beyond our ocean and some seas of dirt, just above the surface of faeces and urine, there is a world of civilized creatures. Physically, they are indistinguishable from us. Out there they have two words that are beyond the realm of our comprehension. Sympathy and

157

empathy! Sympathy and empathy, son! These evolved creatures experience regret for others' misfortunes and hardships; they don't have to experience the pain but still they show sympathy. Son, some even imagine themselves or their beloved ones in the same situation; they put themselves in the shoes of those cursed with sufferings, so to speak; they don't only regret what victims might have endured but also, willingly simulate victims' experiences, anticipating and feeling their emotional states. Out there, those who lack such abilities are called names. Psychopaths!" Hazem fixated at his lit cigarette end sighing out the inhaled smoke. His irises moved up studying Adam's face. Hazem was not sure whether his son was comprehending what he was saying or had lost interest before he added, "You all know a guy who was raped in this swamp of shit. They call him, 'Damaged Ass'. A name the kids in the neighbourhood shout, bullying him. Everybody laughs at him, even you, Adam! Children and adults, alike, name and shame the poor teenager. Ar-Raqqa isn't known for any sense of empathy. In the dearth of sympathy, preying on victims of sexual abuse starts at the moment of assault and follows the survivors to their grave. It changes everything. It makes them unfortunate, outcasts; nothing but victims."

Part III

Chapter 10

The Technique

A mixture of helplessness and anger had become the usual bedfellow of my morning routine. Quite often, it had been a struggle to arise from under the thin covers. I always found refuge in my first cigarette. As I inhaled the smoke, eyes to the ceiling fan, my worries would begin. Reading the news with little energy or hope amplified my sense of helplessness. Admittedly at some subliminal level, I was still a naïve little boy. My highly unsophisticated idealistic subconscious rekindled certain emotions. Beyond my conscious control, my nose flared, my lips pursed and thinned, while my cheekbones and mouth rose as my chin quivered. Staring back at the ceiling fan, a subtle a sense of defensiveness and a forced smirk dissipated all my anger. Letting go of my childhood-entitled fury, I started my holistic process of political, economic, and cultural analyses of the news headlines.

Pushing my elbows against the bed, or to be exact against the mildly painful metal springs, I felt its resistance. As I exhaled, I felt a rush of blood that forced a minor erection.

"Not today", I muttered. Pushing the rest of the thin cover off, I stood up looking at the window, noticing the construction workers on a site close by. I always wondered whether they could see my total nakedness. In few steps, I reached the bathroom sink. After I finished the morning ritual of taking a leak, washing my hands, washing my face, brushing my teeth, and washing my face again, I put on my old pants and walked out to the living room. For some reason I was unaware of, I kept forgetting something in my room, so I kept going back and forth until finally I fetched my laptop and placed it on the small table. After reading all the news on BBC, CNN, and Al Jazeera, I turned to Facebook to read more news.

"It is almost 10.00 a.m., fuck I hate that shit," I mumbled. I was supposed to meet Professor Nora at eleven. Not long ago, I became her ghost author. I had managed to finish her year-long project in a couple of months. Fuck poverty! I only earned three hundred dollars out of her sixty thousand dollar project. Her current grant was even bigger. I had already finished two articles in less than a month. Over many emails, she'd made it clear that I was unworthy of being paid even the minimum wage. My last work had been published in a reputable journal. The latest manuscripts were even better.

It was barely fifty cents per hour. Somebody from the right demographic would be paid nine hundred a month for publishing only two articles a year. I don't know what she was expecting. I'd finished them in a month. Sighing heavily, I was reminded by my father's lifelong saying: fairness is a childish concept.

****

I was feeling angry. Outraged, actually! I figured it had not been a good idea to go to the café. I knew I wouldn't be able to do any writing. I was about to ride my bike back home when I felt a vibration in my pocket. Getting my phone out, I recalled I was supposed to be meeting my buddy, Mike for a cup of coffee. Looking at the screen, I muttered "Of course!"

"Hey dude, it is twelve-thirty. I'm already in Starbucks. Where're you at? It sounds noisy around you."

"I'm sorry, man. I'll be there in no time. Again, I am sorry."

"Don't worry about it. I want to buy an HD cable. Call me once you get here."

"Sure thing. See you soon."

I knew that I should've ridden my bike to the shopping mall. However for some reason I parked it and sat on the corner edge of the pavement. My elbows anchored on my thighs just above my knees. My back bent like an old man without the strength to straighten up. The palms of my hands covered my cheeks and my fingers were in front of my eyes. I noticed that somebody had spat on the road, just by my right foot. Nothingness! I zoned out, sighing. I remained in that state for around ten minutes.

Recalling my meeting with Professor Nora, "Fuck that shit," I murmured with a mirthless grin. I knew it was time to go. It took me around fifteen minutes to reach my destination. In a small alley around a dozen Chinese restaurants' back exits, I parked my bike and handed the guard the fare. *The scent of rotten chicken could be a cure for obsessive appetite.* I was stood corrected though, as I caught a glimpse of the foreign workers taking their lunch by the dumpsters of that putrid alley. I exhaled fully to purge myself of the smell.

Walking from one end of the mall to the other took me a few minutes. Finally, I caught a glimpse of the barista's Pan Am Welcoming Smile.

"How are you sir," she asked with a saccharine-sweet smile. Making eye contact I said, "I am no sir.

Nevertheless, I am fine, thank you. What about you?" As though her programmer had forgotten to wire her with an intelligent reply function, she proceeded to ask for my choice of beverage.

"Three shots of espresso, a glass of room-temperature water and a tall-size Americano", Mike jumped in, placing his hand on my left shoulder.

Looking up, due to the height difference, I smiled, "You know me well buddy! I apologise for my lack of punctuality. As they say in my town, an Arab is never on time. It is on me man."

"How are you?"

"I have been better. Yourself?"

"I am fine. Our diving trip was amazing. Would you like to see?" Without further ado, Mike started to show me the pictures on his phone. The locals seemed as though they were taking a part in a "Free the Nipple" campaign. The photos were like the ones people use as desktop backgrounds. Strangely, I had no interest whatsoever in the subject, though I thought it would be polite to enquire about the details of the trip. Things like the locations, attractions, and the like. Mike was excited to answer my questions, giving me a lot of unnecessary details. He looked overjoyed to be sharing his good experiences, even the difficulties. Over the course of his tales, my verbal and non-verbal gestures conveyed nothing but interest.

Trying to keep my cool, I felt the urge to smoke. I stood up and looked toward the patio before asking, "Would you like to smoke? Second-hand smoking, of course!"

"Ha, ha of course!"

Mike followed his prolonged tales by enquiring about my wellbeing. I wanted to reply, *I had what might qualify as a bad day. I guess you are aware that I am a researcher of some sort. Researcher on demand! Fuck that shit!* Instead, I tried to repress my obvious fury. I had the urge to clarify, *a number of incapable and lazy-assed lecturers and students pay me to write articles of their choice. See, poor people don't have many choices; we do what we have to do.* I wished I could've cut the foreplay and confessed that I worked as a ghost author. I was about to spit it out and explain, *among my clients, I am known for being fast. What takes an average researcher months to finish, I do in weeks; sometimes just a matter of days. For that reason, researchers, in fact mainly professors, have been hiring me to finish their year-long projects in no longer than three months; sometimes, in only few days. One time, I had to finish a book chapter in two days; the submission was within the assigned deadline. It's been a dry season and I felt sufficient desperation to take one of my worst clients back. I had a meeting with her this morning. Courtesy of service providers like me, the fraud has moved to a bigger office. It might sound rich, coming from me, but I had to wait thirty minutes because one of her Malay students decided to visit her during our designated appointment. It is all about priorities! Her student also happened to be one of her 'co-authors'. She did not even do the submission herself. You gotta be loyal to your own, I guess. For a long time I have been consumed with libertarianism. I thought entitlement and privileged treatment only led to laziness. But who am I to judge? I am only a cheap ghost author. The funny thing is, her student gets paid for doing absolutely nothing. Actually, demographics matter!*

I pushed my back against the chair splat, straightening up, and inhaled the smoke as my head faced the ceiling of the smoking area. I had to say something. Mike was studying me, expecting a story.

In my head I argued, *see the thing is, I am not the victimising type. Anyways, I have to admit that it has been tough recently. As you know, back in my home country things couldn't be more tragic; too many people have died and the butcher's knife is sharper than ever. The societal fabric of my country is very much decimated. As somebody put it, the country has become a bitter cocktail of tyrannical brutality, communal sectarianism, and terrorism. I can't even start to imagine how impossible life has become… my family is going through a tough time. The toughest I can imagine! With that in mind, I have to attend to their needs, although I am not in a good situation myself. I am facing many difficulties as it is. Nothing compared to what they go through on daily basis, of course. Despite the fact that my father likes to believe otherwise, their ultimate achievement has been to stay alive. I remember once asking him about how shitty things really were. To that question he responded that there were those who have been suffering more. He recounted the ordeals of some of the millions across the country who had it worse. God forbid, father pleaded, fearing the loss of one of my siblings. What frightened him the most was the off chance of any of them getting radicalised. In the face of that fucking calamity, I would tell him to be realistic and that there is no god! He always laughs things off. For in a life of misery, one has to maintain some sense of normality.*

As you see, I had to be there for them. I mean, in a material sense. However, I am penniless come the fifteenth of the month. Being somebody's ghost author has so far been the only way to secure extra cash. But again, even during peak seasons, it is not enough. I hate doing it! But fuck that shit, being poor has stripped me from being at peace, constantly having to go against my so-called ethical code. That said, I've had to make peace with it. After all, I wouldn't do this for myself. I am supporting a family living through the worst humanitarian crisis of the twenty-first century. It is wrong but I can't afford right. And by doing this, I am hurting myself the most. I have to let go of any sense of recognition, leaving me with just the guilt of crossing the lines of my ethical code.

You see the accident of birth counts for something. I accept who I am. I accept my situation. That way, I can get shit done. I could've cornered myself and licked my wounds until the cows came home. However, with that chip on my shoulder, I'd have chosen to swim against the current of shit. This way I knew there'd be fewer nights that my family would go to sleep hungry. It is all about perspective! Be the self-loathing villain or be the righteous victim. Dare you try to be both and you'll end up consumed by fighting yourself against yourself. You would definitely lose touch with reality and end up in a limbo of some sort. You would end up licking your wounds until cows starved to death. You would lose all the battles and be destined to lose the war.

Instead of arguing the raison d'etre behind my agitation, I used my technique. Answering one of the universe's most deceiving questions has been very tricky. The three-worded question of, "How are you?" implies that the person saying it is interested in a sincere answer. I knew better than allowing

Mike to open that Pandora's Box. I remember telling him, *I have been better*.

There was something about the look in his eyes that urged me to come up with something wordier. I regarded Mike highly. It was the way he carried himself. I couldn't recall a time he had ever made a racial remark. The way he took care of his wife always amused me. I remembered the time when our Norwegian friend labelled Hitler a strong leader. Mike went bananas on him. As a German, he did not hide the national sensitivity of the subject, let alone, Hitler's evil doings. He'd also taken my side on multiple occasions. I recalled the time he even supported my take on homophobes.

Mike noted, "You look off man! Is there something wrong?"

Looking him in the eyes, the lies came naturally, "Emm, I wouldn't say I had a good day. I guess you noticed the green lines on my laptop screen."

"Yes. You told me that it is still under warranty."

"It is actually."

"Why don't you take it to the service centre?"

"That's what I was trying to say. I went this morning. It is so fucked up."

"What happened?"

It started to get busy at the café's smoking area. Around the mall there were few banks and offices. The industrial zone was a ten-minute drive. The café got very crowded during lunchtime. The noise often become annoying. I didn't know why some parents kept bringing their toddlers along to that not-so-spacious area. As I noticed the flow of customers, I asked Mike "Would you like a walk outside the mall?"

Mike happily welcomed the idea and stood up, "Of course! I really need to exercise more. I am putting on some weight."

"I don't know whether that counts as exercising. You should come with me to the gym."

"Ha, ha. I should. My wife keeps telling me to tag along with you."

"Please do, brother. It is good for your back."

During our walk out of the mall, Mike said, "Please keep going." I was thinking it over. Exhaling the smoke of the newly-lit cigarette from my nose, "I don't want to bore you with all the blah blah blah," I said. He grinned, "I am really interested, please go on!" Looking into his eyes I muttered, "Alright."

Mike placed his hand on my left shoulder, as the space was barely enough for one person to walk through. Not long ago, the mall management decided to make the walking space VIP parking. As we strolled, the cars had kept coming our way; we had to keep several paces apart from each other. After being interrupted for the umpteenth time we decided to stand by the central zone's gate. Mike chipped in, "You were saying?"

"Yeah. I went to the service centre this morning." I paused for few seconds, folding my hands behind my back. I was in no doubt that Mike was confused. He asked, "Are you okay?"

I smiled, trying to hide my despair, "Yes, I am! I was distracted by the cars. That's all. So in the service centre they told me that the warranty doesn't cover damage to the screen, especially in the case of bad usage."

"Oh, that's lame!"

"Yeah! Forget about that buddy. By the way, the other day I couldn't help but hear that your in-laws are coming to Penang. Man, I have no god but I'm gonna pray for you."

"Ha ha, good one! I'll tell Tania what you just said."

"Please don't!"

"It is funny, she'll like it. Don't worry!"

****

I rode my bike back home. It was 9.30 p.m., Malaysian time. South Korea was an hour ahead of us. Jennifer was an early bird. Despite the next day being a holiday, I couldn't help but finish my work early to spare her the waiting; I knew she wouldn't go to sleep until I made that call. I took off and reached home in ten minutes, give or take. I lay on my bed, connected my phone to the internet and dialled her number.

"Hello Jenny."

"Darling, darling, darling!"

"Hey sweetie! How was your day?"

"I came back home early. I finished work on time. I am happy! What a simple person!"

"That's good. That's good sweetie. Have you had dinner?"

"Of course! My mum made a Chinese meal. It was spicy. So I'm sure you can imagine my tummy is huge. I am sorry darling I know you don't want me to get fat."

"Jenny, you are skinny. Besides, I've never asked of you to be a certain shape. I like you the way you are sweetie."

"Really?"

"Yes."

"How was your day?"

"Just normal. Nothing special. I woke up, went the mall, got my coffee and started working. Nothing special actually. It was just a normal day. Same daily routine. What about you Jenny? Tell me more."

"My senior officer gave me around fifty bucks, as a lunar New Year gift. He drove me back home. I was so surprised."

"I saw the photo of the envelope that you messaged me."

"I gave it to my father. He was happy. As you know his business has not been going well."

"That was good of you sweetie."

"Talk to me. Tell me about your day."

"Sweetie! My day was just a normal day; nothing out of the ordinary happened. It was like yesterday and probably like tomorrow will be."

"It is okay?"

"It is."

"Talk to me. I sense that there's something wrong. There is something you are not telling me."

"Nothing is wrong Jenny."

"Your voice doesn't sound like it."

"Sweetie…"

"Please talk to me."

"Okay. I don't tell you everything. I don't want to. You broke up with me three times after I opened up to you. You won't get it and you'll end up blaming me about something else. Then, I have to apologise. Sweetie, I have a fucked up life. I have minimal control over anything that happens in my life. Last time I started to explain some of the minor difficulties, you gave up. You know with all the responsibilities on my shoulders, my family, the war, terrorism, sectarianism, and all the fucking shit I have been enduring… I am sorry but I am afraid that you won't be able to comprehend it. I think it takes somebody to go through the same experience to understand and relate to how I feel. See, I know you are an optimist. I know you choose to be positive. I simply can't. You got angry with me when I made the remark that as a Syrian, I am worth less as a human being. I am presumed guilty and when proven innocent, such findings are, often, neglected. You know what I mean. Embassy staffers look at me as if I am an ISIL operative. Less of a human, that's how I coin it. You rejected my terminology. Here is the thing sweetie, I also reject it. Though, I have to explain myself clearly. I am affected by my work and study. Everything I write follows a scientific method. Accordingly, after locating any issue of concern, I research all the facts surrounding it. Extrapolating on that procedure, I make a list of hypotheses. My hypothesis is that we are all worthy, we are all equal. I refuse to surrender to the notion that the accident of birth makes a person more or less than anybody else. Following this so-called method, I have to test my hypothesis. That is to say, based on the analyses of the obtained data, I determine whether my thesis is supported. Now methodologically, I have to reject the hypothesis when past, present, and future analyses unveil contradictory findings. Sweetie, I am not a good researcher. That hypothesis has been rejected more times than I care to count. I guess I am insane! I have been doing the same thing over and over again and every single time expecting or wishing for a different outcome. See the fact of the matter is that I love you and I am willing to do whatever it takes to save our relationship. To save us! However, I can only try. Try my best and as hard as possible. I don't know to what end. But I know it's a battle I am fighting against too many odds. Sweetie, you know the outcomes of a few battles and I have to bring up that your immediate reaction to each was to break up with me."

"I am sorry."

"Don't apologise. I do understand. Listen! Given how devastating my circumstances can be, many emotions and modes have over time become too luxurious. Grief and depression are just too pricey. I firmly believe that the sum of our experiences manifests in an evolution of some sort. In my hometown there is a saying that translates to, 'one's ordeals make one's skin thicker than that of a crocodile.' This evolution has given me the strength to keep going forward. When shit comes my way, I step over it and keep going. Going forward. Maybe just going astray. Astray, but forward. That might be an evolutionary necessity, but it comes with some side effects. See, while getting over negative emotions takes an extremely short amount of time and effort, experiencing positive emotions is getting harder. You might think it is difficult to be me. Actually it's not! As I said, my circumstances elicited this evolution. You know me, I am a social creature. Given my social needs I developed a technique. As

177

you know, for the last three years I have been facing problems that would make the strongest people I know lose it. Except for some of those who have had it as bad as or worse than me. That said, there are small and minor issues I face; a bad experience at a restaurant; a friend being late; feeling homesick, and the like. However, notwithstanding that, the sum of the aforementioned experiences doesn't take me over an emotional threshold, they can be used to sustain social interaction with people around me. The experiences serve a purpose. So when real shit happens, I hide behind those smaller incidences because they are the ones that people can handle. They allow me to maintain my friendships with people. Evidentially, it works. I am afraid to say that from time to time I use this technique with you. Though, I really hate doing it. You are my girlfriend and you of all people should get me. That's it. That's all."

"Has anything happened today?"

"Have you heard any of what I've been trying to say?"

"Yes."

"Are you sure? Can you tell me? Just to make sure there's no misunderstanding."

"You told me, that unlike those you are acquainted with, you want to be truthful with me."

"That's not all that I said. That's just what I wish to do.'

"Be strong darling!"

"What?"

"Darling," Jennifer said laughingly.

"It's not funny. Anyways, I've said a lot. If I keep going, you're going to misunderstand me. Then, you'll get angry with me and then I'll have to apologise."

"Darling," again she laughed.

"It's not funny."

"Be strong! Be strong darling!"

"I am very strong. I am the strongest man I know. That's not the point. Sweetie, you told me that you have been practising a song to sing me. Can you sing it?"

"It's not important. Now is not the time."

"Come on sweetie! You asked me and I answered. Besides, I didn't say anything wrong. Did I? Why are you angry with me?"

"I don't know!"

"Sweetie I hope you know that... You know that I have been fighting so hard against all the odds separating us. I know that, insofar, I've failed too many times. I am willing to keep fighting. I just hope that you are too. I have my doubts but it's one of these times when I wish to be wrong."

"You have doubts?"

"Yes sweetie. Recently, I've been facing a lot of hardships. I guess more than you care to remember. I'm sorry to remind you but it's practically impossible to forget those experiences. When shit started falling, you gave up on me. Twice in less than ten days. I understood why. Probably, I would've done the same if I were you.'

"I love you darling."

"I love you too sweetie. Are you going to sleep any time soon?"

"Yes darling. In ten minutes."

"It's getting late. Good night and sweet dreams."

"Good night darling."

****

I'd taken on Professor Nora as a client again. My job tasks were pretty simple. Write articles so she could fulfil her grants' requirements. Recently we'd had some sort of disagreement regarding my payment. Out of her desperation, she had hired me again, shortly before her grant reached its deadline. In almost a month, I finished two articles. She thought they were not enough. It took an average student a semester to finish one. However, she wanted me to finish three. It was only for three hundred ringgits a month. To deliver the manuscripts, I'd worked no less than sixteen hours a day. An average research assistant working for a lecturer with a grant, got almost eleven thousand dollars for writing two papers, annually. The articles didn't have to be exceptional. It didn't even matter if they ended up published in a spam journal. Me on the other hand, I had to produce them at Scopus level, to say the least.

Professor Nora thought that I needed to finish three articles per month. I tried to reason with her, but didn't have much luck. When I confronted her with the standard rate, I was belittled by her reply, "Buy the one with the cane." It was an old fucked-up Arab saying. It is to do with buying the best slave. Trying to hide my fury, I clenched the edge of my nails against the palms of my hands so strongly that they cut through the flesh. Still, I couldn't help but ask, "How is that related?"

"It is not the point," she raised her tone. "What is the point?" I calmly demanded, knowing that I had too much to lose. I couldn't risk my PhD. I had to pay my dues. There was too much at stake.

I stared at her eyes, hoping for enlightenment; my eyes did not blink. I waited silently for few moments, trying to push the slavery remark out of my mind. Even if it was unintentional, I was offended. I thought it over and over, but I couldn't get what she was trying to say. I contemplated every aspect of our arrangement but still, that phrase did not make any sense. She wasn't a native speaker of Arabic and she might've misused the saying. In any case, she had a mind of her own. I couldn't see an excuse for what she said.

Finally, she spelled it out. The entitled lazy-ass had the audacity to raise her tone, look at me furiously, lecturing, "I know why you took this job. You told me that your family is in immense need for the cash. I am aware of your country's situation. Given your nationality, I am certain that I am doing you a favour. My husband told me about your many attempts to secure an opportunity elsewhere. Not in this country! How many times have you been rejected for visas? By the way that's a rhetorical question and thus, you don't have to answer it. You should've been more serious. I am a busy woman. I don't deserve this. As you said once, 'Do no good, nothing bad comes in your way.' You need to push yourself harder. You need to do more..."

I interrupted, "Professor, I cannot do more! I wish it was that simple. I've been spending no less than thirteen hours a day working. You see, I am trying my best here. Maybe it isn't enough. You know why I need the money so bad. Just to avoid any misunderstanding, I just want you to know that I haven't asked for any raise."

She yelled, "Esh esh, enough! You are getting me angry! I don't need this!" I stayed seated, hoping she'd ask me to get out of her office. I was kind of hoping she would sack me. She moved her head slowly, avoiding any eye contact. I couldn't help but be infuriated by her sickeningly sanctimonious smile. "I have a solution," she said. I was all ears waiting to hear what she had to say.

Without dignifying my existence with a look, she said, "I cannot pay you." It is hard to surprise a very pessimistic person, like myself but I admit she managed to make my jaw drop. In shock, I felt compelled to say, "But we didn't make any agreement regarding the number of articles per month. Last time, I had to submit two articles at the end of each month. You didn't say a thing when I started working for you again. I just assumed…"

She stopped me again, "Esh esh, I did not say that you can speak. This month, I am not going to pay you. Don't let me down in the next two months and you will get paid. You've put me in a difficult situation. I promised the head of our department to give him three articles. His assistant is on maternity leave and he's really busy. Scratch my back, I scratch yours! He is the head of department and every time I apply for a grant, I need his consent."

"Honestly," she continued. I zoned out. I just couldn't listen to her anymore. I kept pretending to hear her out. After some time, I noticed that her mouth had stopped moving. She stared at me for few minutes before I said, "Very well! Six articles in the coming two months. I will get paid after delivering them."

Loudly and impatiently, she ranted, "You people are troublemakers. That's not the deal. You will get paid after the articles get accepted and published."

I thought, *I was supposed to wait three months, more or less, for a manuscript to be reviewed before having to get any editorial decision. Once accepted, a manuscript might take up to a year to be published.* It was only then that it hit me, *Not only had I crossed my ethical code but I had signed up to a slavery contract.* As it dawned on me, I failed to figure a way out of the heavy chains I'd placed around my neck.

A sense of self-loathing started to overwhelm me. *My people are risking everything in the pursuit of dignity and freedom*, I weighed on that fact. I was left with no doubt that I dishonoured the memory of those who had risked their lives so that people like me could have the very basic rights of freedom and dignity.

Facing Professor Nora, I was anxiously trying to figure something out; a solution to break the chains. "Professor Nora, I have a better solution," I spoke softly. Studying her, I was without any doubt that she had no interest in anything I would say, but I needed to make things clear to her. I argued, "Professor, I admit it is entirely my fault. I should've worked harder. I should've worked more. I cannot deny that you've made many compelling arguments. Therefore, I should discipline myself so as to avoid future mistakes. In two months, I promise to deliver six manuscripts. I will be on time. As you know, my proposal defence is approaching. As such, I won't be able to do more. In the interest of reconciliation and out of your kindness, I hope you can find it in your heart to forgive me. Last but not least, you don't have to pay me a thing. "Fair enough," she murmured.

Chapter 11

Learned Helplessness

At home, the slow water ran and spilt through the blooded knuckles of my shivering hands. My bathroom door was open; I could see my whole body on the mirror opposite. I stared at my naked reflection and remembered Jennifer telling me that I was "built like a brick shithouse", and the first time she touched my chest, she told me that I was "rough like an animal". Even at five foot nine, I've been called brawny. Sami thinks it's because of my warm, tan complexion. With that skin tone, I can get lost in the midst of Latin Americans, Mediterranean, and Pakistanis. I showered, the water slowly running from my hair to my feet, as I readying myself to go to work. But all I could think about was Jennifer: her slender, soft body; her innocent, pretty face; her fruity voice.

We were the total opposite of each other as though we were from different planets; a pessimist falls for an optimist. Richard Flanagan, in A Narrow Road to the Deep North wrote that "A happy man has no past, while an unhappy man has nothing else." Jennifer rejected the notion; she was a firm believer that everybody deserves an equal shot at happiness.

For in experience, the delusions of faith are unveiled. I am sure that at some point in my fucked-up life, the floating emotion of happiness has made some appearances. However, tragedies have left more lasting scars with an intimacy that has crystallised into a lifelong bond. After all, Flanagan spoke the language of a guy whose core endeavour was to have fewer troubles than a girl who lived for nothing but the pursuit of happiness.

The code of one of the Syrian armed forces implied punishments were collective while rewards were personal; I lived by a different code. For me ordeals were matters of classification and thus, kept on a need-to-know basis. Pleasurable and happy events were shared. So it followed that, since, when shared, emotions became amplified for me, and contagious to others, it made sense to imprison bad experiences in my heart.

****

I knew that I wouldn't be able to do a thing. I looked at some articles and ended up checking Jennifer's profile on Facebook. I hadn't planned for our relationship to start; I'd avoided all of her signals. I'd played as dumb as dumb comes! If it wasn't for Caroline, I wouldn't have even met her. She and I were close during her time on the island. As the daughter of a priest, she had some strong opinions. Nevertheless, I enjoyed our little theological debates. For some reason, she fixated on her perception of me being a Muslim. Even after I told her that I had been an atheist for life, she argued with me, on the basis of her presuppositions of a tanned Middle Easterner. Our affairs were purely platonic and whenever she got herself a man, I lost touch with her. I never knew why!

I respected Caroline's wishes and when she called, I made myself available. I never heard from her after she left the island. Social networking wasn't my thing. I seldom appeared online; when I did it was almost always by mistake. It was around a year after Caroline had left the island that we had a conversation. She was staying in New York and wanted to tell me how much she missed life in Malaysia. Jennifer was a close friend of hers. Caroline asked me to help her get by. Through a number of emails, Jennifer and I arranged for a meeting once she landed on the island. I friended her on Facebook before she left South Korea. She looked younger in person.

****

There she was, a petite, hyperactive woman; talking to three people while collecting some files. She didn't notice me at first. Once her brown eyes caught a glimpse of mine, her pale face lit up with the most pleasing smile I'd ever seen. She was all business, a little uptight but it didn't matter since I only wanted to familiarise her on how to get things done. I have to admit that there wasn't much that I could offer. She was one of the most organised women I'd ever met. On the bus to the café, she showed me this envelope. In it she had arranged printed advertisements of rooms she liked, with contact information and everything; it also included her plans for a week with maps and budgets. She had it all figured out. In the café she gave me a number. It belonged to a customs officer in the airport. Jennifer had had an issue with her luggage; it wasn't the last time though. Every time she came to the island, a delay in collection occurred. That day the officer had told us to go there after 7.00 p.m. Meanwhile we met a few friends, took our lunch, and bought a few things from the mall.

"Would you like to join me for a cigarette?" I pointed to the café patio. Jennifer looked shocked and in a tone of agitation she noted, "I don't smoke!"

"I know! I meant to continue our conversation outside. I guarantee you, the view is better from there. Ha, what do say you?" I gave her a grin as if it would persuade her. I opened the door and waited for her to walk out. I tapped a cigarette against my lips and offered her one; from her seat she gave me a face that clearly said, "Fuck off." A belly laugh escaped from me while studying her expression. Trying to collect my breath, I teased, "Take it easy madam, I am just messing around!"

"Ha," she gave me the profile of her face.

"Jennifer, take it easy! Tell me now, are you tired? I can take you to your guest house…"

"No, no. I am fine," she waved a hand in front of her face and smirked. She thinned her lips and continued, "It's just that everything is in that bag; my cosmetics, clothes, books, your gift. Are you busy? I don't want to bother you though."

"Oh, you're asking me something! You lost me at gift."

"My brother said that I should buy you something…"

"Jennifer, Jennifer," I pursed my fingers' tips. "I am kidding. You're not bothering me at all. I was worried you might be tired. I am not planning to work today. Remember, I offered my help. Besides, I haven't gotten to know you, yet. Tell me, why Malaysia?"

"I've worked for the last five years, non-stop. I had no option, I had to. I guess I've missed out on a lot of things in life. Think of it as a vacation so I can figure out my life ahead." I could see that she was forcing the words out. Though, I had no doubt that they were sincere.

"Hey cheer up, Penang is a good place to decompress." For a few months to a year, the place is great. If you're a Caucasian, you get treated like royalty. Korean and Japanese likewise. *She will love it. She'll make a lot of local friends in no time.* I reckoned they'd paint her the picture: Middle Easterners are dangerous folk with their cocks over the shoulders, on alert to attack. In our bags there are all tools of misogyny. We are not to be touched. We are to be feared.

Being a tanned Arab comes in handy in socialising with the Malay, but not the Chinese, should you be Muslim. Still you fall short on the list of peoples' values. But being a tanned Arab infidel, you are lowest of all lows. Lower than cats for the Chinese Malaysians; lower than dogs for the Malay. Of course, I wouldn't dare to generalise the observation, even in my head. It was just my limited personal experience. And I would not say that you could not have a lasting friendship with locals; I had had the pleasure of meeting some bright-minded

192

individuals. However, having been on the defence long enough, I'd been overwhelmed with a desire to change the status quo. I'd managed to elicit a change in the attitude against my kind in my own circles. Admittedly, I'd avoided such urges on many occasions. I'd often found myself weak in an endless struggle against a deeply-rooted culture of bigotry. For me the island had long been branded as a place of exile. But for Jennifer, I was confident that she would like it here.

Jennifer sighed, "I have my doubts after my experience at the airport."

I averted, "Come on, these kind of things happen anywhere. I am sure you'll love it here! Besides, it's a chance for us to get to know each other."

"Right, right, you're right Mister Adam…"

"Drop the 'Mister' please. Unless, of course, if you prefer me to address you as 'Madam'."

"Madam," she grinned and continued, "No don't, Adam." Calling me by name sounded heavy and forced.

"That's better Jennifer! So what did you do? I mean for living?"

"I worked at a cosmetics packaging company in Seoul. We dealt with different suppliers and distributed our products around Asia. I handled the Chinese market."

"Oh, that sounds good. So, do you speak Chinese?"

"Yah, of course! What about you?"

"Before coming to Malaysia, I worked at a college. Here," I looked around to indicate I was referring to the island, "Many things. All boring stuff. You know, I am still doing my PhD. So do you have a family?"

I realised that the question sounded a little odd as she began to crack a laugh. "Everybody has a family," she smirked and continued, "but if you mean whether I am married or emotionally involved, I am not!"

"You mentioned your brother, any other siblings?"

"No, just the one. You?"

"Now, five sisters and two brothers."

"Oooh, your mother had given birth to eight…"

"Actually, nine."

"I am sorry…"

"Don't worry about it, it was long time ago."

I suggested we go inside. It was a hot day and the sun was slowly approaching us. "Would you mind if I worked a bit on my laptop?" I asked. She didn't mind. She was a very polite lady. She paid attention and was full of gratitude. After skimming the news headlines, I gave her a look. I couldn't fail to see her exhaustion as she started to doze off. She made these soft snoring sounds. I thought it was very cute. It hit me that she had arrived the night before and still hadn't made it to bed. *She couldn't have had even an hour to rest.* I worked on my thesis for few hours.

Regardless of how soft her snoring sounded, it woke her up few times. She would crack open her eyes, look around, close her eyes, and snore again. The time flew past as I fixated on some theory of unconscious emotional reactions. It was already quarter to eight. I tapped Jennifer on her shoulder and gave her a grin as she opened her eyes.

We took a cab to the airport, got her luggage, and took another cab back to the town. For most of it we didn't talk. Though, whenever we passed a street, I'd tell her the name and the attractions. Her luggage was quite heavy and I carried it to the third floor of her guest house. "Jennifer you must be starving," I said. She nodded in agreement. I added, "Let me wait downstairs. I'll take you to an Indian restaurant. It's famous; there is a whole section about it in Lonely Planet."

"Let me decorate myself first!"

"Ha ha, you mean fix your make-up!"

"No, decorate myself," she thinned her lips and made this angry-kid face.

We walked through a few alleys of old Georgetown. "This is the cheapest place on the island if you want to get some beer," I pointed at a place called *Anterabangsa*. "Here we are," I announced our arrival at the restaurant.

"I am starving," Jennifer rubbed her skinny tummy.

I couldn't help it but notice her studying me eating. With a mouth half full I asked, "What's up?"

"Slow down, Adam. Let's enjoy our dinner! Are you in rush or something? Am I boring you?"

"Ooh," I felt embarrassed. "I'm sorry, force of habit," I justified.

"I am sorry; it's just that I used to be you!"

"What? Were you a guy who was born in the wrong body? I am ok with that, just so you know."

She stared at me for seconds before she belly-laughed and I could see the tears drop from her eyes. I tried to keep a serious face until the upper corners of my lips started to quiver, cracking a laugh. We noticed the little kids at the next table staring at us like old men bothered by our childish outbreak. Jennifer had this thing for kids. I swear, regardless of gender or race, she loved them and they loved her back. She talked in toddler tongue to them. I was not sure whether they got what she said but those old-men-looking toddlers started giggling.

"Do they have beer in here?" she asked.

"No, this is an Indian Muslim restaurant, I am afraid not."

"Are you?"

"No, I don't believe in the guy, girl, or whatever it might be. And if it does exist, I am not a big fan. You?"

"I believe in family as the only divine, sacred thing."

"I like that, having faith in family!"

I walked her back to the guest house. She wanted to check out the next day. I knew her luggage was heavy and she needed some help to get by. The next day she moved into a room in a Chinese woman's house. We both kept things formal. However, I'd taken the initiative of checking on her every now and then. I invited her out few times but never only the two of us. One day, I messaged, "How are you? How are your studies? I hope all is well." She replied, "Why?" I wrote her back, "Just checking on you? I thought that's what friends do!" She didn't write a thing. The next day, while I was working from the café, she came and stood opposite to my table. It took me a while to catch a glimpse of her angry face.

For several moments she stood there in silence. She might've been waiting for me, hoping that I'd be able to read her mind. I was no psychic though! She crossed her arms, folded them, and gave me that deadly stare. She berated, loudly, "Who are you? What do you take me for? I am a woman, not some helpless child!" I looked around as the people in the café started to study us. I gave her a grin and said, "It is my fault! Can you take a seat please?" "I didn't mean to offend you," I continued.

"Jennifer, what can I get you?" I pointed to the nosy barista who seemed to be entertained by our quarrel. Jennifer's face turned slightly red, and she pressed her elbow against the table while leaning her forehead against the back of her hand. "I'll choose for you," I lowered my face so she could see my eyes.

As I waited to be served, I couldn't help but recall the last time we'd been together. It was in one of those upscale areas. For me, every time, I went there, the beauty of the ocean, the imperial architecture and the yachts brought bad feelings, reminding me of my limits. We had gone together to meet the guys over there. Our friends had left earlier. On our way back to the bus stop, she told me about her ex-boyfriend. Actually, I brought the subject up. She briefly recounted their affair. When I enquired about the reasons that had brought their relationship to end, all she said was "Promises are important. It's okay if you cannot deliver them all. It's enough to try." She was talking about her former boyfriend, but I knew she was telling me something else. I played dumb to keep things formal. It's not that I didn't desire her then. My past, if anything, proved that I inflict people with nothing but heartbreak. Once I got there, there was no going back. I didn't want to lose her. In the back of my head, the only true voice I could hear was, *she's too good for you.*

Every time I looked at her, a gracious grin masked my face. I handed her the drink and seated myself. I kept observing her. She broke in, "I just humiliated myself, no?" Thinning my lips as I struggled to hide my smile, I nodded sideways. I could see the confusion in her eyes, "No, no, just a simple misunderstanding; that's all," I clarified. The awkward silence couldn't have been louder: *say something, say something, anything!* While I collected my thoughts, she stared at me. "Jennifer," I chipped in and studied her face for moments, unable to come up with anything to clear the air.

Finally, I was able to articulate myself. "Listen, Jennifer," I said, "we are both strangers in this country. I just thought, as a friend, I should check on you from time to time. I meant no offence, though. It's just the way I treat my friends. I just wanted to assure you that you can count on me, as a friend. I know you can handle things on your own, I am just offering help, in case you need any."

She broke in, "Adam, friends only message each other on occasion, like Christmas, New Year, not to check on them."

"Oh, come on Jennifer. Friends should be there for their friends!"

"Not in Korea!"

"I didn't know that. I'm sorry if I offended you. It was not my intention. Let me make it up to you! Have you ever tried Mexican food?"

"Yeeees." It was one of the longest yesses I've ever heard.

"I like Mexican food. What say you, I treat you for lunch?" She just stared at me. "Fine, let's go," I invited. Over lunch, we talked about many things. She watched the news. We found ourselves drifting from the conflict in Syria to Obama's job act. After lunch we parted ways. I didn't contact her for weeks. I thought it would be better that way.

I was restless on my bed when I finally got her call, the first since that lunch at the Mexican joint. It was late and got me worried. She blubbered, "I need to see you now!" No questions asked, I called a cab. I stood by the elevator of her block before messaging her to come down.

I watched her as she emerged. She was wearing that pink tank top that had a painting of a toaster with a headset plugged into it. The shirt showed her bewitching little arms; still I hated that fucking top. Her beige mini shorts revealed the beauty hidden by those stupid jeans of hers. Her tearful eyes were red, leaving me with wondering, *did I do something?* I put out a gentle hand, almost touching her shoulder blade, and walked her to a marble seat by the entrance to her block. She sat so close that her arm was a breath away from mine. For the fraction of a second it touched mine, some sort of heated, minor electrical shock pushed mine away. Those brief almost unnoticeable touches raised in me some sort of masochistic desire I never knew existed. Suddenly, all I wanted of her was to toughen her grip on my chest and press her hands so hard that her finger nails cut through my rough flesh. As I pushed away my dirty thoughts, Jennifer broke in, sobbing, "Do I look like a cheap whore?!"

"What?" I chipped in, "What happened?" Ashamed and angered, her eyes were unable to hold her tears. I watched as she placed one hand on her temple while the other wiped both cheeks. I offered her a cigarette and whispered, "Take your time!" Her reaction was a mixture of a gape and a high pitched laugh. "No thanks, that's not the solution for everything," she replied to my silly offer.

"That's better, smiling suits you better."

"Thank you," she muttered and gave me a feeble grin.

"So Jennifer, I'm all ears. Why don't you tell me all about it?"

She recounted, "There is this guy from my class..." She went silent for a while before adding, "We usually study together. Yesterday..."

I could see that it was hard for her to talk about it. I put a hand on her shoulder and assured her, "It's ok you can tell me anything." She pulled the phone out of her pocket and murmured, "See for yourself!" The opened message read, "I like you. I'll give you RM 100 to have sex with me." I was in shock for a moment, with no idea what to say. I guess she could see that I was dumbstruck. She broke in, "He is from Jordan. His name is Islam." For some reason, I hissed, "Islam!"

"Why? Do I look like a cheap prostitute?" she demanded an answer.

"It's not about you Jennifer. It is not! He is a bad person." I could've spoken my native tongue, saying curses like a waste of human spirit, anus mouth, and assed-faced-fuck. But all I said was the shithead is a bad person. I gasped, "You are a decent woman. I know some good Jordanian people. But this guy is an idiot. In what world could anybody say something like that? Don't you dare entertain the idea that it's somehow your fault! I know a lot of half-men who have no clue whatsoever on how to treat a lady, let alone show affection. Jennifer, listen to me, it is not your fault. I'll deal with him, just leave it to me."

"Thank you," she whispered, holding back tears.

"You think you're cheap," I broke in after moments of awkward silence and I continued, "let me tell you a story. I think it was my second day in Penang. I wanted to buy an SD card. My roommate told me to get it from BG. You know the mall near your institute? So I took the bus, reached the mall, and bought the SD card. I wanted to take the bus back home but I didn't know which number it was. A man was standing by the bus stop. He looked in his late sixties. I asked and he told me which one to take. He was waiting for some bus but I didn't know which one it was. I noticed his intense look at me before he asked, 'Can I touch your arm?' I just went, 'What? Why? No!' He said, 'I give you fifty.' So you see, I am cheaper than you."

"Come on Adam, you can't be serious. He offered you fifty for a touch."

"That's right, fair enough!" We laughed it out.

I got Islam's number from her phone, assuring her that I'd deal with him. I watched her disappear through the elevator before I called the fucking douche.

"Hello," I spoke English.

"Allo"

"This is Islam, right?" I queried.

"Yes, I am Islam."

"Good for you!"

"What?"

"Listen to me, you piece of shit…"

"What?!"

"Just listen, ass-face. Don't speak!"

"What? Why you say? Who are you?"

"Listen, just listen! I am a friend of Jennifer's." I only got his attention after saying her name. He then stopped mumbling some English curse words.

I continued, "So now that I've got your attention, just listen! I saw your message…"

"I didn't…"

"No, you did. I didn't say that you could open your anus mouth. I don't know what century you come from, but here in this one, women are not bought with money…"

"I didn't…"

"Stop," I sighed impatiently, "just stop fucking talking. I have an offer; you think about and let me know what say you. Say, I give ten ringgits and I get a blow job in return. No teeth…"

"You say shit, you fucking Nigerian Nigger."

I had no idea how he could've mistaken my accent for a Nigerian. In a severe tone, I continued, "You fucking racist smug…"

"You fight?!"

"What? Sure!"

"Tomorrow at 12.00 p.m. by UPS's mosque…"

"Sure!"

He just hung up the phone. I didn't think I would find him there. I walked toward the mosque, the closest I've been to a place of worship in years. A tall guy was standing a bit far from the mosque's gate. "Islam," I pointed at him. "Yes," he anxiously replied. I rushed to him and stopped close, facing him. Without a word, I found the back of my hand bitch-slapping him. I knew that I took him by surprise which gave me the alpha dog's edge. I couldn't make out his face, was it anger, fear, or just simple, plain confusion? Quickly, I spun my hand and raised my arm. In response he took a step back. It could've been just his subconscious mind that forced that sort of cowardly impulsive reaction. He trembled, falling on the ground. Staring down at him I put a finger in my nostril. Looking him in the eyes I harangued, "Dare you talk to her, dare you whisper her name, or even look at her; I'll fuck you up." I left

Islam sitting on his ass, scared shitless. I assured Jennifer that he wouldn't get in her way anymore, without telling her a thing about our encounter.

The next day I asked her out to town. This time, it was only the two us. I knew that I desired her, but my intentions were purely platonic. We strolled for hours around Georgetown. We talked culture, politics, and art. She talked about her parents and brother's fiancé. To most of it, I listened. I asked a few questions, keeping her entertained. Foremost, I struggled to keep her on topic; her. We ended up in an Italian joint of my choosing. I could tell that Jennifer didn't like it. I figured, it was a little bit pricy for the both of us, and I couldn't afford her favourite white wine. She seemed a little flirtatious walking through the narrow allies by Love Lane. She kept giving me hints of interest. She smiled and elbowed me to look at couples. She laughed at my sarcastic jokes. She even held my hand. On my part, I pretended that I didn't notice. On our way back, she apologised for dressing so casual. I assured her that it was fine. That night she messaged me, "Thank you. I needed to get out. I really enjoyed our time out. Let's do it again tomorrow."

The next day we went to the beach. We walked through the tent-like night market. It was full of pirated DVDs. The counterfeit handbags and watches shouted, "We are poor imitations, we are fake, don't buy us!" We both hated it. She wanted to take some seafood. She picked a food court by the beach. I don't know what had got into her; she looked a bit out of it. When I sat by her side she requested that I move a bit further. I thought, *I might've misread the signals*. I kept my cool, telling myself that it was just a platonic, friendly night out. I figured, *we should head back home after dinner*. Before I could make any suggestions she asked me if there were any nice bars, by the beach and far from the crowd. I knew of a place called *Bora Bora* which fitted the bill. At the bar, we picked a table on the sand with an enchanting panoramic ocean view. She talked about her friends, her mother's former job in the military, and her brother's work in Japan. Mostly though, she explained how much she had missed out on living, having to work her ass off so she could support her brother's studies and the back-breaking cost of her father's surgical operations. Although I had already liked her prior to this new understanding, hearing her tales, I felt a deeper connection. I made a few sarcastic remarks, but for the most of the night I listened.

I noticed Jennifer studying my face. I thought, *there might be something wrong. Maybe she was buzzed by something at the restaurant.* She muttered, "Adam!"

"What is it Jennifer?' I asked.

She hunched, sighing. I guess it took her some courage to articulate herself saying, "I would love you if you were Korean!"

I was all, "What!" Except, I didn't say a word, it was all in my head. I'd never used *that* word; it always sounded so foreign, unnatural. Coming from my mouth, it would have been more fake than the fucked-up counterfeits of that night market. Jennifer was saying something but I was so consumed, drifting in and out of memories of former affairs. Here I was hearing the word; except I was not Korean. Denied love! I realised that I had no chance whatsoever.

****

I recalled previous affairs, "I am afraid to tell you that I am in love with you and you're too stupid to realise my love," Veronica had whispered after our quarrel. Back in Syria, Seba who I hadn't even touched, muttered, "I am terrified! I think I love you." Even my Iranian booty call had once said, "I cannot be open about my love to an Arab." I'd never once heard a plain, *I love you*.

****

I just waited for Jennifer to get bored and call it a night. Instead, she wanted to sit on the sand, right by the water. It was quite far from the bar. We just sat there, gazing at the ocean. She wore this gracious smile. I suddenly became aware of her studying my face. It was a look I couldn't fathom. There was something about it that urged me to place my hand over hers. For in that enduring look, I found the courage to move my hand to rub her thigh so roughly and without caution. Our mouths were too close; I inhaled the air out of her soft lips. We kissed! She tasted different than any other women. And that taste made it all worthwhile.

****

The next time was a thing of magic. For in the only divine ritual of mankind, your past, present, future, who you are, and who you aspire to be are altogether captured in that which is only natural. On top of her, I was her only true god and I was her only connection to creation. Beneath her, I was a faithful worshipper, for she was my only true god. She was the prey; she was the predator. I was her loyal follower; I was her only leading figure. She had possession of me; she was all mine. For she was a mysterious god; I was an uncertain subject whose faith was the only means of filling her desires. This divine paradox was the bridge to mirror our souls.

The reflections of two flawless gods strengthened our conviction, lengthening the journey of our utmost gentleness and aggression toward the fulfilling sweetness of its inevitable destination. We were there but not quite; embracing our moaning gods; ready to cast the most satisfying feeling known to us, yet denying it. My supernatural ability to repress the inescapable was derived from the incomprehensible logic of my faith. Our resolve to deny our submission to the climax of pleasure and joy was weakened by the limits of our evolved species. Stronger than my ancestors from the animal kingdom, I fought for a bigger window of time in heaven until my animal started to take over. I knew she couldn't see her reflection all the time. She lost sight of it once and wanted a second glimpse. As her worshipper, I obeyed. Then, god wanted more and I couldn't halt the prayers until seeing, hearing, smelling, tasting, and touching her commanded me. My vision went blurry, but I resisted. I fought it, but then the reflection almost disappeared. I fought so fiercely against my animal and defeated him, seeing a clearer, yet still cloudy reflection. My struggle won, over my battles against my human, seeing the reflection of both gods; me and her. At last, on her third signal, my animal took possession becoming a starving monster, readying his fangs to prey. In that very moment, I was a god, a man, and an animal, inflicting indescribable, breathless pleasure, announcing the end of our night-time mass.

The night before, at least the early part of it, had been catastrophic. I had exclaimed, "My life is so fucking complicated. I am afraid that I will disappoint you, hurt you. I have a miserable life, things you wouldn't begin to understand..." Without a word, she dressed herself and opened the door. I tried to follow her and explain myself but she insisted that I leave her alone. I was surprised when she called the next day. "Adam, are you married? Do you have kids?" she asked. I went, "No, what, why..." She interjected, "Get us some dinner. I am coming over for the night. There is nothing we cannot work out."

I told her about the war, the family, the misfortunes, and my shortcomings. I explained everything. I showed her the skeletons in my closet. She wasn't scared easily. Her answer was, "I am a grown women and I can decide on my own. I have a mind of my own. I accept you and want to be with you."

Jennifer's friends tried to influence her with their poisonous opinions. We survived Caroline's offer of finding her a better man from Korea. We went through Jasmine's doubts of the "malicious intentions" of Arab men. With her, I overcame my emotional shortcomings; I learnt how to show affection. We took care of each other. Actually, she took care of me in ways I couldn't have ever imagined. Throughout I often reminded her of my situation and my responsibilities. Something that had become so redundant. All I wanted was for her to accept me and my situation, not a futuristic, improved version of me.

I remember a time after an invitation to Yamen's place. On the way to the bus stop we saw a homeless man sleeping on the pavement. I was broke and had been rejected by many embassies with my expiring passport. A while back, I had forged an extension; a measure taken after visiting UNHCR and bribing the Syrian embassy staff many times. I never believed in hope. On that day, I couldn't have been more pessimistic. Studying the man, I announced, "That could be me one day!" There, at the bus stop, she sobbed, "Why, why, why..." I tried to calm her down but everything I did only added gasoline to a burning fire. After I managed to stop her, she went all silent on me. On the bed, she whispered, "All I want is to have two babies and share my life with you." I fancied that more than anything in the world.

We even survived that night. Finally, we came to an agreement. That was, there were forces beyond our reach and we owed it to each other to fight so fiercely that we'd end up together. Jennifer tended to get overwhelmed, I couldn't blame her, but she always managed to snap out of it. We survived the distance for over nineteen months. She had, of course, moved back to Koreabut had visited me on the island three times; the longest she stayed was a week. We talked every day, sometimes twice a day.

I knew she was very busy. *Three trips to the island, I have to make it up to her*, I decided. Koreans, apparently, have this festive week during the Chinese New Year. I thought it would be the best time to pay her a surprise visit. And maybe put a ring on her too. *Definitely, do that*, I intended. So I went to the Korean embassy with all required documents, yet I was denied a visa. It was on the premise that my application was incomplete. I enquired, "What can I do?" and was told, "Check our website!"

"But I did," I replied.

"We cannot assist you, please let us deal with other applicants," the officer ordered.

I'd no doubt that it was my nationality.

Via a Skype call, I told Jennifer about my plans. I even knelt and proposed to her. She eventually accepted. I was happy, happier than I had ever imagined possible. Jennifer had wanted to get married and start a family way before my proposal but it was the romantic gesture of the whole thing that aroused that emotion in me.

Things started to get serious and I had to check for all kind of arrangements. I needed to provide the court with an affidavit and my birth certificate. They both needed to be issued by the Syrian embassy, which meant that I had to go through the fruitless blackmail once again. Even with a valid passport, I still couldn't get them. I told Jennifer everything, except for forging the Syrian embassy's extension. After I had finally sorted things out, I told her about that too. She went bananas on me; she told me that I was a selfish and irresponsible prick. She broke up with me over the phone. I tried to contact her but I had no luck. I thought I could reach her through Caroline. I sent her a message on Facebook, "Can I talk to you. It's about Jennifer."

She replied, "What is it now. I am tired of the both of you."

"I am sorry but I haven't talked to you in years, let alone about my relationship with Jennifer."

"What is it?"

"Can I call you?"

"Just say it here!"

"It seems that I am bothering you. I am sorry to get you involved."

"What is this? You say you want to talk. I don't understand this."

"Okay, Okay. I love your friend. I have managed to deal with some tricky issues. I want to tell her that it all worked out."

"Stop lying to her."

"I haven't lied to her once. What are you talking about?"

"You want to make her miserable. She is happy here. She doesn't need war!"

"War! I don't understand what you are talking about. She is happy with me and that's all I want for her."

"Where are you going to live? I know you are Syrian, you cannot get anywhere."

"Maybe I cannot go to the US but I wouldn't take her to Syria."

"Just leave her. She'll be happier without your problems."

"Okay, I got it. Thank you. I have to hit the road."

"Just don't make her hit that shitty road with you."

"Okay. Thank you for the help. I need to go."

She sent couple of messages that I left unread. For some reason, Jennifer called me before I had reached the motorbike parking. I explained the solution. She didn't object much. In a few days, we went back to normal. That is, accepting each other and happy to be together. Then things got difficult again. Jennifer informed me that she'd already sent a letter of her resignation. Simply, I asked, "Why didn't you inform me before you made such a decision?" And of course we ended up arguing about what kind of decisions to share with each other. I asked her to wait and not to ruin her livelihood, not just yet. She saw it as cold feet on my part. From that day onward, I noticed some changes in the way she talked to me. Most of our conversations seemed to end in nothing but putting too much blame on me. I bore the brunt of her frustration.

That week she was on her last trip before leaving the company for good. She told me she'd been working there a month to train her replacement.

Two days before her return from that, she resolved to come to the island, get married and then maybe we could plan for our immigration to another country; somewhere where it would be possible for both of us to find jobs. Then she wanted us to have babies as soon as we had got there. I tried to reason with her that we needed to settle down first. She agreed. On the day of her departure she asked for some time, and that she would talk to me once she got back to her home. I gave her the time and waited a while longer. Then, without explanation, she wanted to end it. I called countless of times. For my calls, I got no answer; for my messages, there was no reply. She finally broke the silence saying, "I want to see the world and explore other options." She told me that, for some reason, she felt lucky and happy. She even went to this island in Korea; an island she claimed, "The best place for couples and newly-weds." I tried to reason with her even after that. But my endeavours were fruitless. In the face of many hardships, I was helpless, refusing to accept the new status quo.

****

I don't know what came over me. When you ride a motorbike too fast, your eyes water. They can't help but shed some burning tears. So, there I was, on the bike, riding as fast as it could go, despite the blurred vision. The speed pushed the drops to my earlobes; making their way through the back of my neck to my shoulder blades. I wanted it. I didn't slow down. My trembling, weak body needed the venom of it, all out at once if it were only possible. The lump in my throat and the quivering of my Adam's apple had been escalating, suffocating me of breath. The ache in my chest, just above the right nipple, had been buzzing in me for days. Sometimes, I felt two pulses beating one after another, at a quickened pace. I didn't know, it could have been the smoking; except, it was not. Exhaling, my lungs forced a husky sound. In my head, it sounded like roaring that would vibrate the closed windows of the speeding vehicles. It felt like my chest was releasing the excruciating agony, signalling its maximum intake of pain. I rode to the bridge that connected the island and the mainland. I knew nobody there. The bridge was high and long and the wind was strong; I struggled not to lose my balance.

I'd never understood the structure of the mainland. It was like a group of small towns of high-rise buildings and bungalow houses, separated by nothing but empty jungles. I was heading there. I sought a shoulder off the road and far away, with no town in its immediate vicinity. Taking the left I entered three of these wastelands before I reached the one I wanted.

I lit a cigarette and footslogged toward the woods, quite far from the road. I glanced toward the road, making sure that the bike was still visible. I had no sense of direction. Jennifer had often said that the GPS in my brain was somehow impaired. The bike was my compass. I knelt on the ground. The grass was wet and the patches of reddish soil were muddy, seeping through my jeans. Smoking my lungs out, I thought this ritual might help. After all, there was nothing else that I could do to change the current state of affairs.

On my knees, I couldn't help but remember these animals that underwent an experiment. I am not sure when it happened but I sympathised with the poor things anyways. It was when a group of scientists decided to electrically shock the unsuspecting creatures without giving them the chance to flee the punishment. They continued to be punished over the course of weeks, or months, I could not recall. Then, the scientists decided to change the conditions of the experiment, allowing the animals a chance to escape the punishment. They found that they just kept taking the punishment. From there comes the term, "learned helplessness".

There is another story I heard many times in Syria and Lebanon, in which any person with an operating cell in her or his brain can regard as fictional at best. The story goes that a French or British influential interior minister, actually I cannot remember his position, before the First World War wanted the public to revolt against the head of the state. He figured that he should humiliate citizens in order to elicit rage against the leadership. So on the entrance of each city he placed a number of guards and for any male citizen to enter the city, he should be fucked by a guard. A blow job wouldn't cut it.

The mastermind of the operation's patience grew thin and he decided to check what was going wrong with his plan. Behind a long line of people, he queued. A fight broke out between two men. He thought it would be a good chance to incite anger against the leadership. He queried, "What's up?" One of the men went, "the asshat left the queue half an hour ago and now wants his place back." So, the man shook his head disappointingly. He thought, *here I assumed that they'd revolt against the state but instead they are fighting for who gets to be fucked first!*

Except in my case, there was no scientist to reverse the conditions of the painful experiment at some point in the foreseeable future; there was no interior minister to stop the unwritten law of being fucked at every turn. I admit, in learning helplessness, I've been one of the worst students. Broken as the burning drops crept out as each couldn't wait to catch the other; my voice was caught in my throat, I found myself choking up lines from old songs:

Trouble...
Trouble, trouble, trouble, trouble
Trouble been doggin' my soul since the day I was born
Worry...
Worry, worry, worry, worry

Worry just will not seem to leave my mind alone

I am a man of constant sorrow

I've seen trouble all my days

I bid farewell to old Ar-Raqqa

The place where I was born and raised

For thirty long years I've been in trouble

No pleasures here on earth I found

For in this world I'm bound to ramble

I have no friends to help me now

It's fare thee well my old true lover

I never expect to see you again

Throughout the songs' lines, my mind flickered the images of my brother's disfigured face; Zain lying dead underneath his rapist and above a pool of blood; my second-youngest sister's friend's dismembered tiny body; the hole in the back of my cousin's head; the Jordanian pilot dancing as he burnt; all the beheading scenes; the stoned women of Syria; the flies on the big tummy of the Somali baby. With every blink the images haphazardly repeated themselves. Suddenly, my mind started a game of fixation. All I could see was my mother kneeling and slapping her face with hands full of dry, brown soil; my father's strong grip on my shoulder as he moaned; Zain mother's animal-like keening; the Iraqi woman from the news, face to the ground, asking god where the fuck was he; the Syrian father carrying his dead baby looking up as though god was going to give him an arsenal of relief. Then, for some reason, all I could think of was the scene of Jennifer sobbing and asking me, "Why, why, why…"

Refusing to submit to a state of helplessness, I stood with my arms stretched open, reaching a tree at each side. I pushed and howled as the ache rose in my chest. "Fuck, fuck, fuck, fuck!" I bellowed my desperation and rage. I released my hands and shouted until the vein on the left side of my neck almost exploded. "Fuck you Bashar, fuck you

223

Baghdadi, fuck you Putin, fuck Ayatollah, fuck Nasrallah, fuck al-Maliki, fuck al-Qaeda, fuck Obama's red lines of cowardice, fuck Ed Miliband, fuck SNC's Muslim Brothers, fuck Jihad, fuck terrorists, fuck racists, fuck the Kardashians, fuck me, fuck me, fuck me," I punched the poor tree with every fuck. My hands shivered and the red drops slowly departed the knuckles to reach the grass and the muddy soil. Out there in the jungle, breathless, the anger got slowly replaced by a smile. Slightly relieved, I thought, *I cannot afford the whole day off.*

Chapter 12

Homophobia: Questioning Empathy and Evolution

Sleeping in a new bed has always been a struggle. I am also not the most tactile man on earth. The usual nightmares and the sleep-late-sleep-less routine had made it hard not to be self-conscious the first night in her bed. She also had to wake up early, at five thirty in the morning. Cats have never been my best friend. That fucker with the foot fetish couldn't have been more annoying. There was also the surge of after-sex energy and the nicotine rush from the smoke that followed. It was our second time in no more than seventy minutes but it felt like I could do a full body workout routine. My brain was still at its normal functioning capacity; I could talk science, philosophy, politics, or anything. However, pillow talk was not my thing. Sheila by far was the smartest and most intelligent woman I'd ever met. I enjoyed talking to her and the more we talked, the more I came to respect her intellect.

She gave me a look of permission to go for a smoke. On her enormous balcony, I got two of her fancy chairs and seated myself on the one to the right so the smoke wouldn't bother her, should she decide to join me.

On our first date she paid interest in my research. We talked art, psychology, aquaculture, foreign affairs, theology, philosophy. I wanted to know what she liked. She told me about what she disliked. I guess it was a mixture of evolutionary-subconscious-relational-compatibility signals and an occupational hazard. She was a researcher too. I have to admit that I believed in the notion that dislikes were as important, if not more, than the likes. And differences outweigh similarities in the pursuit of a lasting intimate affair. But still, her interests were part of the equation. I pressed on, getting them in the picture, though I didn't get much to go on. We both talked. For six hours we talked. We never had a single awkward moment of silence, not any that I was aware of.

My PhD lasted longer than I could've anticipated. My examiners lamented that they didn't get the psychological or political aspects of it. One said that she wasn't into politics and found any subject of that sort boring; the other internal examiner claimed the difficulties of following through without having any statistical background. The chairman wanted me to state that politicians from the American Republican Party were stupid! The external examiner had never heard of any research utilizing secondary data and given that I had never been to the U.S., regardless of the statement of the research problem, the selection of the context was not justified. I knew none of them were from my field, my supervisors included. I thought the viva was a session in which a candidate had a chance to defend some arguments; evidently, I was wrong. I was told that I was angering one of them. Another was showing verbal and nonverbal signs of annoyance. I was told to shut up and instructed to respond to comments in that manner. I had to listen to anti-American sentiments. I had to listen to nonsensical conspiracy theories. I had thought that as a candidate following a rigorous research methodology, valid scholarly justification was required once a notion was posited. I knew I had to suck it up like a man and wear a fake smile. My defence was four hours and seventeen minutes of self-restraint. I waited for half an hour so they could take dinner and then ten more minutes to get their verdict. Everything they asked had already been included in the research. Yes, I had to do some cosmetic changes, but nothing serious enough to be labelled as major or needing to wait for the minimum time until resubmission.

It was already quarter to seven. My second date with Sheila was set to be at six-thirty. I was already late. I was furious but I didn't want to cancel. I called and apologised. I asked for more time and she was generous enough to give it to me. It was also rush hour; it took me ages to get through the bottleneck. I hadn't slept the night before. My eyes were red and I looked like shit. I made it there nonetheless. To my surprise she had waited.

I was not the most punctual man on the island but still I couldn't help but feel like a douche for being an hour and a half late. I explained and didn't excuse myself. She gave me a get-out-of-jail-free card. She claimed I could only get two. By the end, I had collected a full deck. By the fourth of July, we had been seeing each other for forty-two days. Through that period, I came to realise that she was too good for me and I was out of her league.

If progress in life was measured on the basis of your achievement and self-realisation, I was in no way Sheila's equal. Maybe I was only smart enough to realise how intelligent she was. Finances aside, she was in a stable place in her life. Sheila also gave to those in need. She had volunteered in Africa for two and half years and spent some time teaching in Nepal. She spoke French and had a master's from some posh school in the UK. If I had to brand her, I would have to include liberal, independent, strong, hard-working, sophisticated, tactful, and supportive. She was all that and more. The woman had a stable job, could travel anywhere, and was able to make future plans. Finances considered, well who am I kidding; her rent was double, if not triple my income. I was out of her league!

That said I had learned not to make a decision on anybody's behalf. That was their right and I could not take that away. Without any exaggeration, I opened my closet to show her my skeletons so she knew what she was getting herself into. Things were going so fast and so well, the thought of losing it all scared me. We were so fucking compatible. We communicated and came up with every possible scenario. We decided to give each other a chance. Well, she gave me the chance! I had no reason to doubt that she accepted me, with all my baggage. Still, I was overwhelmed by the skeletons of my past. However, it was her decision and I needed to let my guard down to have any chance of living.

Her intellect aroused me in ways I'd never experienced before. I could say what I wanted without having to explain it or dumb it down. We didn't agree on many issues but I was liberated from misunderstanding with her. And I craved for any conversation. Conversations often were the foreplay of longer debates. And the debates were more sensual than anything I'd ever experienced. And I liked and yearned for the experience. And with greed I wanted to get more and more of it. And the experience aroused in me anger and fear. And the anger was directed at my helplessness in my endeavours to put my skeletons to sleep, or stop them from growing, to say the least. And my cynicism of her resilience in facing the shithead of my skeletons scared me. And the chorus of my doubts called for building higher walls to prevent disappointment. But the experience was overwhelmingly fulfilling. And the sensation became an addiction. And my addiction urged me to topple the walls. And willingly I made myself vulnerable. And I thought, it was a small price for that high.

****

Sheila loved to host and she was a generous one. She was a good cook too. Even as an expat, she maintained her national traditions. For the fourth of July, she invited four friends of hers. Suzan and her husband were on the list. On our fourth date, Sheila had wanted me to meet some of her friends. I think she wanted me to be vetted by Suzan. Knowing my evaluator now, I would trust her opinion too. Before going to the expatriates' dinner, I was feeling somewhat intimidated. Suzan and Matthias, her husband, were from a social class that I have come to label as "smothering". I wouldn't be able, even in my wildest dreams, to associate with people who had achieved that much in life. It's not that I have anything against people of different classes but rather the relativity of personal status. Competitive creatures, human beings are! I put myself on high alert, knowing that I was being vetted and, well, having to socialise with people of high intellect. And it wasn't that I didn't want to have such acquaintances. Nothing aroused or excited me more than being challenged intellectually. But still, I was being vetted by people from another planet. People who only see my kind after our boats have capsized in the Mediterranean before making our way to their countries. People who would, at best, look at my kind with pity. And I hated pity. But I was there and I chose to be there and I thought, *while self-conscious, I have to keep my cool and keep an open mind*.

The small talk was not that bad actually. In fact, I enjoyed it. At the same table, there were a number of people, of whom Suzan was the most interesting. Sitting there for an hour without a cigarette, I knew I needed a smoke to continue keeping my cool. I gave Sheila a look and graciously told her of my desperate need for a smoke. Suzan wanted to smoke too. She told me on our way out that she wanted to talk to me. Out of the restaurant we started to inhale and exhale the smoke rapidly.

"So Adam, how did you find the dinner? Sheila told me about your research. It sounds interesting!"

"It was good. Well I am glad that you think it's interesting. My examiners beg to differ!"

"What are you actually trying to do?"

"I developed this brand of sorts. It is inclusive of two blocks of emotional experience, namely, the implicit and explicit. I also study the impacts of a number of forces on the dual dimensional construct. The main thesis is that the brand is predictive of voting behaviour. Furthermore, being able to elicit changes in that variable is posited to influence one's choice of candidates. Now, the findings suggest a high predictive power. Its development also accounts for a number of ways to elicit changes in the dual dimensional brand, and thus, voting choice."

"In other words, manipulation!"

"Yeah, more or less." We drifted from one topic to another; from sleep health to sexology. Before going back to the restaurant, Suzan noted, "Sheila is a great woman!"

"She is," I replied. Suzan was Sheila's closest friend on the island. Sheila considered her to be her support system. She was the person to seek in times of crisis. A person equipped with amazingly sophisticated reasoning and who had acquired an undeniable ability to disambiguate the roots of complicated conflicts. Or at least, I thought so. This was my impression of her and the more I heard from and about her, the more I felt that I was not alone and that there were plenty of my kind out there. For in being an abomination of existence, or having that perception of one's self, a man cannot help but have some sort of confusion and anxiety at meeting one of his kind.

****

I was excited to see Suzan again. It had been a while since we met. Sheila knew all her guests' dietary preference and made sure all were met. Over dinner, the conversation flowed across a range of topics. They say no news is good news but while that week had been so bloody, it had also marked a win for civilised societies around the world. The supreme court of the USA had voted for marriage equality. Suzan was excited by the news and congratulated the American people for finally recognizing such inalienable rights. I was distracted by something and found myself hearing Suzan talking about those who had to undergo sex change operations, despite not wanting that specific change of identity, so they wouldn't get punished by their governments.

I added, "For those living in countries like Iran, many resort to this option without necessarily wanting to be identified as men or women. Shadi Amin, a political activist who fled to Germany, talked a lot about gay and lesbian ordeals and having to undergo sex reassignment surgery with 'little real choice' in the matter…"

Suzan, studying me, "How on earth do you know about that? Not many have interest…"

I found myself out of my comfort zone. I didn't need to lecture anybody. I was liberated and accepted, yet this unfamiliar situation was unsettling. Anxiously, I interrupted, "Well, I do!"

Sheila clarified, "that's Suzan giving you a compliment!"

I got the compliment but I still I thought, *how on earth did a guy from Ar-Raqqa, now the de facto capital of ISIL, develop such a view?* On a subject where I often show the sharpness of my fangs, it felt weird to have a shared belief with everybody at the table. I recalled the two occasions on the patio of my usual café. I remembered my forcefulness and aggression during the first and my fury during the last.

****

At a simpler time when worries were merely material, I went to the café to read the papers. Jamal, my Iraqi friend, soon joined me for a smoke. He was a world-class conspiracy theorist. The fact that I kept up with the latest socio-political events had always been a conundrum to him. For to him, in conspiracies lay answers to the most complicated questions of all, be they political or theological. As shown through that map of the least sophisticated logic, all roads tended to lead to the Mossad.

In the mantra of shared hatred and placing the blame on Israel, our cowardice to face the barbarity of our heads of states was replaced with a divine purpose. Contemplating the manifestation of the eradication of hatred I often concluded, *the entirety of the Middle East's theocracies and dictatorships would be replaced by total anarchy*. We would be left with nothing, as our brotherhood of hatred was the only bond known to us. Enculturated in the malarkey of that demagoguery, forces beyond our control and comprehension seem to deceive us into a less harmful and satisfactory logic as opposed to placing some blame on ourselves and thus, having to act to reverse that state of affairs.

The blind faith in some half-assed conspiracy theories lines up with the logic of having to believe in something with no questions asked. It gives us peace and comfort. As simple as I was, I found that resorting to this absolute nonsense was the root of all our problems. It was a road of willingly-learned helplessness, for no action could make a difference, thereby no action was needed. We might as well have bent our backs with our hands stretching our ass cheeks, waiting for any perpetrator to penetrate us.

Over that cigarette I asked Jamal about his research progress. His answer was detailed, giving me more information than I cared to know. Chemistry was never my thing. Observing Mike and Daniel coming toward our table, I felt relieved as I could finally bring his lecture to an end. My German friend Mike was very close to Daniel. Mike called Daniel "The mayor of expats' companions." He was Norwegian. Daniel claimed that there was an art to being an unemployed companion.

Daniel laughingly asked "Adam, what's wrong with your friend?"

"You mean from yesterday? Is it Mustafa?"

"I don't know his name, but yeah, the one from yesterday."

"Oh yeah, he is a homophobe!"

"What happened?" Mike enquired.

"Mustafa and I were sitting at that table," I pointed to one by the corner. "Two ladies then came and took that corner table. They were transgendered Malays. Mustafa freaked out! He kept looking over his shoulder as though they would rape him. I didn't want to move to another table but he took my cup along to the one at the far corner away from where the ladies sat. I guess there was some sort of an event yesterday. A few minutes after we had changed our seats, the patio was full of transgender people. Mustafa couldn't get why some people go through sex reassignment surgery; he would readily deny them the identity they desired."

"He didn't notice the new ladies behind him as he was preoccupied by his fear of the two sitting at the far end of the patio. I asked him why was he scared and what he thought they would do to him. He didn't admit his fear. Instead, he said that they were disgusting and unclean. However, I knew he was paranoid so I decided to press him, asking if he'd feel dirty surrounded by transgender people. He said absolutely! I continued pressing to see if he felt unclean at that moment. He claimed that he didn't feel that way because we were far enough away from them. So I thought, *fuck that homophobe.* I didn't know how he would react if he realised that the patio was packed with transgender people. I knew he would be frightened but couldn't anticipate what action he would take. So I pointed out that while everybody in the patio was transgender he still didn't feel unclean. That was the moment Daniel was heading into to the café. Mustafa looked at the rest of the people on the patio. He looked back at me. Then, he stood up and looked at me again. He was speechless. One of the ladies looked him in the eyes and flirted, 'How are you handsome?' I have to say it was funny studying his facial expression and his process of dealing with fear. In the end, he mustered all the strength he could manage, stomped a couple of paces before tripping over his own feet. Everybody laughed, including me."

Mike and Daniel giggled as Jamal added, "Gays are disgusting…"

I interrupted, "I don't get it. What is it about gays that disgusts you?"

"I don't know. Two men having sex is unnatural. It is disgusting!"

I started, "You don't know…"

Jamal interrupted, "I finished my military service before the American occupation, right after college. We had to spend a few months in training camp. There was a young pretty guy who had his training with us. You know there are no women and furlough was banned during training. Three big cadets befriended the pretty boy. They lured him to go with them somewhere. They fucked him in the ass. Before the training phase finished, he committed suicide. It's better for a gay to kill himself; if he were my son, I would kill him."

With my face resembling the typical expression of Robert De Niro, I turned to Daniel and Mike. Then for moments, still wearing that face, I stared at Jamal as though to ask, "Why? What? How?" I placed my arm on Jamal's shoulder and said, "That's fucked-up man! Where do I start? Let me see. The three guys fucked the pretty boy... Shit man, I really don't know where to start. They raped him, right?"

"Yes."

"Fuck that shit. So you don't know whether or not he was gay."

"It doesn't matter."

"How come?"

"He will be gay!"

"Is it because he was raped?"

"Yes. I read a study that guys who get raped end up being homosexual."

"What?! That's fucking stupid. I have been hearing of that half-assed study for ages. I actually tried to find it and I had no luck. However, since you seem to have read it, may I get the title?"

"Actually, I heard about it."

"Oh, now you just heard about it! So let me be blunt here, there is no such a study. You might've heard of it but that is no proof. On the off chance that there is yet another one of those studies that give idiots a free pass to ignorance, how do you know it's reliable? You know it doesn't matter. I thought you were explaining to me your disgust of gays…"

Jamal broke in, "Yes. Gays bring shame on their family. Two men having sex is disgusting and against our beliefs and social values. If my son was gay, I would spare my family the shameful and undignified living."

Daniel breached, "There are treatments for homosexuality…"

I interjected, "Do you mean some sort of hormone treatment?"

"Don't get me wrong, I have a lot of gay friends. But yeah, some course of hormone-based and behavioural therapy."

"So, did you tell your 'lot of gay friends' about it?"

"No man, that's rude!"

"Rude because it isn't right?"

"I don't know man."

I turned to Jamal and I said, "The guy from your military training was a victim. I, for one, believe the way our region treats victims of rape, be it men or women, is something to be ashamed of. It is more humiliating than some Stone Age tradition that tells you what you can and cannot be. Punishing victims in the name of honour! How fucking nonsensical is that? It just sounds ludicrous! Back to the main issue, which is of course your dis of gays. I have a number of questions here. I don't want you to go off topic…."

"Can I say something first," Jamal pleaded.

"Sure!"

"My father's friend recently came back from the UK. His son moved there in 2003. Obida was his son's name. He wanted to resettle his father over there, as his mother had passed and he was an only child. However, Obida lived with a black nigger! His father kept telling him that he should ask the housemate to move out. You cannot feel comfortable around blacks. After a while his son told him that the black nigger was his partner and that he loved him. His father was humiliated and devastated. That's very tragic! Not only he is gay, he is in love with a black nigger too."

"I don't know which is more tragic; your racism or your homophobia. You would rather kill your son than accept what should be within his right..."

"Talk is cheap! What if it was your brother or son?"

"I have no kids. But I assure you that if that happened to me, it wouldn't change a thing. It is not my life, not my choice. Foremost, I won't dictate what kind of life he or she might choose to lead..."

"You know our society..."

"I do. In fact, I acknowledge it as an obstacle, but not an obstacle for me. Look, killing is too extreme. Let me reason through some other options. As a father yourself, I assume you want the best for your children. You desire their success and happiness. Maybe you want them to have a better life than yours. But you need to consider that they will make choices and decisions you might not approve of. None of us is right all the time. I know it would be fucking hell for them to lead any sort of life in our region, should they be gays or lesbians. Nonetheless, it's their life and being a parent doesn't give anybody the right to imprison her or his kids in a pretentious life, a miserable life. If her or his wellbeing, livelihood, and happiness are what you are concerned about, then killing them isn't the answer. If it's an overwhelming societal battle that your kid wants to fight, which is what it would be if they stayed in Iraq, support them. If they want an easier time of it, facilitate your kid's exit strategy. If you don't have what it takes, try to strengthen your spine. If you cannot take it, tell your kid to leave that shithole. But whatever the case, please don't kill your kid."

"Did you believe that I would kill my kid? Do you think I am that kind of animal?"

"I certainly hope not."

"I think advising them to leave the region is the best choice. It might not be something they can control. Maybe it's biological."

"Whatever brings you peace. But no killing please!"

"Hahaha, okay, okay, no killing."

Mike, Daniel and I kept chanting, "No killing please, no killing please, no killing please." The fourth time around Jamal started chanting too. On our way out I asked him, "Do you know that gay means happy?" Shocked he exclaimed, "What?!"

****

It was 2012. Yamen told me that he was bringing over to the café his new roommate, a guy from my town. This be would the first time I was to meet Sami. Bob and I were talking theology before the guys made it to the patio. After the introduction, I didn't say much; I merely listened. The guys asked him a few questions; I didn't feel the need to say anything. Sami's language was vulgar and he was easily agitated. He told a lot of tales; mostly about the conflict. He often reminded us that it's hard for us to know what's really happening in Syria as, being in Malaysia, we are so far removed. The first time he said this, I let it slide. The second time I still just kept it to myself. Sami then claimed that love is childish and he wasn't in high school. He said that he wanted to marry a woman who he had only talked to five times over the phone! Then, that became three dates and nine calls. My thoughts go out to her; whoever she might be, I truly sympathise. *After three years of my conditioning him, he won't marry without love.* His latest version of the now old love story was that they stayed together for over a year. In Syria for over a year, you must be kidding me!

The third time he repeated the mantra that we were not there and had no idea what was going on in the country it consumed all of my patience - it was the way he assumed a lecturing position. He would always drift from some half-assed tales to teaching us politics 101. Irritated, I couldn't hold it in any longer and stopped him, "Can I ask you something?"

"Yes."

"So you said that you don't believe in love?"

"Yes. I am twenty-five."

"I know your age now. But how do you make such a claim without having been in a relationship? Of course you can love from a distance but you haven't had a real relationship ever. A few calls are not a relationship. Maybe she is not the one!"

"Love comes after marriage."

"So love is not only for children."

"There are steps. Everybody lies and when they marry, you know it. I am sure you realise that. You have been outside Syria so long that you have forgotten who you are."

"Ah, I see. I wouldn't marry somebody that I doubted, let alone without knowing that person to start with. Forget about that. I want you to clarify something to me; if you don't mind of course."

"What?"

"I will take that as a yes. So you were arrested right?"

"I was in a demonstration in Ar-Raqqa and got arrested."

"Right! So Yamen told me that you've been here for nine months. The first demonstration in Ar-Raqqa was a month ago. Did you really get arrested?"

"I don't lie. I got arrested. You think the news is always right. You haven't been there so you don't know. And I didn't say it happened in Ar-Raqqa…"

"Sure. Of course it didn't happen in Ar-Raqqa. You don't need to speak so loud. You need to calm down…"

"You come down."

"You mean calm down. It's C.A.L.M."

"You are loud. What is this Yamen?"

"Okay man. You keep repeating that we don't know what's happening over there because we are, well, not there. Are you superman?"

"What?!"

"I will take that as a no. Otherwise, I would ask you to end the unrest and bring the villains to justice. But you are not. So let me be clear. You know what happens in your household only if you are there. You can only see as much as you are witness to. You don't have super vision or any abnormal ability. When you were in Ar-Raqqa, you heard the same news about Darra, we heard about it here. Nonetheless, it's February and you have already been here for nine months. The uprising started on the fifteenth of March, 2011. It went violent around July of 2011. Two months after you left…"

"No…"

"Take it easy man. You are right… Not actually, but you need to calm down."

Sami didn't say a word for a few minutes. I changed the subject, "Let me get you a drink. Where are my Raqqan manners?!" No thanks received of course. He just asked me where the sugar was. I pointed to the table by the door. When he came back, I noted, "Sami it is nothing personal. It's just a discussion. We discuss this way."

He studied my face before he asked, "Do you know Hasan Akruma?"

I replied, "Yes we were…"

"He was killed a few months before I left Ar-Raqqa."

****

With the stigma around drinking in old Ar-Raqqa, I sought friends' places to get my occasional sip. Faysal's apartment was my hangout during the winter of 2007. I was his senior. After a glass or two, he'd trash my whole city from our cultural heritage to our current fashion trends. He was from a coastal city. And well, Ar-Raqqa was labelled as a city of backwardness among Syrians from other cities. I often heard that predisposed perception by other Syrians. That is, people in Ar-Raqqa reside in tents and commute using camels. The thing is, I never saw a camel. Compared to other cites, Ar-Raqqa was average; neither the richest nor the poorest; neither the most liberal nor the most conservative; neither the most nor the least developed.

Faysal was in love with this girl from college. He had a funny way showing it though. Huda wasn't dumb, ugly, or a whore; three words he commonly reduced her to. She was really fucking sexy, smart, and elegant. Her father was some public official in the city. Whenever Faysal had had too much drink, his affection toward her couldn't have been clearer and she obviously loved him too. But one

248

cold night, Huda messaged me, inviting me to meet with her. I told Faysal that I was going to see some lady friend. She told me to come over as she was home alone babysitting her brother's kids. By the time I got to her place, the kids were already asleep.

Thinking about it now, having sex scared is quite satisfactory. Maybe, having it under such conditions made it more sensational. On top of me, I demanded, "Can you call your folks? It's getting late and I am afraid…"

"Don't worry," she assured me. Her mother had told her that it would take her no less than an hour to be home. *Sweet*, I thought. She had the most amazing ass I ever seen. I had the pleasure of watching her get me an ashtray from the living room. Lying down by my side she asked, "Adam, do husbands give their wives oral sex?"

"I am not sure, but from what I've heard no!"

"Why?"

"I think it has to do with some idiotic cultural connotation. Somehow, guys I talked to find it shameful."

"Are you shameless?"

"I don't think so. I just give a good head"

She cracked up, "You think so?"

"Huda, can I ask you something?"

"I like that you ask if you can ask. Of course!"

"Don't get me wrong, I like what we have but I am wondering about something. You can deny it, but you and I know it's true. You and Faysal have feelings to each other; it's clear. Why don't you both…"

"Both what?"

"Have sex!"

"It goes without saying that you and I have no potential."

"Please go on."

"My family wouldn't accept you. You come from that part of the city. Your family doesn't even own a place."

"Okay. Not that I am proposing, but what about you?"

"I am sorry but you cannot afford the living I am used to."

"Fair enough! But then why are you having sex with me while you are in love with someone else?"

"A guy in this country would never marry a girl he can have. With you, I know there are no expectations. It also takes ages between the time you get engaged to getting married."

"But your future husband will know that you are not virgin."

"Not actually. I have a plan. Have you heard of hymenorrhaphy?"

"Yeah of course. Smart thinking."

On my way out, I saw Edrees. He knew I'd seen him, but I pretended to be oblivious. I moved a few paces away, but couldn't help turn round when he shouted my name. "Fuck," I muttered. I was scared that he would tell. I think he was visiting somebody in the neighbourhood as his family could in no way afford a square metre in that part of the city. "Adam," he kept repeating my name. "Edrees," I replied. We kissed on the cheeks, "It has been ages," I said.

"Yes it has been"

"Are you busy? Do you care for a stroll?"

"I am not actually."

"I am craving for a lamb's tongue sandwich. Please join me!"

"Sure, why not? I actually want to thank you."

"Thank me for what?"

"If it wasn't for you and Hasan, I wouldn't have finished the seventh grade."

"It's nothing…"

"No it's not. You guys stopped everybody from bullying me."

"School was full of mean kids."

"You were both good guys. You were very strong. Thank you."

"I don't know about good and strong but it was the least I could do. Speaking of which, I lost touch with almost everybody from secondary school. How is Hasan by the way?"

"We're still close. You know, I thought the bullying would stop after school. I was wrong. Hasan has always been there for me. He got married last summer."

"To whom? What does he do now?"

"Their neighbour's daughter. She and her parents came back from Australia. Quite a rich family actually! He owns a small business. After his father passed he opened kitchen appliance store. It's a good business. He always looks out for me."

"He is a good guy."

"Adam, do you know that I am…"

"A homosexual?"

"Gay."

"Yes. I knew before I left school. At the beginning I thought you were weak and kids took advantage, bullying you."

"Would you do the same if you knew then?"

"Do you mean, would I still stop those guys from hurting you?"

"Yeah."

"I think it goes without saying that you were a trouble magnet. It was a jungle, not a school. They smelled weakness and bullied you. I didn't like mean kids."

"You didn't answer my question."

"It wasn't you being gay that made me take your side. I just didn't like how they treated you."

"Do you hate me?"

"Why? Because you're gay! The answer is no, I don't hate you. I have no business to tell you what is right and what's wrong."

"Do you think it is wrong to be gay?"

"I think it is for you to decide who you want to share bed with. It's our people that don't accept it."

"Yeah tell me about it!"

****

Before Sami told me about Hasan's fate, the last I had heard of him was from Edrees in that winter of 2007. It took me few moments to process the news in 2012. "How was he killed?" I asked. Sami smiled before recounting, "His twink friend got him killed."

"Twink is an awful word. What happened?"

"Do you know the faggot Edrees…"

"That's another vulgar word. Can you please tell the story without being so fucking judgemental?"

"What the fuck man? Why do you have to be this way? I am just telling you a story you don't know."

"My fault…"

"He is a guy who likes to be fucked in the ass…"

"Man, please be respectful. They were both friends."

"Do you want to know what happened?"

"Yes, please."

"Edrees has a Kurdish friend. So the Kurdish guy and his brother asked Edrees to join them fishing by the old bridge. After the fishing trip, he went to Hasan's shop. Hasan knew that Edrees had allowed the Kurdish guys to fuck him. Anyways, he went after the Kurdish guys. The older guy stabbed him in the abdomen. He died on the way to the hospital."

"Shit," I murmured as I observed Sami intently with a fury that I couldn't fail to hide. Hasan had known that Edrees was gay; long before I did. Edrees told me so. Sami's judgemental version of the story didn't make any sense to me. *Edrees' so-called friends must've raped him and thus, Hasan went after them*, I thought.

****

I have the habit of contemplating the evolution of my so-called moral code. I had myself convinced that if I managed to figure what led me away from the sheep, I would be able to influence others and bring them to what I ascribe to be right. Seeing the sickening methods of ISIL executions, of those they label as gay in Ar-Raqqa and Mosel, one could only wonder whether psychopathy is to blame. The Russian thugs' campaign of humiliation against their gay countrymen suggested some support to the aforementioned notion. If psychopathy was the disease, then empathy might be a remedy. Putting oneself in another's shoes, allowing a sip of the tragedy of being different, might open one's eyes to the aggression against that group of people. In the anticipation of that aggression lay anger towards aggressors. And that anger was derived from the exposure to the threat. Yet, the threat was there for being nothing except what you were! Not being able to change yourself would bring frustration to anger. For in the absence of justice, the two states were amplified. And here came the question, *what to do about it?* Should I call the demagogues the bigots they are! Should I prevent their abuse? Or should I take no action as an action? *But no action ain't an action,* my conscience shouted out loud.

It wasn't only ISIL and thugs; it wasn't only a Middle Eastern disease; and psychopathy wasn't its only root. Being a homophobe implied being threatened. The fear of exposure to homosexual people might lead to a number of attitudinal and behavioural responses. The most clichéd was "fight or flight". One can clearly see the harm the aggressor causes when they choose fight as a means of reducing this anxiety and fear. I was inclined to believe that this kind of emotion was a socio-cultural artefact as the trend was not global. Our value system was at the core of it. I could see that the system was hard to alter. Yet I went further to claim that the equation was not just exposure, value system, and then fear. There were plenty of things between. Our species evolved and such impulses were not initially given by nature. Regulating these impulses might take a while but it was what separated us from the less evolved species.

Chapter 13

From Behind the Telescope

My earliest memories were of me feeling saddened by Fadi leaving for school. It was winter and I was wearing these girly pink gloves that my mother had bought from some thrift shop. I wouldn't say I had much of a childhood, but however short it might've been, it wasn't the best or worst of times. Thinking about it, my college days weren't much different. I don't have much to say about them either; except of course for the two tiny scars and that urgent trip back to Ar-Raqqa. A part of me has always been intimate with tragedies, without allowing them to overwhelm and define me. Maybe that resilience was not some inherited willpower; but rather my own evolution, forging me into one who wouldn't break under pressure. Maybe I have been broken all along.

Absorbed in the scene of Sheila's cats jumping over each other, I couldn't help but mutter, "Fuck!" Rubbing my shoulder, she asked, "What?"

"The cat's brought up some old memories," I replied.

****

Awakened by the sound of somebody knocking on my door, I was taken by surprise to see Uncle Khamees on my doorstep. We have never gotten along. As I tried to invite him in, he cut me short, "Put something on, be quick! It is urgent."

I yawned, confused, "What is…"

"Just wear something, I will explain on the way."

This cannot be good, I thought rushing to my room. On our way down he harangued me for not getting a cell phone. At first I figured my uncle had some business in Aleppo, *he wouldn't make the trip just to see me, let alone to urge me to tag along with him*. It didn't hit me that some serious shit had happened until I saw Meqdad leaning on his taxi by the entrance. "What the fuck is going on?" I looked my uncle in the eyes demanding an answer. "Nothing, my mother was at the hospital. We couldn't get hold of you yesterday. She's not well. They already took her back to Ar-Raqqa. She asked for you."

"Oh, I am very sorry."

Studying my uncle's empty gaze through nothingness between Aleppo and Ar-Raqqa I concluded, *she is long gone*. Over the new bridge looking down at the Euphrates River my uncle made no sense noting, "Your father needs your support, now more than ever." *My grandmother was old, so however tragic, my father's not likely to need me to help him in grief,* I thought. so I suspected it wasn't my grandmother or my father, but I couldn't figure who it was. When I got out of the taxi my uncle broke into tears, "Sorry, sorry, sorry. Your brother passed." I heard what he said, but something else caught my attention.

My mother emerged, from the door, faltered and fell to her knees. And all I could hear were her howls reduced to some buzzing sound. And all I could see was her falling scarf, her hands reaching the ground, and the soil covering more of her face each time she slapped her cheeks. I took her hand and led her home as if dealing with a tantrumming child. My wailing father grabbed my shoulder and I turned to him as my mother stared on and all I could think of was my parent's pillow talk that summer night when we all had slept in the courtyard.

Their words echoed in my ears, muting their ceremony of grief. Their tears were like waterfalls, landing on my face. I didn't bother to wipe their pain from my face. All I longed for was that fucking pillow talk. They were like "Fadi is this," and "Fadi is that." They couldn't have been more proud. I kissed my father on the forehead and my mother on her cheeks.

"There are a lot of people who want to pay their condolences," my moaning father noted.

"I'll take care of that," I assured.

****

"I guess you know that I am not a cat person," I whispered in Sheila's ear as I continued, "On a summer night, I suppose it was 2006, I was sleeping at my parents. I was awaked by a strange sound. I figured it was coming from under the table by my mattress. I actually woke my mother up to take care of them! I mean to get them out of the room. Long story short, my mother managed to get a kitten out from under the bed. The mother of the kitten attacked my mother, howling at her. She was forced to put the kitten on the ground; I suppose she got scared. With her mouth the mother grabbed the nape of the small kitten's neck and scurried out of the room. At that sight, I could see the drops coursing down my mother's face. Tearfully she murmured, 'Why didn't I have a chance to save my baby?' I couldn't say a word to her."

Observing me Sheila asked, "How is she these days?" Kissing her on the forehead I replied, "With the conflict and a life of constant loss, the poor woman has never had a break." With a hand over my face, she added "And what about you?" I

262

thinned my lips, forcing an automatic reply, "I am fine!" She knew that I didn't want to end the night recounting the tales and aftermath of the conflict.

In light of my distanced telescopic exposure to the mayhem, I refused to plagiarise others' personal tragedies as my own. There is an authorship in misery that costs more than empathy. Often I'd found myself dumbstruck in failed attempts to simulate that particular unfamiliar dolour. After all, no one takes pleasure in being possessed by a wailing father collecting the decapitated head of his innocent six year old. Even on the hinge of a willing attempt at full empathy with those cursed with such catastrophes, one had to have a superhuman emotional powers. I could not, in any way, claim the ability to relate to those who have been forced to swallow the never-ending bitter and poisonous pills of our inherited misfortune. Yet that excruciating pain in my chest seemed to elicit a state of agony in me, even from far behind the telescope. It could have been my tribal gene amplified by the ripple effect of the falling, moving in me what was left of my humanity.

****

Tunisia had a spiral effect over Middle Easterners and North Africans everywhere. The revolutionary movement had somehow awakened many to their long-endured abuse. The Tibetan-style one-man protest ignited a burning desire to reclaim a long lost sense of dignity in all of us.

Before the middle of March 2011, I hadn't even in my wildest dreams thought my people would chant, "Enough!" That said, Tunisia gave me some hope. I thought, *I might be able go back one day*. I had this fantasy of my mother asking me to come back. Her last words in August 2008 were, "Never come back. I lost one, don't make it two."

I understood then, it would break my parents and kill any opportunity my siblings might have, should I get caught. Uncle Khamees had been detained for the fifth time. The forty-seven-year-old had spent more time in the cage than outside; he wouldn't change it even if he could have spent the rest of his life free. My unlawful actions were not anywhere close to his, not by a long shot. If it wasn't for that head of Deir Al Zor's intelligence police, I wouldn't have raised any red flags. Jamea Jamea was the name of that asshole. He was demoted to that position after the Syrian troops had to leave Lebanon, where he used to "serve."

During college, then after graduation and even throughout my teaching career in that college, I'd earned some extra cash selling home-made copies of audio disks. There were no copyright laws against it. For some reason, Jamea Jamea hated Rock n' Roll. He'd led this campaign against those dealing and using that "drug". He deemed an appetite for that genre as satanic. I alerted my parents that things might go south after one of my clients got detained. With the ordeal of my uncle in the picture, they couldn't risk it. It was a no-brainer as we concluded that I should leave the country. I didn't realise the troubles I had caused then. My father had to jump through many hoops, paying the way of my exodus in bribes.

My master studies were completed in June of 2010. A classmate of mine desperately wanted to celebrate my last day in school. Although I hinted that it would be more convenient the following day, I couldn't change her mind. She said she wanted to watch a movie with me. Deprived of sleep, I couldn't help but snatch forty winks during the advertisements. Half way through that teen vampire movie, my vibrating phone saved me.

I went all the way down to the parking lot where I lit a cigarette before calling the unknown number back. It was from somebody in Saudi Arabia. I only knew two people over there; an uncle and a friend. Hearing his voice, I realised it was Uncle Hamad.

"Hello my child" Uncle Hamad began.

"Hello uncle, how're you?"

"Thank god. How were your exams?"

"Good! Today was my last."

"I know your father told me."

"Okay…"

"Your father asked me to wait until you had finished…"

"Wait for what?"

"It is more serious than you think."

"What are you talking about?"

"Do you know Jamea Jamea?"

"The motherfucker!"

"How is your daughter?"

"What?!"

"It's okay, you can tell me."

Laughingly I replied, "Why wouldn't I? If I had a daughter, I would tell you about her."

"It's just, me and your father, through a friend of a friend, paid some cash to sit with Jamea Jamea…"

"And?"

"After you escaped, the police confiscated your belongings."

"Like what?"

"Your computer, books, and documents."

"I see."

"They found something on the hard disk, even after you had formatted it."

"Okay, what is it?"

"There is this opposition website where you wrote some articles."

"Oh. It was nothing. I thought... I mainly cited some of the hate speeches of the neighbouring mosques. Besides..."

"It doesn't matter. So are you married?"

"Enough with that. I am not married and I don't have any children."

"The report they showed stated that you are."

"Okay, that's not right."

"Is anybody paying you?"

"I earn my money. No uncle, nobody is paying me anything. Can you please cut the foreplay? Please cut to the fucking chase."

"The report…"

"Yes the fucking report."

"We read the whole thing. It says that you are married to an Asian American. Initially she was your boss…"

I couldn't help it but break up in a belly laugh for a moment before noting, "What movie was that? I am sorry, please keep going."

"It's serious…"

"Again, I am sorry, but this is hilarious."

"Your boss worked for the Chinese and Americans and you worked for the Mossad."

"Is it because my boss was an Asian American? So, she is a double agent! I know all roads lead to the Mossad but a *triple* agent, that's something new. China! I am sorry uncle but this is too fucking hysterical."

"The report continued that you got married to your boss and both of you are paid by foreign agencies."

I just laughed helplessly before sighing, "Ooooh. I apologise uncle. I am deeply sorry to disappoint you. Listen, I led a very interesting life in that report. I have to say there is not much action happening around here. I am penniless the fifteenth of every month."

"You know you cannot come back."

"I know."

"Your father wanted to tell you but he is afraid that his line is tapped."

"It's okay. Thank you for letting me know about it."

"Just one more thing, you are already charged."

"A shocker, spit it out uncle!"

"You are charged *in absentia*. The court concluded that your crime falls under 'weakening the national spirit'."

"Do you mean sedition?!"

"I don't know, it says 'weakening the national spirit'."

"Whatever the fuck is that? I would say very merciful for a triple agent."

"Please be careful. A few months back your father was arrested. Somebody reported you cursing the regime and calling it Iran state-sponsored terrorism."

****

Before the uprising, my compatriots and I often entertained ideas of possible courses of events. Mine were very pessimistic then. "It will take over five years to topple Al-Assad," I asserted to Kareem. The guy was a know-it-all generaliser. He wanted to assume leadership of our compatriots. He was double my size, but with his high-pitched voice he couldn't intimidate a fly. Kareem came to the mall once, wanting to walk back home; something Syrians do. We love to stroll. I was tired, but didn't mind. The way back to our neighbourhood cut through the high-rise buildings, to bungalows, to a dimly-lit area by the beach, and to the darker emptiness between the woods and the highway. By the beach I noticed a band of bikers watching us. I didn't think much about it and continued on the pavement by the woods. It was there where two bikes stopped, facing us. Two guys on the back of each bike rushed towards us with their machetes. I tried to be diplomatic, and out of stupidity resisted giving them my backpack. As I was trying to talk my way out of it, I held one of the thug's wrists. With a kick of adrenaline, I found the strength to twist the arm

270

holding the machete, trying to gain possession of it. I hadn't noticed the rest of the gang sprinting toward us. With two pulling my backpack, I found myself on the ground counting the kicks. All I could do was to save my head from their targeted attacks. If it wasn't for a nearby vehicle's startling horns, it would have been more than twelve stitches on my head.

I couldn't look around for Kareem, not until they had made a run for it. Lying on the ground, I moved my head in both directions, trying to catch a glimpse of him. Then I realised he had just run. I didn't blame him; I guessed his survival instinct must've just kicked in. His place was twenty minutes away, closer than mine. With my injuries, it took me thirty.

Humour is all about being taken or taking someone by surprise. The sight of Kareem holding the squeegee standing by his condo brought forth my helpless laughter, causing painful coughs. It was then when I recalled how scared the Indian Malaysians had made him. He would try to avoid an alley with any Indian passers-by. *There'll be no action movies dramatising tales of Kareem's courage,* I thought. The shivering self-proclaimed Hercules didn't say a word. "It's okay," I assured. It was a good job they hadn't managed to take my wallet. I studied him trying to avoid paying the taxi fare by the hospital's entrance. I couldn't help but stand for a few moments, gesturing to him to pay the driver before finally telling him, "Take it easy man. I will pay it." For whatever reason, he avoided me afterwards. I heard his version of the story from an acquaintance. It was very much the same, except he'd switched roles with me. I cannot not recall an occasion in which I have hurt him in any way. Regardless, trashing me behind my back was something he mastered.

Kareem was certain. He thought it was a matter of months before an uprising would take place in the country, claiming, "The Syrian people will act decisively to bring the Al-Assad era to a halt."

I admit, even with that revolutionary spirit, it was almost impossible for him to escape the conditioning of Al-Ba'ath Party's books of patriotism. Indoctrinated by the long course of conditioning, the nation was promoted to be at the centre of all regional and global affairs. Furthermore, Western powers were asserted as malicious in their endeavours to exploit the 'wealth of Syria'. Kareem and Yamen had an unshakeable belief in the aforementioned conspiracy-based oversimplification of the world order, which was an insult to those with functioning brain cells. Before things went south between Kareem and I, in the presence of Yamen we

272

had had plenty of political discussions. In the wake of the Egyptian January 25 revolution, Kareem claimed, "Soon it will be us."

"Impossible," Yamen interjected.

I wondered, "Why is that so Yamen?"

He preached, "There is a common denominator between Egypt and Tunisia. It's about their ideology, reliance on the U.S., and relationship with Israel."

"Bashar Al-Assad is also a friend of Israel," Kareem cut in.

Yamen had this sickeningly sanctimonious smile whenever he talked about Iran and Al-Assad. I recognised it as a sign of ideological victory. I thought, it's a *Shiite versus Sunni kind of thing*. He wore that mask of unreasoned supremacy to ridicule malarkey and facts alike. For in him there was a Shiite common sense that served a higher purpose. Observing Yamen's nonverbal counterargument, I argued, "I have no access to classified information and I don't have the experience to intuit that friendship. I actually think Al-Assad is one of their nemeses in the region."

Kareem also wore Yamen's ridiculing mask of intellectual supremacy. Bothered by his idiocy I collected my thoughts, "Emmm," and continued, "well, I guess I've already hinted at my lower level of intelligence. That said Yamen, it seems to me that your opinion is very much shaped by Al-Assad's rationalisation. I mean his interview with the Wall Street Journal. Your president first wanted to distance himself from the uprisings in Tunisia and Egypt and then ended up claiming that Syrians won't follow the trend. He claimed that the Syrian regime, with all the difficulties facing the country, satisfies citizens' ideological aspirations as opposed to those of the Egyptians."

"You read it," Yamen wondered.

"Yes, but what appears to be the case is that you and your president are distant from what is happening in Tunisia and Egypt. He was right on one thing; he should have stuck to talking about Syria exclusively. Neither in Tunisia nor in Egypt have I heard calls for ending ties with the West, let alone establishing a stronger relationship with Iran. Watching what's going on, the sum of demonstrators' grievances is merely internal. To be exact, they are trying to bring an end to their states' repressive regime. What I hear is 'No more abuse of power'. At the core of it, people are demanding the end of autocracies and economic referendums. But of course, Syria has to have immunity in the face of this disease. A shocker, Israel has to do something with it. So Yamen, a client state of Iran or not, you cannot escalate your abuse of power and expect people to keep praising your grace."

****

Moayad moved to Penang days after Yamen, Kareem, and Mustafa registered at the university. I was their senior in time on the island. None of them had met each other before the day Yamen made it to my place. Some Iranian lady had given my number to Kareem. Before meeting him, I asked Yamen to tag along. When I took them to the office of higher education, Mustafa was waiting his turn. Kareem and Mustafa had both attended an event at the Syrian embassy while they were staying in Kuala Lumpur. During his first year on the island, Mustafa distanced himself from our compatriots. We knew about Moayed from my Jordanian housemate, Sameer, who had given him a ride to school. He called him a child. Sameer told Moayed that he shared an apartment with a Syrian. My housemate was a generous dude; he offered the new guy the empty room in our apartment, until he found a place. Meanwhile, Yamen and Kareem had been looking for a flatmate. Although Mustafa wasn't too keen on their place, I decided to make an introduction. They offered him a discounted rate for that windowless room; a price he couldn't turn down.

Kareem was the alpha dog in that rented apartment. Even Moayed and Yamen called their place, Kareem's. The guys had their differences and I often found myself hosting each separately before mediating their conflicts. While Moayed didn't let a thing slide, Yamen took all of their bullshit. He was and still is the least confrontational creature I've ever come across. I had no clue why he strived to please everybody; everybody but me.

My Norwegian and German friends wondered whether they should kiss Moayed's hand. He would shake their hands with the tip of his fingers, gently with the back of his upward. He was so soft that he would make the most feminine lady, in the stereotypical sense, look rigid. I didn't know if he was aware of it. Hearing his drawn-out teenage girl-like voice ranting how men should act manly never failed to bring a few moments of silence that in turn ended with long repressed belly laughter.

Moayed's father was some toothless official in Al-Assad's government. During the time of Hafez Al-Assad, he was a member of the parliament and was then promoted to leader in the national party committee. Before Bashar Al-Assad inherited his father's monarchy, Moayed's father was demoted to a "key". A key was not an official position. It referred to a person hired by a powerful official, serving a proxy role for those seeking the corrupt system's consent, be it legitimate or illegitimate. Moayed aspired to that kind of power; in his own words, "There is nothing better. It grants you respect and people's love. People will, literally, do anything to please you; invite you to major events and buy you expensive gifts." I had the habit of ridiculing that status fucking quo, "It's like being arm-candy!" He would interject, his limp hand dangling from his weak wrist, "No it's not like that. It's like you are up here and they are down there."

I often added, "It's like a modern day prince. Or to be blunt, that's what it means to be a man in power in that corrupted shithole. People don't respect you; they don't looove you. You stand between them and what, sometimes, is theirs." The guy was a classic example of those attaining such positions.

****

After the Syrian regime retaliated viciously and repressed the peaceful protestors I thought, *Al-Assad will lose his self-proclaimed support.* During that phase, emotions were tense. When the killings started and footage of the atrocities made it to the online sphere, it was hard to talk about anything other than the unrest.

For hours, every day, I'd drift from major news channels to social media. Frowning from behind the screen, my place had become a haunted refuge; for in brutality there was indecency greater than that in pornography. On occasions when the sin was committed, the disapproval of those invading my privacy was cast.

Lost in the mayhem of Daraa, I pronounced the honour and shamelessness of my kind. That child looked just like me when I was his age. He was tanned and rough. He wore the cheapest of all clothes. He could've been me. His moaning father could've been mine. And just like that child, I wandered around that ghetto of mine; I'd played ball and enjoyed the outdoors. I'd also worn those cheap old second-hand football jerseys. I'd seen my father coming and leaving. He would ask me to be careful.

I believed that child's father was not any less than mine; or at least I choose to believe so. I could've been that child. He could have had a brighter future than mine, notwithstanding his upbringing. My father could've been that wailing, broken man, with a hand down against my shoulder blades, raising my torso. That saliva could've been his; it could've been his, falling with no care, not that he would've given a flying rat's ass about swallowing it. And the other gentle, trembling hand could've been his; it could've been his hand, shaking, trying to hold my nearly severed head from falling. That disfigured face could've been mine. And that flowing crimson could've been the spill of my blood, stripping my father of his last drops of sanity.

That video of Daraa's child affected me in so many ways, arousing rage in me. Seeing him breathless, lying on the ground and then raised up by his howling father brought forth in my afflicted soul an urge to inflict pain on the walls of my messy room. The yells accompanying the punches had my usually loquacious flatmate worried about my wellbeing. Seeing the bruised knuckles of my shivering hands scared the guy into a state of speechlessness. The regulating tactic of venting the fury of my helplessness became a ritual. As time passed it became a habit. Upon seeing me in that state, Jennifer confessed, "I'm scared of you." Although I explained that my anger was not directed at her and the only entity enduring my aggressions were the poor walls, she felt frightened by that repeated scene. My guess is that she wanted me to talk about it; she desired to be a part of that intimacy. I wanted to get her involved; she wanted to comfort me and I needed the help. But I couldn't burden her. I had to repress my urges in her presence. But I didn't have the resolve to relinquish my ritual all at once. It had just become a practice of solitude. But such a window of opportunity had become too slim, having to share my room with her. Even so, I had to persevere to put my urges to sleep but they kept on accumulating, overwhelming me.

Riding my bike across the mainland highways, I glimpsed toward the woods. They were deserted of mankind. They were divine and sacred. They were holy in the absence of my kind. Those drives were willing sacrifices to lessen my burdened, overwhelmed soul. It was like praying in a place of worship rather than at home. It was like going to Sunday mass; except I was the priest and my soul would call Sunday whenever urged to cast away the curses of mankind.

Sheila called the ritual a support system. She had her own. It was Suzan. After telling her about mine she wanted me to have a human-based one. She wanted to be it. And again, I'd started to change it. Still, I am trying. But in the back of my head I knew, I would relapse and go back to the woods.

****

In Ar-Raqqa we had our ways of showing respect to the dead, be it a relative or a neighbour. We would build a tent in the neighbourhood, or hire someone to do it. It had to be big enough to host no less than seventy of those paying their condolences. The tent was for men and the house of the deceased was for grieving women. Thinking about the custom, I realise it was our method of grief counselling. Of course that only applies for the tent. Close male and distant relatives, friends and acquaintances, colleagues or classmates, and those who had endured similar or greater tragedies practised that therapeutic course of support.

The first day started with paying respect after the burial. For the second day, those close to the departed were pressed to recount the tales of those gone. Some had to be harangued to take part. I have witnessed those outraged by admonishments for not making a contribution. When such anger was articulated, those closest to the one displaying the outburst would force him to leave the tent. An apology was required and a kiss on the cheek would be given by both as a sign of letting that episode slide. By any means, those grieving were pressed to recount their tragedies. On the third day, the tent was dedicated to those who had endured the same or worse misfortunes. In turns they would speak out about their sips of pain. They would recount from the start; the date, avenue, cause, and aftermath. There was a dramatization of the toll their depression took on their beloved ones. No matter how it started, it always ended up with, "This is the logic of life and thus you should go forward." From the fourth day onward, people would bring up all kind of topics; they would even tell jokes. At that stage, those close to the deceased were urged to talk about anything but the tragedy. There was a lot of praying too, a part I always escaped.

Women had a wholly different experience. It was a celebration of endless moaning. On many occasions it lasted long after the tent was removed.

Neighbours had to show respect. Lowering the volume of music was part of it. A wedding ceremony within the next seven doors was taboo.

For me, the rules of engagement through social media were analogous to those of my real world. As a fool, I thought that the whole purpose of the tool was to transmit experiences, opinions, and events based on one's actual life. I struggled to reason past the incongruences that many had shown.

As the stream of footage kept showing my people's early pursuit of dignity and freedom, I tried to show my respect online as the seven-door rule didn't apply to Facebook or Twitter.

I still vividly recall the day my ritual failed to sufficiently repress my outrage. It was months after Al-Assad's first speech. Even I hadn't expected him to ridicule everybody calling for dignity. I didn't think he would go so far as his atrocious retaliation, laughing in the face of those demanding the very least of recognised existence. I stopped to give some cash to Yamen. Moayed had been sitting with him in the living room. They insisted on sharing some of the Syrian coffee that Moayed had brought from his last visit. Over that cup of coffee, Yamen pressed, "Smile man."

"After watching the news, can you?"

"I just finished watching the Syria news."

"You need to teach me how to deal with it."

Moayed butted in, "What happened? I don't read the news."

Yamen clarified, "Some fabricated Aljazeera movie."

Sighing my irritation, "You are not in a battle with fucking Aljazeera. Enough with your conspiracy bullshit. Anderson Cooper responded to your president's ambassador in the United Nations when the latter claimed everything is just a, 'Foreign conspiracy against a sovereign nation.' So I am going to use his line:

Have all the human rights groups been wrong; all the countries now imposing sanctions, all the brave people inside Syria daring to stand on the streets with dignity and call out for basic freedoms, are they all making it up? If so, it would be one of the biggest conspiracies, biggest lies the world has ever seen, which makes Bashar Al-Assad history's greatest victim.

I added, "Come on man! What if Hezbollah and the Iranian-sponsored news channels had it wrong?"

"I would blame those taking their children to demonstrations."

"First, the two-year-old in Lattakia was not demonstrating and yet the people you defend shot her in the eye. But even if her parents did take her, not that I would encourage it, she and her parents are victims and Bashar's army is first to blame."

Starting from the moment I opened my mouth, Moayed was anxious to say something. He looked at me and spoke softly, "Even Americans call Obama Mr. President. He is our president. Why do you keep calling him by name only." I loathed Yamen's poisonous smile. It'd resembled the one Al-Assad used when he mocked those calling out for dignity and labelled them as armed gangs and terrorists. But I had to keep my feelings to myself.

Looking back at Moayed I vented, "A child, among many, taken to prison, then, tortured. And no that wasn't enough! They had to cut his penis. Even after all of that barbarism, his little body still showed the burns of their cigarettes. And all you care about is the title of your psycho president. Let me put it this way, when he stops imprisoning children, killing children, killing civilians, and mocking them afterward... But actually, even then I still could not call Bashar a president."

Yamen was distracted, looking at his phone. "Adam," he questioned, "why couldn't I tag you?"

I knew what he was talking about but the image of that little boy was so overwhelmingly gruesome that it took me a while to respond. I bought myself some time, asking, "What?!"

"I wanted to tag you in the pictures from our last dinner but I couldn't."

"Yeah, about that. I have to accept that first. Just an FYI, I won't."

"Why?"

"Well, it's not in me to disrespect the departed."

"What do you mean?"

"If my neighbour passed, I wouldn't turn on my stereo on the highest volume."

"Take it easy man. It's Facebook."

"That's even worse. I have to show respect to the dead."

"I know how to show respect."

"Of course you do!"

"I do!"

"Whatever brings you comfort. I, for one wouldn't call, "Wohooo! I am happy to be me," respectful. It was on the day your best friend was killed. You are friends with his brother on your Facebook. Even his father talked to you on the same day."

"It wasn't on the same day."

"Actually it was. I was with you then."

"No you keep forgetting."

"Yes I have dementia!"

****

Right from the start it had become clear that the Bashar Al-Assad regime wasn't like the British and thus, the Syrian people couldn't be Gandhi forever. Starting from Daraa, the shit had been too gruesome to swallow. Mothers wailing over their departed children and spouses; fathers howling the eternal loss of their babies; soldiers jumping on those shouting out the indecent word, "dignity"; adolescents dragging the bodies of the fallen, risking being shot at in their endeavour to grant the deceased a dignified burial; chaotic mayhem; and had been slowly dawning on me over the last few days.' Al-Assad and his loyalists denying the braves' existence. Al-Assad maintained his stance, putting the blame on terrorists and armed gangs. Yet at the time, those mysterious outlaws were civilians with a stomach to endure abuses that I never imagined could exist.

You would expect a dictator to justify his brutality or to carry it out quelling his enemies without any explanation. But what had long puzzled me the most was his supporters. What could it be that made sane men and women take the side of that power-obsessed psychopathic maniac? I admit at some intellectual level, I was curious and fascinated by that conundrum. I craved for their thoughts and justifications. I wanted to know whether any possible validation could exist. And what could it have been to make the blood of their countrymen and women so cheap. *Are some people predisposed to violence; are they morally corrupt; were they successfully conditioned by Al-Assad's ruling party; are they that naïve; do they know something that most of the world doesn't?* I'd asked myself. Of course conspiracy was the initial popular theory. But I figured if you kept pushing the right buttons, you would get to the root of it.

Al-Assad's worst enemy then was his own media aids, from top to bottom. They made it easy to counter those nonsensical conspiracy impulses. While gruesome and real, it was funny when Al-Assad's foreign affairs minister presented a video. It sickened me in ways I wasn't aware of.

Feeling the branch pressed against my cheek I turned right and then to the left. I wasn't in pain and all I could see was two bearded behemoths; one holding the stick and the other laughing. Terrified and in agony, I woke up, out of breath, recalling the nightmare, the boiled oil that had been poured on me, from head to toe, then catching a glimpse of my naked fried chicken-like skin; just like in the video. The one presented by the foreign minister, who couldn't speak more than two words a minute at his best moment, be it sad or happy. The video that was real, except not from Syria. That one that had been taken in some Lebanese village, years before March 2011.

Yamen spent almost all of his days on Facebook. He wanted to marry so badly that I figured his childhood dream career must have been to be a husband. "Come join me for a cigarette, I am a real person," I pointed to the patio and added, "please leave your phone inside." He smiled, "She is a real person, thank you."

"Yamen I want to ask you something."

"No politics please!"

"What can two Syrians talk about other than politics? Besides, what is more important at the moment?"

"My fiancée," he smiled.

"She is not your fiancée yet! So let me ask you a very simple question. After all of this, how can you keep supporting Al-Assad? Really, why?"

"Al-Assad is the only true leader. He is standing against the whole world. He is a key in the resistance movement. Tell me who else is standing with the Palestinian people?"

"You know that he's so ruthless that even the leadership of Hamas denounced him."

"But you're against Hamas."

"But you're for Hamas."

"That's not true."

"Come on man! Do you want me to get my laptop and show you the video? Even more, your beloved Hamas claimed that Iran sent them faulty missiles."

"It's just politics!"

"Indeed it is."

"Look the opposition will sell it all to Israel."

"If you mean peace, I certainly hope so. But that's just wishful thinking. Nevertheless, we all know that the political opposition, who are not very representative of the Syrian people, are led by the Muslim Brotherhood."

"Fuck those assholes."

"Well, first I am happy that you're using the words fuck and assholes. Coming from a guy who couldn't say 'butt' when I first saw him, I am glad that I am wearing off on you. I don't understand, if you like Hamas that much, how come you hate the Muslim Brotherhood?"

"What do you mean? They are not like the Brotherhood in idiocy."

"Actually, they are the same. Hamas is made up of that brotherhood in idiocy. You can look it up!"

"Politics."

"I don't get it, are you admitting that politics is too complicated for you or are you justifying your dissonance as political?"

"You know what I mean."

"Honestly, I don't. But for the sake of the argument, I'm gonna assume it's the latter. In a political sense, why is the Brotherhood good in Palestine and bad in Syria?"

"They are fighting Israeli in Palestine. In Syria they are terrorists."

"Actually, one might argue the label is in reverse order. Just to be clear, while the umbrella ideology of Muslim Brotherhood is not deemed terroristic, I am still against them. But that's not the point, which I will come back to later, of course."

"Of course!"

"So it's the good ol' I-hate-them-more-than-I-love-you; except in this case your hate towards the Israelis outweighs the life of your own people."

"It's not like that."

"It actually is. So you are against the opposition because of your hate towards the Israelis."

"Because of our collective struggle as Muslims; you wouldn't understand."

"I don't have to be a Muslim to understand. But forget about my lower level of intelligence. Unfortunately, even if the opposition wins, there won't be peace with Israel. Remember, you agreed that the strongest among the opposition are the Muslim Brothers. An ideology that your beloved Hamas is actually affiliated with."

"I told you, you won't understand."

"Yeah, you keep telling me so. I promise you if you explain it to me, I will try my best to understand. Is it to do with the fact that you are Shiite and pledge your loyalty to Iran…"

"I am Syrian, just like you…"

"I am glad to hear that. But still, why the hypocrisy?"

"Hypocrisy?!"

"Yeah! You are against the Muslim Brotherhood anywhere but in Palestine. Do you support a secular government?"

"No that's against my faith."

"Why, in the case of our country, do you label all Sunni-based groups as terrorists while you refuse the label to any Shiite-based terrorist organisation, globally?"

"It's not like that."

"It's absolutely that."

"Al-Assad will stay in power…"

"Okay."

"My people come first after his. He allows us to practise our ritual, open our Islamic centres, and permits Iran to support us."

"But for the others it's not the case. I mean Sunnis. Just imagine for a second that Al-Assad is gone."

"Palestine…"

"Enough with the Palestine nonsense."

"It won't be the same to my people."

"What? Are you afraid they might be treated equal to the majority of the country?"

"Iran will never be part of the picture."

"So it is about Iran. You just claimed that you are as Syrian as me."

"You wouldn't understand."

"Of course I wouldn't. But here's what I do understand: you would rather your country was decimated than cut ties with Iran. By the way, I wish that what you are terrified of was the case, though still I highly doubt it. Maybe I am wrong! Are you secretly in love with Al-Assad? I mean in the sexual and emotional senses."

"What the fuck, man?"

"The fuck is on the issue you are trading for thousands of innocents. I mean for the sake of the country's stance on Palestine; which I have to say, sadly, could be the same position any successive government could take; which means that you support that asshat of a dictator for no apparent reason. The other reason, you would rather children are slaughtered in the arms of their mothers than a probable loss of ties with the terrorist republic of Iran. Or maybe, it's so vital that no Sunni should be in power that it justifies the genocide of tens of thousands of people."

On that balcony I could see the ocean if I stood on my tip-toes. Moayed handed me some wine. He'd started drinking and wanted to share his cheap red with me. He was so phony that he'd started to drink and smoke cigars just so he could claim the self-image of what he recognised as men with some sort of power. I have to say, at this point in our exchange, I didn't bother to question him about it. After a sip or two he gave me a look as though he already wore the skin of a tycoon, trying to force a thicker voice, "Maybe you wonder why I support mister president Bashar Al-Assad?"

"Okay," I knew I shouldn't say more; he would spill it out anyways.

Moayed placed his soft hand on my shoulder and continued, "You know…"

"I want to know but it's too hot out here and you know I don't like it that you're so handsy."

"You know I hate gays! I am a Syrian, not a faggot."

"Syrian or gay, I just don't like it. Anyways, you were saying."

"My father is very powerful…"

295

"You mean he used to have some power."

"With my father's connections, I won't settle for less than the highest managerial position at any governmental department."

"Okay."

"A guy like me can never get something like that without this influence."

"Oh, I am really surprised that you acknowledge that. What influence?"

"I mean my connections."

"Oh, I see. So you support your president because in that corrupted country, a guy like you can be somebody."

"Why can you not say Mr President?"

"Ah?! You don't mind me talking about you as though you are not qualified to do shit but still all you worry about is your president?"

"I have very good potential."

"I bet you do."

"I am not an idiot like Yamen. You know, we call them pawns. So you see, you cannot blame me."

"Yamen may be an idiot and a pawn of some Shiite doomsday prophecy but, man, you are one sociopathic asshole. Your materialistic interest comes before the lives of hundreds of thousands of people. If all Al-Assad's people are like you, I am proud to be your enemy."

"Do you know what I like about you?"

"What!? Please take offence and don't like a thing about me."

"Really, that you say whatever you want to my face."

"Actually, sometimes I say things behind your back. Bad things often."

"Ha, ha I still like you."

"Sure!"

****

Ever since we shared our first apartment, Sami had been a couch potato. For someone who would leave home only to get supplies, I had always been amused by his strong take on Malaysian culture. Sleeping until every cell in his unused vessel screamed in agony *hungry*, the beast would open his eyes to devour our leftovers. Stuffed and glued to his laptop, he found time to lecture poor souls in the

Middle East, most of whom I recognised from college. On the sound of my keys reaching the lock, he would start his tales. But not on that day. As he emerged from his room, I smirked, "I just called all the hospitals in the vicinity. I was about to reach out to the precincts."

"Why what happened?"

"You weren't in the living room."

"Ha, ha you think you're funny."

"You can't blame a guy for trying."

"I was skyping with Faysal when I heard you come in."

"Whatever happened to him?"

"Actually he is still on. He wants to talk to you. Should I bring out my laptop?"

"Yeah, by all means."

Sami got his laptop and handed me the earphones. He grabbed himself a cigarette from my pack after I had lit mine. On the screen, I caught a glimpse of Faysal. Exhaling the smoke, "So Saudi! It has been a while."

"Yeah I was surprised to hear that you are staying together. I told Sami that you're an acquired taste and it is okay not to like you."

"So Saudi, how did that happen?"

"My brother managed to get me a visa. I left the country last week."

"Oh, how was it? Foremost, how is your family?"

"You have no idea. They ruined the country!"

"Who did? Do you mean Al-Assad and his Shabiha?"

"Not actually. Al-Assad is the only choice for now."

"I see, are you a Shabih now?"

"Either against Al-Assad or Shabih!"

"No, not actually, but you said that Al-Assad is the only choice for now."

"I wouldn't choose those villagers over Al-Assad. They fucked the country in ways you cannot start to understand."

"How come? They've been shot at, bombarded, imprisoned, and tortured for longer than I had ever thought possible. I don't want to assume, are you for or against Al-Assad?"

"Neither!"

"Can you explain?"

"Have you heard about the 'Third Wave'?"

"They don't even have a website. I thought they were only a Facebook group."

"It's the only movement that puts the country first."

"What do they stand for?"

"They are against the destruction, and for peace and development."

"So what is their solution to end the chaos?"

"It has to be peaceful. Not this way. Not through the empowerment of villagers."

"Please correct me if I am wrong. What this 'Wave' stands for is that all of those people who have been fucked for calling out for freedom and dignity are ignorant villagers; they are destroying the country. The only viable choice is Al-Assad."

"Exactly! And the political elite are the ones to handle the advancement of our nation, through negotiation not anarchy."

"But it all started peacefully. People in Daraa didn't demand the ousting of Al-Assad."

"You think so."

"Actually, I am confident enough to say I know so. I am not sure whether the people who pleaded to the head of intelligence in Daraa to free their children are villagers; all the people who came were from the city of Daraa.

"Daraa is not a city."

"It is, actually. It's official. But even if it isn't, were all the people in Homs, Aleppo, and Damascus villagers? And what if they were! Are they lesser citizens; lesser human? And who are those never-heard-from political elite? Where were they when Al-Assad killed the first hundred or the first thousand? As far as I am concerned, Al-Assad's government made it a point to persecute all of those against his party's ways."

"The government should handle the negotiations."

"What government? What negotiations? Are you saying that Al-Assad has to assign his own people to negotiate with him a solution for the mayhem they created?"

"It doesn't work through violence."

"Well, have you witnessed your daughter, sister, and mother getting raped and continued to do nothing but chant freedom? Have you endured Al-Assad's assault taking a toll on you and everybody you love and still waited for him to assign this invisible elite of yours? Man... Tell the fathers who have collected their children's body parts that they are villagers and freedom is exclusive to people from cities. Tell them that as long as they are against Al-Assad, they are ignorant..."

"Take it easy man. I just said my opinion; you are like them."

"You mean the ignorant people who are dying so you and I can live with some sense of dignity?"

"Dignity?! You really know nothing."

"So, if you are that close-minded why don't you just say that you are for Al-Assad? Just stop deceiving yourselves that you are on the right side of history. Villager or not, fuck off!"

****

Watching the slow decimation of my homeland had smothered me in a state of helplessness, arousing in me the desire to do something constructive. Far from it on this tropical island, I cared for the departed and those howling over them. From behind my telescope, I'd found myself sniffling and swallowing the dribbles, preserving my Eastern manhood. Seething

302

and chained in a cage, I sipped more and more from that inflammatory river of anguish. Infuriated in the realisation of my cowardice, my fists found refuge in those defenceless walls before I turned to the woods. There and just ahead of bringing my ritual to an end, I had a moment of clarity. In those seconds or so, peace was made with the realisation of the fact: *I am nothing compared to the braves; I haven't survived their agony for my overwhelming guilt to keep building up; I am witnessing their cleansing and I am choosing to watch; my guilt is an admission of their sacrifices but even with the rage, I am taking no action and no action is nothing.* With that painfully painted reality, I asserted to my conscience that *I owe it to the harmed to help, assist, or care, at the very least.* The least is something, even if equal to nothing in the physical struggle of people. But in doing the least, it would be a grave offence to the greats of my kind to have myself to claim to have acted.

Abdo had a friend who was close to Kareem. They were all from Aleppo. Kareem and I hadn't met each other for quite a long time then. It was my phase four for him. It had taken him longer than Yamen to make it to that category. Kareem had the habit of befriending people, getting close to them, and then, for unknown reasons, trashing them behind their back and cutting all ties with them.

Yamen had meant to introduce me to Abdo, a few months after my twenty-ninth birthday. On that night I'd had more rage than it usually took to start punching walls. On that night, I couldn't.

Abdo was a behemoth, making Yamen look freakishly small. After Yamen made an introduction, the two of them joined me for a smoke on the café patio. Yamen instructed Abdo to recount his first conversation with Kareem. He gave Yamen a look as though to check whether it was a good idea. "It's okay. Adam knows Kareem and they are not on speaking terms anymore."

"Why?" Abdo enquired.

"Long story! Just leave it for later. I am intrigued, please do tell."

"Kareem welcomed me when I arrived at his place…"

"It's actually their place," I pointed to Yamen.

"Thank you," he gave Yamen a gracious look.

"Two days ago, during my first night at their place, Kareem came into the living room and sat by the couch."

"He was sleeping on the couch," Yamen interjected.

"Yeah, so he asked me why was I here."

"Do you mean at their place?" I asked.

"No, he meant in Malaysia. I told him, like him, I am here to further my studies. He said I should have stayed in Aleppo."

"How come?"

"He told me that I should be ashamed, running away from the fight like a coward."

"Do you mean that he wanted you to carry arms against Al-Assad?"

"Yes!"

"Then, why is HE here?"

"I asked the same question."

"And what did he say?"

"He told me that he is away from the country for a reason."

"What would that be?"

"He said that he is part of the revolution. He is in Malaysia because, should the regime know of his involvement, his whole family would be targeted. He is in more danger in Syria than any fighter. And he holds a vital role in the opposition and it's critical that he continue his work from a safe location."

I gave Abdo the serious face before attesting, "Well, actually... emm, it is the case. Kareem is in charge of bringing the international community together to face Al-Assad's military. You can see why it's critical to keep him safe."

"Really!?"

"Yeah, why would I make that up? But please don't tell anybody" I bit my lip so I could keep myself from cracking up. I added, "Man, it is no joke. If you tell anybody, his family would be in grave danger. Kareem is a brave man; one of a kind. He is too humble... keep it a secret!"

"I am sorry I didn't know. I won't, I promise you brother."

"It is okay, just keep it between us."

"Of course brother. Brother, I need to buy some groceries."

"Please go ahead. We'll be here whenever you come back."

Yamen asked Abdo, "Do you want me to join you?"

"No, no, it's okay."

Once Abdo left, Yamen mocked me, laughingly trying to copy me, "Kareem is in charge of bringing the international community…"

"Your new friend is so gullible. I like it."

Maybe there were other Syrians, far from the homeland like me, who found sympathy and care insufficient. I compensated through my ritual, which might not be a global regulatory tactic. Maybe there were those who found refuge in deceiving others into equating them with the braves. I questioned myself on the phenomenon, deducing, *it doesn't work that way*. For one, assuming others do their rituals to counter their state of discomfort, then deceiving others of that fallacy is merely a matter of communicating a desired self-image. Facing the conflict within us should call for more than wearing another's skin, claiming their triumphs, and understating their sacrifices in the pursuit of a stronger desired recognition. For a ritual to bring comfort, one has to be lulled into a false sense of security. But this requires an element of self-deception, which is a blasphemy against the souls of the braves who departed for us to be dignified free. It also makes you somewhat psychotic. Extrapolating on its danger, one should question the folie a deux epidemic, as the shared psychotic disorder is contagious. It could be social media borne.

Part of Sami's nightly tales were the ones of Shakeeb, his friend during college. He had left Ar-Raqqa shortly after Sami. I saw him speaking about his proclaimed ordeal on a major news channel: how he was imprisoned and tortured, his escape from Al-Nusra and ISIL, and Al-Assad's bounty on his head. Hearing him, you would assume that he was public enemy number one. Studying him on television, I murmured, "Nobody could sell a lie better than him." Shakeeb was also a drug addict. After things started to go south in other cities and before ISIL became an acronym, he took one of the migrant boats to Greece, before making it to Germany. From there he started a Facebook group with the name "Rights of the Free". He promoted it as an existing political movement that countered ISIL. Sami called it a movement and sometimes considered it a party. For the delusional activist Sami had asserted himself to be, you would expect him to know the difference between secularism and democracy. Like Kareem, he had communicated more revolutionary endeavour as opposed to those, back in the motherland, risking their livelihoods and dying for a free and just Syria.

****

After work, I'd come back to find Jennifer waiting with everything in order. She'd made the Korean cucumber noodles I liked. There was no cake. We both were almost broke, so a gift was off the cards. Before going to our room she graciously noted, "I know you want to watch the news. I am going to the room and whenever you're done, follow me."

On the eve of my birthday, all major news channel headlines were the same. And they all were on Syria. Sunk deep in an unfamiliar wretchedness of my unfortunate species, I hadn't dignified Jennifer's soft breaths over the nape of my neck with a look. Aljazeera didn't blur the gruesome aftermath of the Ghouta chemical attack although it was appalling. I switched to their website before moving to the-next-to-the-real-thing social media screen. I needed to prepare myself. Before witnessing the highest dosage of hysterical mayhem, I caught a glimpse of Jennifer falling to her knees, collapsing in despair. I would have been down by her side, if I wasn't on that couch.

Lying on an unfinished floor, the toddler's mouth kept expelling foam. The trembling hand of the keening man scanning the scene with his phone had captured less of that white substance on many shivering boys and girls; men and women had it too. Others had froth dripping down from their lower lips. The doctors and nurses on their knees wailed as though their almighty would have mercy on them, or dignify their pain at the least. On a large gurney three unconscious babies, who couldn't have been more than few months of age, hadn't a soul moaning by their little toes.

And then, the fucking buzzing sound found its way to my ears. The last time I had heard it had been about eight years ago. That awful sound meant haunting throes; it was yet another scar.

Moving my heavy head around, it seem as if a strong magnetic force was pulling my eyes back to sip more of that bitter bedlam. The fucking fly didn't just have the pleasure of hovering over the late teen in convulsion; it had to keep landing over the strange-looking-iris of his eye. The mother, who almost ripped her veil to cover her departed family, had transmitted into me a force, tightening my grip on Jennifer's hand. In excruciating agony, a yowling man's cough kept breaking his high-pitched wails. The soaked cleaning sponge in that male nurse's hand dripped continuously as though it was mourning the deceased. Dissolved in tears, Jennifer rose to kiss me on the forehead as if that affection would relieve my aching soul.

I had to take her to bed. Strong as she was, witnessing that calamity for the fourth time would've broken her. Upon our entry, she rushed in to put out the melting candles that were arranged in a heart shape. Speechless, I stood by the bed before lying down over the uncomfortable bed springs, I watched her take off her robe. I should've told her how stunning she was, wearing that black lingerie. Instead, I thought, *she must have borrowed some money from somebody so she could make me happy*. After she changed into her blue sweatpants, I invited her to sit by my side. Gobsmacked on that bed, we stayed awake for hours. At the end of it, I think she closed her eyes just so I could leave the room without guilt.

I thought the twenty-second of August would qualify as a global mourning day. Evidently, the world didn't give a flying rat's ass. Insofar, my species' life expectancy had fallen by twenty-seven percent. The country was described as the humanitarian catastrophe of the twenty-first century. However, the celebrity story of the Zimbabwe jungle cultivated more sympathy than the innocents of my kind. As time goes by you come to the conclusion that the world *ain't gonna give a shit*. That said, I had expected to sense the ache in my kind.

On my Facebook page, I noticed Yamen's post of a smiley face with the phrase, "Feeling happy," as though it was a clarification for old-schools, like me, who didn't get emojis. His communicated emotional state was accompanied by its stimulus, "Green tea Frappuccino. This is the life."

"What a fucking life," I muttered.

Catching a glimpse of Yamen and Moayad just outside the café, I felt the urge to smoke before getting my coffee. Facing the street, I inhaled the smoky air having to turn away from Moayed's shit breath. "Take your arm off my shoulder," I ordered, glowering at his soft hand. Yamen noted, "Somebody got up on the wrong side of the bed! Let's take a seat."

"Do I have a choice?" I asked, irritated.

Moayed enquired, "Are you okay?"

"Have any of you seen the news?"

"What happened?" Moayed asked.

"I think you should see for yourself."

"Don't," Yamen instructed.

"Why not?!"

"Please tell me Adam."

"Yesterday your president's army attacked Ghouta using sarin gas, killing around one thousand, four hundred and twenty-nine people, including no less than four hundred and twenty-six children. It's so fucking gruesome that I cannot even start to describe it. What's your deal with children? Yamen can you tell me who's worse Saddam or your fucking president? You owe it to your people to see the price the country is paying so that your genocidal president stays in power. With what is happening, I have no idea how can you sleep at night. I just want to know what has to happen to wake you up from deluding yourself. Just…"

Yamen interrupted, "It's not our armed forces. Al-Nusra front kidnapped the children from Al-Qardaha." Hearing his counter version of the mayhem made my jaw drop. Repressing my fury, I wanted to listen to their fictitious tale. Yamen added, "The Free Syrian Army attacked them for two reasons. That is, to take revenge and get international support."

Trying to keep my calm, I inhaled more smoke before asking, "Have you seen the aftermath? Is that what you think happened?"

"I don't like to see the videos. Besides they are all fabricated. I am not making things up. You should listen to what Bouthaina Shaaban said!"

"So the videos are not real…"

"Not all of them are real. It's hard to get hold of the real footage."

"I see. For your information the footage has already been checked by experts. And they are not fabricated if you'd like to know. Moreover, you are trusting the word of a terrorist over the rest of the world."

"Not everybody in the government is a terrorist! Please stop labelling respectable people as terrorists."

"Are you taking about Bouthaina Shaaban? The same Bouthaina Shaaban who was involved in Samaha's terror plot?"

"Come on man! You always disregard people who believe in conspiracies. Don't be a hypocrite."

"Excuse me!"

Moayed took a shot at me, "Well you call Mr President's media consultant a terrorist; she is a very intelligent woman. I know her personally…"

"Stop Moayed. You know shit. Have you heard of Michel Samaha?"

"No!"

"Then shut the fuck up and listen! Samaha and your fucking president's chief of security, Mamlouk, conspired to destabilise Lebanon using explosives; they wanted to use Sunnis so they could incite sectarian strife. Phone records uncovered the involvement of the bitch Bouthaina Shaaban."

Yamen justified, "The Mossad..."

"Fuck you Yamen! Lebanese reports called him an undercover police informant. But be it the Mossad, what fucking difference does it make?"

Yamen retained his sickening sanctimonious smile. Mad as hell I harangued, "Does your fucking smile mean that all I just said is wrong? Or does it mean that you are proud of what your government is doing? Or does it imply that you don't give a shit as long as you get the chaos the fucking terrorist republic of Iran wants?"

"You are so angry man!"

"No shit, as you should be. For you it's not enough to ignore the pain your regime has inflicted on our country. And I am not only talking to you. One would rather the decimation of the country for some twisted doomsday theology and the other would ignore all atrocities as long as he becomes some corrupted shithead. Just let me be clear, the way I see it, you are both partners in one of the most atrocious ideological cleansings in this century. And for what? You are not embarrassed, not ashamed. Yamen, you are no different than those who support al-Qaeda.

Moayed, for money and title you would sacrifice the lives of hundreds of thousands. Just admit it; not to me, to yourselves. Because if you knew that, you wouldn't have the audacity to preach your fucked-up, intelligence insulting and fictitious tales. You would know better than to kill and then play the victims."

Yamen gave Moayed a grin and mumbled, "He is angry..."

"I can speak for myself, don't speak on my behalf."

"I am telling him that you are under too much stress."

"I am furious but not stressed. And disappointed that I actually tried to reason with you. You will never change. You are both fixated that no matter how high the price and how many injustices our people endure..."

"Enough Adam. Just remember what you always say."

"What is that?"

"That you are not absolute and you can be wrong."

"Yeah I can be wrong but not on this. You might need to entertain my philosophy. A hint, nobody wants to be you in that situation. I mean living with the knowledge that you're wrong and you've been taking the side of the babies' butcher."

****

Over the slow agonizing torture of the braves and innocents in our motherland, our exposure from such distance left us to either witness or be infected by the hometown syndrome. For in matters of struggle there is the legitimisation of sufferers' claims and in matters of war there is fairness in all unjust affairs.

As the merciless demagogue stepped harder, crushing the throats of the free, their haunting voices called for the only holy prayer. In memory of their sacred remains, those mourning the loss of the free and those inspired by them congregated. In the name of the absolutist egomaniacal tyranny, the masses were forcibly dismantled, caged in the halls of sadists, or put down to sleep, once and for all. Worshippers of the true god, Freedom, across the motherland stood Gandhi-like in the face of the heretic; defiant in their chains, roaring "Enough!" But not all had the stomach for that conviction. The pilgrimage was a privilege of only the braves. Their enlightenment was inevitable in the pursuit of that godly prophecy of dignity. Spurred on by altruism, they endeavoured to show their fellow countrymen and women the light, freeing them from the dark spell of their doomed slave master.

Far from behind our telescopes, we chanted, shouted, we felt pain and rage, we wept. And from the distance some lectured. Overseas and far from the savage claws, those who originated from places of defiance had viewed the hesitation of those in other parts of the motherland as betrayal, marking patient zero of the hometown syndrome.

Sufferers of the illness showed low tolerance to the counter justification of those from towns of heresy, be they on the ground or distanced. Urged on by the contagious disorder, they portrayed the roaring worshipers as hypocritical; shouldn't these worshipers offer the ultimate sacrifice to the cleansing devil? It was as though being violated was equal to faithfulness. Consumed by tallying the beast's selective evildoings against their regions blinded them to his fangs in the whole nation's back. It was as if Al-Assad's regime was Lucifer and the mayhem he caused was their sacrifice to the gods. From their safe havens, they bargained using their hometowns' bedlam. Branded in victimhood, they claimed the rights to reap the fruits of the braves' endeavours.

While the brute fangs inflicted deeper scars, the syndrome showed its next facet. As atrocities resulted in an unprecedented magnitude of decimation, the sufferers cursed the souls of early worshipers. Some only cherished it elsewhere; for Damascus was the oldest capital, Aleppo was in the heart of the country, and Ar-Raqqa contained the unfortunates' refuge. It was the villagers' takeover, they would curse.

Every part of the motherland had its roles and merits; tragedies were agonising, the sane could argue. Those captivated by the prophecy of dignity, from their telescopes, might have wished the struggle to occupy the deserted emptiness of the nation. But really, they shouldn't have wished it for anybody, but acknowledge its presence no matter where.

****

For a long time, I had realised that many members of my compatriots in Penang ranged on a spectrum of political ignorance between wilful and bumptious. However, notwithstanding their shortcomings, they were inclined to have their say in our common, complex misfortune. I also came to witness one of Syria's worst enemies. That was, the overwhelming pursuit of a new deity. It went without saying that

Al-Assad's regime, ISIL, Iran, Al-Nusra Front, and Hezbollah topped the list.

Preaching on the danger of "Allah is Almighty"; I was disciplined for my lack of tactfulness by the faithful and not so faithful. Warning of the exclusiveness of Islamic chants, I was called sectarian as if I had a religion. Sami called me racist and after I argued, "As a Middle Easterner myself and given that Islam is not inclusive of ethnicity, the label was a naïve offence."

"What can I call you then?" he demanded an answer.

"Adam!"

"I mean people who are afraid of Islam."

"Just to be clear, I am not afraid of Islam but of what political Islam might do to our country."

"There is a term, right?"

"Yes, the word you are looking for is Islamophobe. And I am not." Sami fixated on the word until he denounced his faith.

The opposition in exile was another curse that the Syrian people had been enduring. Distanced, and equipped with their telescopes, they'd risen, claiming to be the motherland's salvation. Scared into caves by the savage's claws, they claimed the fruits of the blood-watered seeds of the free. From behind our telescope we welcomed the self-proclaimed liberators. The new elite were as conspiracy-driven, counter-intuitive, and exclusivist as the thug and his entourage had been. The short-sighted juveniles had inflicted their share of scars on those in the motherland and those behind their telescopes.

The Syrian National Council had become our version of "Keeping up with the Kardashians". The Council and its phonies had gotten under my skin, bringing out the worst version of me. The uncharismatic, incompetent representatives brought about yet another paradox to the word "leadership".

On the day Jarba was elected as president of the Syrian National Council, I had to do my due diligence on our new supposed leader. Sami had taken his position on the couch as though his ass was attached to it more than Al-Assad to his father's throne. Using my speakers, the Lebanese comedy he was watching was so loud, people on the mainland would have had the right to complain. In irritation I asked, "I found an interview with the new SNC president. Would you like to watch?"

"Not those idiots … I have no idea why they replaced Moaz Al-Khatib."

"You are right, you have no fucking idea."

"Why do you speak to me like that?"

"Your former 'president' resigned in exile. They didn't force him to leave. If you ask me, they should've ousted him earlier."

"Why? Is it because you are an Islamophobe?"

"No, because he lacked the skill and the stomach to hold such a position."

"He was a real leader."

"Maybe in leading people during Friday prayers."

"You keep saying you aren't an Islamophobe! Did you just hear yourself?"

"I did actually. But for me to support someone, I have to know everything about them. First, your new god…"

"I have a god, don't insult me!"

"I am not insulting you, but for me hearing you praising that naïve figure just reminds me of Al-Assad's diehard supporters."

"He is not naïve."

"What do you know about him before the uprising? Do you know that he was the imam of Umayyah mosque? Of course it goes without saying that he is very conservative. Besides, we all know imams and where they get their Friday speeches from. A hint, they are informed and supervised by the same government he opposes now. I get it; he was forced to preach Al-Assad's messages. I just have no clue how on earth his past experience qualified him for the presidency of the SNC…"

"Just admit it; you hate him because he's Muslim."

"I have been equally critical of all. And just an FYI, all of them are Muslim. The question is why you want to replace Al-Assad with a new deity. Listen, if you must know, on a conference a while ago, Al-Khatib advised Hezbollah to stop terrorising the Syrian people as Hezbollah fighters are Muslims and their blood shall not be spilled. To date, he has rejected labelling Al-Nusra Front as a terrorist organisation. He refused it although they represent al-Qaeda in Syria. That said, he still begged for international support. And when he couldn't get that support he decided to resign. So tell me, how could he be any good for the Syrian people? He is one of the weakest men who has had any power in the history of this crisis. The Syrian brave men and women fighting that asshole deserve more than a naïve delusional imam."

"Go watch the idiot's interview. I am sure you are gonna say he is naïve too as nobody is good enough." Sadly, Sami was right. Observing me sighing he enquired, "What is it with him?"

"He called Al-Nusra Front a group of apostles!"

"Maybe it was long time ago."

"Even so, he lacks the intuition to hold such a position."

"Your standards are so high!"

"Not actually."

"You have to understand that we will deal with the devil to oust Al-Assad."

"Toppling Al-Assad and his entourage might prove hard, but possible. Inviting that cleansing ideology to the country is a bigger crime than the ones of Al-Assad; it will be impossible to eliminate them once they get it. I would say that ship has already sailed."

The Muslim Brotherhood through its gullible liberal front, along with Al-Assad, had paved the way to ISIL, Al-Nusra, and their Shiite counterparts to drag the nation to the gallows. Thinking about it, I had often found myself in limbo with no feasible options. The Syrian people's pursuit of the Almighty in Command also had blocked fruitful debate; it had been either Al-Assad or his partners in the decimation of our unfortunate motherland. I had the habit of saying, "I seek someone who is willing to put the nation before her or his sect and ethnicity; someone with no innocents' blood on their hands." But even then I knew it was a dream.

****

Far from behind our telescopes on whatever side of the war, we had been touched by the agony of our kind; some more than others. With the increasing suffering of my species, the world was touched too. The wealthy of the Gulf region were first to respond to the ache the war had brought. Through some written and unwritten laws, they branded us pariahs. The Gulf region claimed the authorship of the so-called "Arabs' magnanimity". Limiting or prohibiting work visas for the orphaned Syrians who had struggled their way out, the Gulf Arabs displayed their utmost "munificence". Egypt was at times more or less generous in that sense. Of course, those fortunate nations in the West had to compete with the Gulf region's generous initiative; some would say they were the first to label us the unwanted.

When the terrorist regime's infamous figures and institutions were justly sanctioned we, from behind our telescopes, were for some reason denied their services. From banking to health insurance we had been flagged. Dare we do the unspeakable, we would be confronted with a look as though we were audaciously unclean, needing to show regret for our heinous acts. Whatever one's purpose of visit, applying for a visa was the greatest of all sins. For some destinations, we were seen below the rejection's threshold; it was a futile quest to fulfil the unwritten requirements for the sinister Ishmaels of my kind. With the mark on our foreheads reading "Abomination", and in a state of unease we had found a bond. High and dry we knocked on many doors; some appeared to be the mirrors images of our own desperation.

Sami, Yamen, Mustafa, and I had brainstormed, navigating the legal and illegal, and the grey area between both. In the pursuit of a homeland, we sought safety as a priority; we favoured the least insecure of all options. Far from the motherland and on an expiring stay by our unwelcoming host, anxiety rose in the quest of locating our next refuge. There was neither a legal nor a safe choice. There was a wilful departure to the hell the motherland had become; there were boats of death; and there was the UNHCR.

The greed of human traffickers forced in us the most hazardous of choices, yet still a privilege for those who could afford the gamble. The four of us couldn't come up with enough money to grant even one voyage. Begging the UNHCR to make our plight known to the gatekeepers of any land who are made aware of our existence would take more than half a decade. With the exception of Yemen, we were without a recognised partner; deemed to be the disenfranchised. We concluded that putting our lives on hold in this exile was our only viable choice; so we were forced to knock on that closed door.

Only three of us were desperate enough to embark on a trip to the Malaysian capital. It was a Monday. The guards of the UNHCR didn't allow us in. We wanted to enquire about the procedure. When we asked one of those wearing a badge which said "I'm 1 who cares!" we were told, "Syrians only on Wednesday." I pressed "May I...?" but all I heard was, "Wednesday."

On that Wednesday we stood by the gate for five hours before the Syrians were allowed in. It was so hot that Mustafa and Sami got sunburn. Lined up through the fixed barricades, we were sweating from head to toe. There were lines of Myanmarese, Sri Lankan; one was designated to those from the Middle East. There were Palestinians, Iraqis,

Iranians, Yemenis, and Syrians. The Somalis were the smallest group.

We stood there for more than an hour before our counter opened. Standing in the middle of the line, hours had passed and we hadn't sensed that our turn was going to happen. Sami asked the guy behind him, "Where are you from?" The guy looked agitated, even before Sami approached him. "Gaza," he answered and continued, "What about you?"

Sami replied, "Syrian. How long have you been in Malaysia?"

"I am here for a week and I leave in twelve days."

"Where to?" Sami asked.

"I work in Qatar. My friends told me it would be faster to do it from here."

Sami couldn't hide the surprise on his face, "You have a job in Qatar!"

"Yes, I have been working there for almost four years."

Sami looked at me and whispered, "Do you believe it?"

"It is what it is."

"Would you come here if you could get a visa to Qatar?"

"Absolutely not!"

"Me neither," Mustafa replied.

The two guys in front of me had their family seated elsewhere. I thought the Syrian guy's mother and a Palestinian dude's children and wife should be spared the strain of queueing. When I brought it up, all parties agreed. I struck up a conversation with the middle-aged Syrian, "Where exactly do you come from?"

"Baba Amr, Homs."

"Oh, I'm really sorry."

"We are lucky to make it here."

"Why Malaysia, if you don't mind me asking?"

"It's okay. My friends' son promised he'd find me a job in a Syrian restaurant."

"That's good."

"Not actually. The owner hasn't paid us for ages."

"I'm sorry to hear…"

"That's not all. When we arrived here, he promised to get us work permits. We paid half of our salaries for a year to cover the visa cost. He held onto our passports for more than a year. After several months of no pay, we wanted our passports back so we could look for jobs elsewhere. He kept delaying until we fought with him. Our passports had been with him all along!"

"Fuck that shit! I am really sorry. I don't know what to say."

"Just our luck."

"You keep speaking in plural?"

"My mother worked there too. It is not enough for one of us to work."

"I'm sorry. Is that all your family?"

"No, I had a wife."

"I'm really sorry. Can I ask you what happened?"

"In Baba Amr we saw what hell looks like. Constant bombardment! Bombs all the time and everywhere. There was no water supply and no electricity. Nobody could leave or enter Baba Amr." Hearing him sniffling and about to choke up, I put my hand on his shoulder. Observing us, the Palestinian guy sneered, "You Syrians... It's not even four years yet. We have been enduring this life so long that it's become normal."

A younger Syrian in the line interjected, "Sure! Even if all our people are killed we're still less."

"We have been waiting for years and now you are the UNHCR priority. You haven't seen what we have endured."

Avoiding the confrontation of those competing in victimhood, I turned to my fellow countryman, "It's hot in here isn't it?"

"Yeah, it's like working in a Syrian bakery."

"Ha, ha. Yeah indeed! I guess if you'd known, you wouldn't have worn long sleeves. He responded by pulling the collar of his shirt down, unveiling severe burns from his collar bone running down what I could see of his chest. He clarified, "My arms are burned too. They are from the night I lost my wife. I am lucky I have no children!" Dumbstruck, I felt my rage before I realised my guilt. I thought, *if any of us was deserving of a chance, it would be this man; not the guy working in Qatar, Sami, Mustafa, or me.*

****

My family had strived to keep me in the dark of their horrifying ordeals. They had their reasons: those far removed from the agony shall not be burdened with the ache of the suffering. I had to wait for my sister Heela's slips of the tongue. Over the years there had been a lot of those. Before things went south, I would talk to them few times a year. The conflict changed everything. My father had become all upfront emotionally. He wouldn't miss a chance to state, "I am proud of you son." On occasions he would say, "I love you son!"

Two years after March 2011, Al-Assad regime loyalists were easily overrun by Al-Nusra. The al-Qaeda affiliate had enjoyed the help of a handful of other groups. If anything Al-Nusra should have thanked Al-Assad for abandoning the city and the Syrian National Council for being in bed with them at that time.

Heela was in touch with our family more than I was ever able to be. She had more friends in the city. She had spent a year after graduation in Ar-Raqqa and left before Al-Nusra had been overtaken. I was proud of her. Made by Hazem and Warda she grew to be a strong and independent woman. I still remember our conversation after she made it to Turkey. She claimed, "I was smuggled across the borders like Mexicans making it to America." Hearing that line I couldn't help but ask, "Where have you seen Mexicans making it to America?"

"American movies."

"Movies are always real!"

From Syria, Heela had managed to secure herself a scholarship in Slovakia. Unaware of the curse put on our kind, she applied for a visa through the embassy in Ankara. She was asked for the impossible and when we made it possible they were left with no choice but to flat out reject her. However, with the little cash she had, she made it to Egypt, a country very conflicted on who Syrians are. My kind had been welcomed in earlier times, then labelled and treated as outcasts thereafter. During the good times, she enrolled in a master's course with a full tuition waiver only to discover that the autocrats could take back what the theocrats provided. She worked hard all the time but in that nation it was like prising a baby from a vicious lion's fangs. Heela had the lead on reaching out to people from the city after Al-Nusra claimed ownership. Outraged by her naïve friend, she vented, "The idiot is happy! She told me that it felt like the day before Eid."

"How come?!"

"Apparently, they prayed as though it was."

"Yeah, use the mosque to get your word out."

"Exactly!"

Before the savages established their court of injustice, I'd managed to reach my father. Over the phone I asked, worried, "Is everybody fine?"

"We are fine son; your mother, sisters, and brothers."

"What about your brothers?"

"Son it's full of darkness here. With their beards and masks, they are going to fuck this godforsaken city up. They are taking this town to the stone ages."

"What about your brothers?"

"The day Al-Nusra entered the city your uncles stopped the fight. It was another version of Al-Assad. It was fight for me or death. They just brought their culture of death with them and now it has to be everybody's code."

From Heela I got to know of the dangers and costs that my younger sisters had to endure so they could go to school. I had been aware of ISIL's ban on female education beyond the fifth grade, but I had been kept in the dark that they had to take one of the deadliest routes in the entire country. The upside of this torment was that they had something to fight for. I know for sure, I would have surrendered to a state of endless depression, should I have sipped half their agony. Hearing my discouraged tone, my sister Samar deflected, "Brother you've got it all wrong!

You're hearing the bombs and saying 'Fuck.' Deir ez-Zor has better network reception than Ar-Raqqa. You see, I would go every day just so I could hear your voice."

"Fuck off!"

"Without your help, I wouldn't even have this chance."

"It's the least…"

"I love you brother."

"I love you too."

My father's salary hadn't been enough to survive on; two loaves of bread per head for ten days was all they had. Before getting married, Solaf, who was four years younger than me, spent her monthly pay check on the rent for the family's apartment. She too maintained the rule of keeping me distanced and in the dark. She had the guts and the tenacity to go to work until the day ISIL, on the basis of their terrorising misogynistic faith, prohibited this defiant woman from putting a roof over her family.

Movie heroines, or villains for that matter, would use the line that everybody talked before they would have to resort to enhanced interrogation techniques, which is anything but enhanced. Maybe being a teacher herself was the straw that broke that strong camel's back. Escorted by Nyhad, one of my brothers, she rode the bus to the school in the remote village she was assigned to. He had to wait for her every freaking day. After all, he had nothing better to do. Al-Assad's fighter jet had brought his institute to rubbles a semester ahead of his graduation. Without his files and threatened by the arbitrary recruitment of Al-Assad's armed forces, he was left with no choice but to accept his fate. Solaf and Nyhad saved some money walking from the terminal to home. The fastest way was through Ar-Raqqa's clock square.

Having noticed the crowds around the square, they walked head down. I think my mother passed the term to Solaf who described it as "ISIL's plays of horror." The man was high enough that passers-by couldn't help but have a glimpse. He had been blinded, his chin anchored to his left collarbone; dried blood stretching from his right eye to his neck. Solaf froze in terror before collecting the strength to pull her trembling hand to keep the savages from smelling her fear.

I managed to get hold of them the same day. Over the phone Solaf recounted the scene. She added, "There were so many children."

"That's bad."

"Bad doesn't even start to describe it! There was a kid who put sunglasses on the crucified man."

"Ooh that's insane."

"Wait! Some kids took selfies with the corpse."

"Fuck. Oh man."

"Even if things become normal someday; who will these kids grow up to be? What kind of lives will they lead?" Somebody in the background was yelling "indecent" or "one-eyed woman"; in Arabic the two words sound almost the same. It sounded like Sabrina, my youngest sister.

"Is that Sabrina?" I asked.

"Yeah," Solaf giggled.

"What is it?"

"Your sister went to the minimarket by the corner. She cannot walk wearing the burqa. She keeps tripping over her own feet. The shop is a minute away from the apartment so she didn't wear it. In the shop an old man called her indecent. She confused the word with one-eyed woman. She told him that she had two eyes. And then she covered an eye with her hand and kept repeating "one-eyed woman." He pulled her over and slapped her. She said he did it five times."

"That fucking piece of shit! She is only seven. She doesn't even understand the word decent. Please put her on speaker."

"Adam they killed my dog!"

"Who? Wait, do you have a dog?"

"Puppy," Solaf interjected.

"Who did?" I asked.

"ISIL," Sabrina answered.

Solaf added, "We think they did."

Sabrina questioned, "Adam why did they kill my dog. It didn't hurt anybody."

"Ahh..."

"It was white and beautiful."

"I am sorry my love."

"Why did they kill it?"

"They are crazy criminals. They hate dogs. They believe that angels are scared of mirrors and dogs."

Sabrina sniffled, "They killed him because of angels?"

338

"Maybe! I am very sorry my love."

Sobbing Sabrina yelled, "Adam said they killed him because of their scared angels. They killed him. I hate angels."

Far from behind her telescope, the war had taken its toll on Heela. I knew better than to ask resilience of her. After the perceived predisposition of our kind took a turn for the worse in Egypt she had been intimidated and threatened twice to seek a shelter in a different neighbourhood, should she be courageous enough to stay at the mercy of that unwelcoming host. Upon branding my species as a bad omen, terrorists, and indecent, Heela increasingly found she was only able to maintain the existence of body but not that of mind. She worked and studied for too many hours. When she couldn't do either, she endeavoured to know and understand our clan's anguish as though in doing this she would find refuge from misogyny and asininity. Her telescope was better than mine; it had a better angle through which she witnessed more of my clan sinking in floods of endless shit.

I couldn't only count on her slips of the tongue. I persuaded the few acquaintances I knew in the city to encourage her to keep me in the loop. I argued, "Sooner or later I will know what you know; I would rather know sooner. Besides, I don't want to be dumbstruck by some idiot telling me about the fate of my own. I beg of you to be the one breaking it to me." Hearing her recounting the horror, the only phrase I could think of was, *Oh god, what have I done?* Except I wasn't the one dropping the bomb. Heela asked, "Do you know that grandmother Gammeek passed away?"

"Yeah I knew about it."

"Do you know about Uncle Adhamm?"

"Oh please, he is the only Uncle I like."

"Do you want me to tell you?"

"Please do?"

"A week after grandmother passed, he lost one of his children."

"Who?"

"She was born in 2009; you don't know her."

"How?"

"She inhaled some powder?"

"What powder? What?"

"On her way back from school she inhaled this powder. There was this house that was attacked by Al-Assad's air force."

"It wasn't sarin gas, was it? I would've heard something about that."

"No they say it's another chemical. They took her to the public hospital but nobody knew what it was. Uncle wanted to take her to Damascus but she was gone before they managed to get on the bus."

"Oh my... Oh. Somebody should've told me. Oh..."

"Yeah, I am sorry but father said that it's better not tell you."

Sighing I muttered, "I need to know. It is better."

"Uncle couldn't take it."

"What do you mean?"

"He went mad and has barely spoken since."

"Oh, shit," with my free arm, I fought the wall with punches, "Fuck, fuck, fuck."

"Maybe I shouldn't have told you."

Inhaling and exhaling deeply, I demanded, "You must not keep anything from me."

"And..."

"Enough for today! I will call you tomorrow."

"This is about our family."

"Have we lost anybody? Is anybody ill?"

"No but it's important"

"I don't think I can take more… I have to go to work knowing that uncle went mad after losing his little daughter. I should be able to work."

"Okay."

"I will call you tonight!"

After talking to Heela, I needed to hit the road. Instead, I stood on the balcony for an hour looking down at the children playing ball. I smoked one cigarette after another, using the end of each tobacco rod to light the next. Worrying about what Heela had wanted to tell me, I realised, *I will fuck this day up*. I decided *whatever it is, I have to deal with it; and afterwards I must go to work*.

"Hit me with it," I greeted her.

"Don't you want to go to work?"

"Yes, but it would be impossible now. I need to know first."

"Okay…"

"Go on, cut to the chase sister!"

"Except for father and Solaf, everybody else is in Al-Kasra."

"At mother's parents place, why? Anybody dead?"

"No, but they haven't got the money you transferred yet."

"Solaf told me that they couldn't find anything to eat."

"They couldn't afford it and father couldn't borrow from anybody."

"I am sorry I was a little late this time."

"No, thank you."

"I should have transferred it earlier. You know it took me ages to get that money. It's an advance from my clients; I won't earn a dollar for the next two months. All I wanted was to avoid that situation. So why did they go there?"

"Food!"

"Shit, ahh…"

"That's not what I wanted to talk about."

"Shit, please go on."

"There are rumours that ISIL is planning to arbitrarily recruit people from Ar-Raqqa."

"Ahhh, fuck."

"Father is stressed and scared that they might recruit Nyhad."

"Yeah, you don't say!"

"Father is thinking about moving to Turkey. ISIL is everywhere; with the aerial bombardment it's very dangerous."

"The girls are not going to school anymore. Solaf cannot go to work. No electricity and water for days and weeks. I get it, it is so fucking shitty in there! Smuggling our brother Moath cost me over a thousand dollars. After he was sacked from his last job, I had to transfer him some allowances. And my guess is that none of them have a passport. That would add around sixty per cent more."

"Actually father has a passport!"

"As though it would make a big difference."

"I will tell them that you cannot help, not that they have asked."

"Don't. Just tell them to see how many passports they can get using my last transfer. I will take care of it. Even if I have to sell an organ."

"Don't sell an organ…"

"I won't!"

"Do you know anybody buying?"

"Of course not!"

Chapter 14

An Ishmael of Syria

During my last night at Sheila's place, Solaf had called me couple of times before I noticed my phone. It'd been a while since we'd talked and I missed her and her sarcastic takes; something that had long bonded us. Solaf and her husband were staying in Ar-Raqqa. I felt an ache on hearing her voice. It was our first call since ISIL had taken the liberty to cut off the city from the outside world, as though getting in touch with anybody in Ar-Raqqa wasn't well-nigh impossible already. It was yet another fatwa. The savages had gone all 1984 on the use of the internet. Solaf asked, "Have you heard about the latest from ISIL?"

"The internet?"

"Yeah!"

"I did. I've tried to get hold of you millions of times but I couldn't. Frankly, I was waiting for your call. Thank you by the way."

"Don't mention it! I also want you to break some bad news to mother."

"Of course, but why don't you tell her yourself?"

347

"Can you do it please?"

"Sure, just give me a second." Anticipating the worst, I moved out to the balcony and closed the door behind me.

"Are you okay now?"

"Yeah, go on."

"Do you remember cousin Freeda?"

"Mother's second youngest sister's daughter, no?"

"Yeah, she got married almost a year back. Her husband passed away six months back."

"Ah, I am sorry to hear about it! Was she the one staying with us?"

"Yeah she is close to mother."

"I am sorry about that."

"It has been a while and mother knows!"

"Okay, what is it then?"

"She gave birth five months ago."

"Yeah."

"Did you know she is a nurse?"

"No!"

"So she is forced to work daily at the public hospital. Yesterday she was going to the bus station with her brother. She was using her scarf to cover her baby boy. I guess it was quite long. I mean with the burqa and everything. Her scarf was long. It was sunny and she covered her son's face with it. On the way to the hospital, somehow the end of that scarf went under the wheels, dragging her and her son down."

"Shit!"

"I am sorry…"

"Shit, shit, fuck…"

"Listen, her son is gone."

Loudly, I yelled, "Fuck!"

"I am sorry."

"What about her?"

"I visited her yesterday. She is in critical condition. Her face…"

I kicked the wall, "Oh shit, fuck, fuck, fuck." Sheila saw the whole thing but pretended that she was reading something on her laptop.

"Just so you know, I am the one who broke it to her when cousin Abdorazaq was killed."

"Who's cousin Abdorazaq? Is he related to mother?"

"He was her brother's second son. You don't know about him. He was born after you left the country."

"How?"

"What? Oh yeah. ISIL vehicles ran him over. They didn't even stop!"

****

Sheila had been on the road for the last few weeks. She had been spending a little too much time up in the air. She sent me her last itinerary. Flight paths tripled the distance between Sierra Leone and Malaysia. She was in charge of setting up an office over there on behalf of her company. On Sunday she messaged me every now and then. I promised her to give her a video call once I'd made it home.

Over that call, Sheila talked about a feeling. A feeling I have long lived with. She was a people person too. On Saturday night and upon her request, the hotel manager had set up a meeting between Sheila and his Senegalese cousin. It had been years since she last spoke any Wolof and she had asked the hotel manager if he knew anybody in the vicinity.

Over a few messages she told me that the guy was under the impression that she could get him a job. In

350

our video call, we rationalised this was likely to be on the basis of desperation. Sheila hadn't hidden anything, mentioning my name and recounting some of my share of misfortunes in my pursuit to secure a job.

Foremost, we explored the feeling she had. It was a mixture of boredom, anxiety, and loneliness. Back on the island, she had enjoyed the company of her many friends. I assured her, "Whatever that feeling is, it's normal to experience it in new places. It might even make you restless at night."

"Yeah, that could be it."

"Yeah, the story of my life. You see, during college back home I felt like that. In Malaysia, it wasn't always like this."

"How come?"

"Like you, I have the desire to be around people and to be part of their communities. I thought I could make that happen here. I have to admit for a while it was the case. I guess I was more patient then. I just can't do it anymore."

"What can't you do?"

"Keep trying to defy their stereotypical assumptions of my kind. Having to explicitly define myself.

Having to defend my whole species. I mean first being an Arab. It's like being guilty of something. I have to start almost any relationship on the defensive. I have been patient to do it. I remember telling Sami when we moved to a place together that on the island you might have no choice on who you befriend. They say you cannot choose your family. I told him for us over here, it is easier to choose your family than your friends. I've reached a point where I've grown tired of trying to convince people that I'm not who they think I am. I've become exhausted of having to defend my whole race. I've ended up alienating myself. I was never on very good terms with my Syrian clan. But I need to socialise with somebody. Although, we disagree on core issues and no one keeps in touch with the others if they leave this forsaken island."

Eventually we concluded our take on the phenomenon. Before, we said to each other, "Sleep well." Sheila asked, "Have you talked to Nyhad? You told me last time you might've upset him."

"That was over eight months ago."

****

On the night my family made it to Turkey, I made everybody promise to gather in one place so I could see all of them at once. Except for Solaf; she and her

352

husband were in Syria. It had been six years since I had last seen any of them in motion. A video call was not in any way equivalent to a face to face reunion but it was all I could afford. Before that call, I'd danced and sang. Most of all, I was happy. I was full of joy until I caught a glimpse of my family's demeanour. Father looked very skinny, weak, and twice the age of a man of his years. Mother wept before I had the chance to say, "Hello." The grey covered her head and the toll the war had taken on her was clear in her eyes and face. Nobody would ever confuse her as my older sister; she could easily pass as my grandmother.

I spent hours talking to them. Before Nyhad's turn, I talked with Jomana, my second youngest sister. She had recounted part of her tale about their night in the wilderness before something else caught her attention. From behind my screen, I witnessed the whole thing. Distracted by some sound she froze. Silently, I waited for her to continue her story. Jomana's lower lip quivered as she looked to her right and left. I Frowned from behind my desk. I didn't hear the sound of her chair falling to the ground.

Jomana had crouched under a table by the door of the spacious room, sobbing and trembling, as Nyhad made it to the screen. He adjusted his seat, whilst my mother sat by my sixteen year old sister's side. She held her daughter's hand and kept whispering something to her.

Jomana's trauma was in no way Nyhad's fault. I kept my rage repressed for the best part of our conversation. I was aware of his need to build a future for himself. For long, I had come to label preachers of hopeful fallacies in times of calamity as warlords. He had laid down his plans and I couldn't show more disapproval. I wanted to let it slide. But when he made a mention of the UK providing a fast-track resettlement programme that was exclusive to our kind, I just couldn't hold it in anymore. I vented, haranguing him on the danger of hope.

****

Regardless of its varying narratives, the story of Ishmael has always fascinated me. Jews, Christians, and Muslims alike had it that Sarah, the seventy-five year old wife of Abraham, offered her handmaiden, Hagar, to her husband. Hagar was supposed to give them a child. She was a slave with no rights whatsoever. The late eighty-five-year-old had sex with his wife's slave. In a matter of months, Hagar got knocked up. Envious old Sarah went all bananas on her, treating the poor thing like shit. Thinking about it, she must have taken shit to another level that even her slave couldn't endure it. Hagar went AWOL.

Hagar claimed receiving words from God, who persuaded her to suck it to Sarah. As a man for whom faith is absent, I can't take her word for it. God must have been a very bored man with a lot of time on his hands. One, at that time, could only argue, "Why me?" Hagar claimed that God made her a promise that her son would father a great nation. To others, God called that son a "wild donkey of a man"; whatever that is. I can only assume that God loathed wild donkeys. God also wanted the child, for whatever reason, to be named Ishmael.

After Ishmael turned thirteen, God told Abraham, his words not mine, that he would give him another son, Isaac, and that the father was to establish his covenant through the newborn. Abraham wondered, "What about Ishmael?" Abraham said that God had assured him that Ishmael would be just fine; even better than that.

After giving birth to Isaac, Sarah accused her stepson and slave of playing with or mocking her son; we actually don't know whether he mocked or played with his stepbrother. Sarah told her husband to get Hagar, the slave, and her son the fuck out of her sight. A woman known for nothing but the warmth of her heart didn't want the slave's son to share her husband's inheritance; all of the goodies shall belong to Isaac. God was a friend of Abraham; an invisible friend who talked plenty to the ninety-nine-year-old. Whenever his friend got whipped by his wife, he told him to obey.

Abraham, from this point called "the friend of God", freed the two slaves, Ishmael and Hagar, and asked them to fuck off. Not to strip him from having a heart, I should say that he gave them some bread and water. If it wasn't for God, called from this point onward, Abraham's invisible friend, who had given Hagar the strength to carry on that voyage across the forsaken desert, both would've departed the living.

As a woman of honour and virtue, Sarah had her reasons. In her own defence, the slave's son was predisposed to sexual immorality and even violence. On the bases of deductive reasoning and developmental psychology, she feared for her son's wellbeing. Sarah was an admirable woman who put her child first. She didn't want a slave, who also happened to be her husband's son, to claim or share his whipped father's inheritance.

The Jewish traditions have been divided on whether Ishmael was the ancestor of the Arabs.

Some agree with the Islamic narrative, asserting that Arabs descended from Ishmael. There was also a division between Jews and Christians on one hand and Muslims on the other over which boy was nearly sacrificed. Abraham's invisible friend asked him to show faith by executing his son ISIL style; maybe without a mask though. The bible said that Abraham's invisible friend ordered him to sacrifice his "only son Isaac, whom you love." One can assume that Abraham either didn't love his other son or Abraham's invisible friend didn't acknowledge the slave son's existence. Sarah couldn't agree more with Abraham's invisible friend that a slave was not deserving of love or acknowledgement of existence. Muslims claim that Abraham was about to cut his son's throat when Ishmael was thirteen, thus, Isaac was not born yet; therefore, almost slaughtering Isaac was impossible. Whoever that son might've been, I often ask myself, "What the fuck!"

Contemplating the way the story was delivered through the scripture, I couldn't help but remember a number of ISIL executions. In both, sickening agonising acts of savagery were portrayed as touching and beautiful. Just like the speech an executioner of the terrorist organisation had given before stoning that Syrian woman to death. And just like his softly spoken words, describing the poor woman's life in heaven; in idiocy there had been the beautification of the most heinous crimes.

Other than being the name of that unfortunate child, Ishmael also means "a pariah". During my time in college back in Ar-Raqqa, I made peace with being an Ishmael to my own. But even as an Ishmael I hoped that one day I would fit in. I deluded myself into believing that if I tried hard enough, elsewhere I would blend in. I thought I may have been only an Ishmael of Syria. Defeated in my struggles to relinquish that derogatory label, I have found myself at a constant loss. When our collective agony has made all of my kind outcasts, I have found no company. I realise, I am an Ishmael of Syria. Undesired at home; doomed by the rest.

I could've answered Nyhad. I could've just told him my story but I didn't. I didn't explain myself over our first conversation in six years. Last I heard from him was him was eight months ago. Him preaching, "Hopes and ambitions bring us nothing but depression."

In a war-torn country Nyhad was hopeful. In safety, he lost it. And even though he had reached that realisation on his own, I couldn't help but resent myself and feel guilty.

Acknowledgements

I believe that many of us have sipped or are maybe still sipping that bitter dose of helplessness. I know I have! It has been a long and lonely journey. Writing this story has given me comfort – I felt as though I was recounting my tales to someone who understood. When all was said and done, I was not alone in times of crisis. When I have been knocked down so badly that I doubted I would be able to stand again, David Hodges, Ng Kok Meng, Jiyoung Yoo, and Hessam Nejati lifted me up to defy the impossible.

This book wouldn't have seen the light of day if not for the support and help of friends, acquaintances, and complete strangers. I deeply appreciate your contributions, suggestions, and getting the word out. Katherine Suri, Mark and Hilde Burby, David Hodges, Marina Apgar, Ng Kok Meng, Iain Mclellan, Emelia Rallapalli, Mike Suri, and Lacy Nash – I am so very grateful for your generous contributions.

My first readers and critics: Sandra Perkins, Vidya Chariya Sinnadurai, and Katherine Suri. Your invaluable insights, comments and encouragement have helped to shape this novel. I cannot thank you enough.

Many thanks to my editor, Miranda Summers-Pritchard, who ensured that the heart of the story came through clearly. Any remaining inconsistencies are mine.

I appreciate all the time and effort that Judy put in to creating multiple cover choices. And thanks to Lorans Alabood for using his Photoshop talents to weave the images into the front and back covers.

To my future readers: I am glad to share my story with you.

About the Author

Born in the 80s, Asaad Almohammad was raised in Ar-Raqqa, Syria. A member of the International Society of Political Psychology and a research fellow, he has spent years coordinating and working on research projects across the Middle East and North Africa. To date he has addressed a number of psychological aspects of civil unrest, post-conflict reconciliation, and de-radicalisation. In his spare time Asaad closely follows political affairs, especially humanitarian crises and electoral campaigns. He is especially interested in immigration issues. *An Ishmael of Syria* is his first novel.

Asaad can be found and followed at:

Website: http://asaadalmohammad.com/

Facebook:
https://www.facebook.com/IshmaelofSyria/

Twitter: @asaadh84